Photograph by Claire Westwood – L.M.P.A. Reflections Photography

J. M. Colhoun was born and educated in Liverpool. After being awarded two music studentships in Singing and Pianoforte she spent four years at the Royal Manchester College of Music, then completed a Postgraduate Certificate in Education and a Diploma in Teaching English as a Foreign Language.

After a period in education (teaching and lecturing in Music, Drama and Modern Languages), she became freelance, performing solo broadcasts for BBC radio, and acting as a vocal and dialect coach for stars of the stage, screen and radio.

She has written in various genres and now divides her time between writing, performing and composing.

CHANGES

To Will, Naomi, Laura and Glenda, with love.

J. M. Colhoun

Changes

© Copyright 2011 J.M. Colhoun

A RedArrow Paperback

The right of J.M. Colhoun to be identified as author of
this work has been asserted by her in accordance with the
Copyright, Designs and Patents Act 1988.

All Rights Reserved

No reproduction, copy or transmission of this publication
may be made without written permission.
No paragraph of this publication may be reproduced,
copied or transmitted save with the written permission of the
publisher, or in accordance with the provisions
of the Copyright Act 1956 (as amended).

Any person who commits any unauthorised act in relation to
this publication may be liable to criminal
prosecution and civil claims for damages.

A CIP catalogue record for this title is
available from the British Library.

ISBN 978 184433 017 1

RedArrow Books is an imprint of
Austin & Macauley Publishers Ltd.

First Published in 2011

RedArrow Books
CGC-33-01, 25 Canada Square
Canary Wharf, London E14 5LQ

The paper used in this product is grown in sustainable forests

All characters in this publication are fictitious and any
resemblance to real persons, living or dead, is purely coincidental.

Printed & Bound in Great Britain

My husband Will, for his constant love, support and encouragement, without which this book could not have been written.

My daughters Naomi, Laura and Glenda, for their lively interest and enthusiasm for the project.

My illustrator Marianne Birkby, for her lovely artwork, patience and cheerfulness.

The publication team at Austin & Macauley for their helpfulness and efficiency.

And finally, our family cat Tigger, whose feline beauty informed many a passage in this book.

"It is time," said the black cat, "for me to go on to The Great Adventure." She climbed into the wooden casket, roughly fashioned from the logs of an ancient oak tree, and lay down upon her velvet paws, turning her green eyes to the girl.

"Bury me in the forest clearing where I've always loved to be, under the oak from which this casket was hewn. There my remains will rest in the dappled light of day and the moonlit beams of night. At twelve of the clock tonight, my Gifts will become your Gifts; use them well; use them wisely, for the good of humankind. I bequeath them to you with my respect. And my deepest love."

The cat smiled at the girl. The girl smiled at the cat. Then the cat stretched out and closed her eyes forever. Large teardrops fell from the girl's face onto the sleek black fur. She stroked the head with the back of her fingers for a while, then closed the casket gently.

Then she went to the clearing in the forest and found the great oak tree, where she buried the casket containing the body of her mother.

* * *

She lay with her head on the pillow, her heart fluttering.

Waiting...waiting...how will it feel? She fingered the brown velvet choker around her neck, in the centre of which sat a golden disc. On it was engraved her name. It said simply: "KIT".

At twelve of the clock, the church bell began to toll in the distance. As prophesied, the changes began.

At first, an unusual feeling of muscle contraction in the fingers and toes; this gave way to a pulling sensation, as if the bones in the feet and hands were closing together, upwards, upwards, as if they were shrinking in length and becoming somehow lighter in weight. There was an awareness of movement within the flesh, as if muscles were turning, changing shape inside the casing of the hands and feet; an odd *sensation in the fingertips and toes heralded the extension of the nails, which began to curl under from the sides.*

Though her heart beat a little faster, Kit strangely felt no consternation as she observed these occurrences; rather a fascination, a curiosity as to what would happen next. Slowly, the forearm and lower legs started to experience the same feelings as before; the shrinking of the bones, the emerging new positions of muscle and tissue, spreading now to the upper arms and legs. Kit watched in wonder as her limbs shortened and contracted in width. Then suddenly her chest became tight; her breasts began to shrink and flatten; the nipples darkened and decreased in size; she could no longer take in the deep breaths which would normally fill her lungs; her chest and abdomen seemed to move inwards, the movement more rapid than before. She felt somewhat alarmed at the increased speed of the changes. Although her limbs and torso were now more in proportion, the altering states of her heart, lungs and internal organs caused a sudden, quick intake of breath; strange pangs of rapidly alternating sharp and dull pain accompanied their modification. Though lasting only a few seconds, these sensations were more than a little frightening.

As her neck and throat started to narrow, she felt a sudden apprehension that her too large and heavy human head would snap the fragile bones developing within. For the first time since the onset of the mutation she began to fear for her life. The most unnerving element of the entire process was beginning.

A compression of her skull; her heart beat very fast and she felt a sharp pain in her head, as if her brain was about to be crushed like a walnut. Panic threatened to engulf her, but then a strange thing happened. The pain quickly subsided and she began to perceive things very differently. Her heartbeat resumed a normal rhythm; she was becalmed, and it was as if she was an interested observer rather than a participant. Her face muscles began to relax; her eyes began to see more clearly; she was aware of her hearing becoming more acute, and of a more highly developed sense of smell.

Looking down at the altered state of her being, the tiny arms and legs, her diminutive chest and abdomen, she felt a peculiar sensation at the base of her spine above her buttocks. The bones seemed to be pushing outwards, and she felt an odd weight behind her she had never felt before. She was able to move it at will. A tail! No sooner had she become accustomed to this extraordinary idea than yet another amazing phenomenon occurred.

In one sudden fluid movement, her whole body converted to the skeletal framework of a cat. Where once were arms, she had two front legs, which upon her transformation fell gently forward and touched the floor. The feeling of the wooden boards on the surface of her sensitive pads seemed to act as a prompt for the final part of her change to feline form.

It started between the claws of each of her four feet; the small, short hairs which appeared there began to cover her feet; the hairs thickened and became fur, spreading upwards over her legs, around her abdomen, back and haunches, backwards along her tail, and forwards onto her neck and head. It was over. Her metamorphosis was complete.

Kit felt warm, calm, serene. She turned her head to look along the length of her body. A beautiful pair of black stripes ran the length of her spine; tiger-like single stripes radiated downwards over the caramel-coloured fur on her body and legs. She sat on her haunches and curled her tail about her delicate tan feet, with their charcoal black pads. Her tawny tail was ringed in black, graduating to the tip, which was like a soft, sable paintbrush. Her little pink tongue flicked out and licked the fur, creamy gold, upon her chest. How easily did her newly-formed muscles respond to their task!

She stood upright in a slow, graceful movement, arched her back, then padded on silent feet towards the window. Judging the distance perfectly, she sprang onto the sill, experiencing for the first time the satin-smooth glide of muscle *and sinew inside her as she moved effortlessly upwards. She sat down, curling her tail about her once more. Her whiskers touched upon the glass and she blinked in appreciation, revelling in the new-found sensitivity.*

Her feminine and feline instincts became one, and she carefully groomed her silky coat until it shone in the moonlight, purring, taking real pleasure in the sensations she felt deep within her.

She was going to enjoy being a cat.

1723

Little summer flowers of every hue spilled gaily down the gentle slopes of the valley and along the edges of the path into the village of Witlock.

On this morning of June the sixth, although only just after ten of the clock, the sun's heat could be felt on the necks and shoulders of the young farmhands and dairymaids as they went about their chores, and the old folks donned hats to ward off the rays, which for many years had creased and browned their ancient visages.

The heat shimmered; it was still, and save for the odd clank of a labourer's tool, the lowing of cattle, or the song of the birds, there were few sounds to be heard, and tranquillity reigned in the little hamlet.

Shortly before twelve noon, the skies suddenly darkened, and with the thundering of the horses' hooves, the clouds poured forth a deluge, lightning forked in the sky, and four horsemen came to an abrupt halt outside the inn. Their black cloaks swirled in the rising wind, and they dismounted, striding purposefully to the door of the tavern, their black hats sodden at the rims, their faces grim with intent.

From the instant the door opened, the landlord's heartbeat quickened. The Witchfinders had arrived.

They did not delay their task.

"Bread, cheese and ale – and some information, Innkeeper."

The four sat down at a table and the speaker summoned the trembling landlord with an imperious gesture of his hand.

Old Josiah swallowed, and approached the men with fear in his eyes. The leader of the group spoke again, his sharp eyes narrowing in his gaunt face.

"We come to do the Lord's work."

"And for this we will need sustenance," said another of the party, "so have your good woman bring us platters, while you, landlord, bide here to tell us what we need to know." The lips of the fat man slid into a cruel smile.

"Be sure to bring the best and the freshest " he indicated the leader with a movement of his plump hand "for this is Matthew Greer, most famed of all the Witchfinders in these parts."

The innkeeper nodded and turned with trepidation towards the plump young wench who now approached the table.

"Your good woman?" said the third member of the foursome, a smirk upon his bearded countenance.

"M-M-My granddaughter," stuttered Josiah, and added nervously "a good, God-fearing girl she is, my Alice."

The men looked at one another. Josiah and Alice exchanged glances, and Alice quickly dropped a curtsey and hurried towards the kitchen.

The men directed their attention to the innkeeper, who sat down at their bidding, twisting his old, gnarled fingers, by now very ill at ease.

"It has come to our attention," said Matthew Greer, leaning over the table towards the old man, "that there dwells in these parts a young wench, of eighteen years or so. She lives alone – save for the company of what is evidently her familiar..."

"...a wolf," interjected the fat man, and added with relish, "obviously no usual companion for a young maid."

"...of no husband, and neither father nor mother to guide her in the path of the Lord..."

"...a maid who by all appearances seems to be engaged in the Black Arts. We need exact knowledge of her whereabouts."

The four men spoke with a dark, eager urgency, and Josiah's old heart raced in fear. He knew the young woman of whom they spoke; a kindly girl who had a way with all creatures, and as far as Josiah knew, an orphan, recently come to live on the outskirts of the village. She made a living from her hand-made craftwork; woven baskets, whittled wooden bowls, platters and spoons. A witch! Josiah shook his head in disbelief at the thought. He wished no harm upon the wench, and though fearful of these men, his own good heart and sense of justice bade him reply:

"I know of no witch hereabouts, sirs –"

"Landlord," interrupted Greer, with menace, "we will do the Lord's work, of that you may be sure –"

" – one way or another." The fat man's mouth smiled, but his eyes did not.

Old Josiah followed Greer's malevolent stare, and saw that it fell upon his granddaughter, now approaching the table with a tray of food and ale. Josiah's heart leapt violently in his old chest, and the look that Greer turned upon him near froze his blood.

Alice dropped another curtsey, and as she left the table, crossed herself.

The gesture was not lost upon the four men, who looked at one another in a meaningful way.

"There are some witches," said the bearded man pointedly, "who would have folks believe that they are good, God-fearing women."

"Such blasphemy!" said the small, sharp-faced man who sat on the right of Matthew Greer. He bent forward and looked hard into Josiah's countenance and began to chew on his bread. The others commenced silently eating their food; not for an instant did they take their eyes off the old man.

Josiah did not mistake their inference. He feared so for his Alice, the words spilled forth like millet from a sack.

"There is a wench to be sure – she lives alone outside of Witlock though, just on the border of the wood, yon. In a tiny cottage close by it – a quarter hour's ride from here or so."

The men rose as one at his words and made for the door of the inn, leaving their food and ale unfinished. Their hunger was no longer for victuals.

Josiah's heart, once full of fear, was now leaden with remorse.

* * *

A squirrel ventured towards the outstretched hand of the young woman as she knelt outside her cottage door. The girl held her breath, keeping her hand as still as she could as the little creature timidly approached. With a swift movement the proffered nuts were stolen from the upturned palm, and the squirrel raced away with its prize, leaving the girl's hand empty, and her heart full. Oh, the privilege of being at one with nature, in harmony with living things!

She thought about the night before, when the grey wolf came to her door. How he waited in the shadows, took the meat she threw to him from her doorway and ate it hungrily, advancing a few steps nearer than he had on previous nights. She loved the wolf. He was old and he was tired, probably too tired to hunt for himself, but now his eyes were bright with trust of her, and she longed to reach out to him, to put her arms about his neck, and to stroke the fur that had seen him through the harshest of winters. But she kept her distance, not wishing to frighten him away, biding her time. He in turn crept closer upon each visit; last night he was but six feet away from her. The lass smiled as she thought of his beautiful face and his large, intelligent eyes.

She turned in surprise at the approaching sound of horses' hooves. From the forest? She was not aware of any wild horses there, yet – no! Not forest ponies, but four strong black steeds, bearing men all dressed in black. Before she could collect her thoughts, the four men had dismounted and surrounded her. One look at their faces set her young heart pounding.

"You are the wench who lives alone here?"

"Yes, sir," the lass managed, shrinking from the speaker, whose girth was as great as his breath was stinking.

"You have no menfolk at all?" The bearded one raised his eyebrows and peered at her through narrowed eyes.

"None, sir." She turned her head to answer him as they circled her, scrutinising her in such a way as made her feel very uncomfortable.

"I see no cross around your neck here, girl," said the

gaunt-faced man, his fingers icy upon her throat, causing her to shiver and her skin to crawl.

"She has no cross, but instead a wolf, 'tis said." The man's voice was as sharp as his features.

By now the girl was tremulous with fear. Upon the words: "She be our witch!" she almost fell into a faint. She felt herself swept up onto a horse's back, the rider's breath upon her neck, the movement of the galloping, and the swirling of the countryside feeding the sickness within her.

* * *

"A silver cross!"

"You like it, Mother?"

"Where did you get it, son? Come on now, tell me, Jed." The woman held the young boy's shoulders and looked into his eyes.

"I bought it. I bought it for you. You said you always wanted one."

"Darlin' Jed! Where would you get money to buy such a thing as this? We barely scratch a livin' from this little chicken farm – we've no money for ought but the necessary...a silver cross!" She shook her head and pleaded with him anew.

"Come on, Jed, there's a good boy. I couldn't wear the Lord's cross around my neck if I thought it wasn't honest come by."

"But it was, Mother. I earned the money, to be sure. A gentleman on horseback asked me if I could furnish him with some information. Well! I said I would help if I could. He asked me if I'd seen anything different around here of recent times."

"Different? What d'you mean?"

"Well, anyone new hereabouts. Or anythin' unusual."

"Well, there baint anybody new in the hamlet, is there?"

"No, but when I was up in the forest a few nights ago –"

"What was you doin' there?"

"Stalkin' a deer, that's all. Anyways, I saw a girl while I was there. I was just comin' out of the forest – I'd lost track o' the deer – too quick for me – an' I saw this girl, like I say. She was feedin' a wolf."

"A wolf? Are you sure? Folks don't feed wolves, they kill 'em."

"I know. But she was feedin' it. I just watched for a bit, through the trees. I don't think she saw me. Then I come on home, for it was gettin' dark an' I knew you'd be a-frettin' if I wasn't home before dark."

"True enough, I would've. An' you say this gentleman paid you?"

"He did. Two florins."

"Two florins!!"

"Enough to buy me a ride to Newtown and back to buy your crucifix. I knowed you always wanted one. Now you 'ave one."

"Oh, Jed! Jed! Well, I never! Oh, you *are* a good boy!"

* * *

The silence in the courtroom was deafening. Even those villagers of a garrulous disposition sat like statues on three sides of the room, their eyes fixed upon the four men at the long wooden table, as they confronted the maid. She was tied at her slender wrists and ankles and sat on a wooden bench facing her accusers, her heart beating violently, her face blanched with anxiety. The Meeting House had never before been host to a Witch Trial, and all but the very old, sick, or weak were present this day of the hearing.

"We are gathered here to do the work of the Lord. The accused, one Catherine Woods, is on this day of the sixth of June 1723, charged with being in league with Satan himself, through the vile and contemptible practice of Witchcraft."

There were gasps and murmurs from the assembled company.

"How plead you?" Matthew Greer leaned forward and the crowd turned their eyes upon the girl.

"Sir," she replied in a low voice, barely audible, due to the dryness in her throat, "I am innocent."

There were mutterings amongst the villagers.

"*We* shall be the judges of that," sneered Greer. "Let the questioning commence."

"With whom do you reside, Catherine Woods?" asked the bearded Master Tavistock, looking directly into the maid's eyes. The long, black lashes lowered a little, then she raised her eyes to him and said:

"I live alone, sir."

"Is it not unusual – nay, unseemly indeed, for a girl of eighteen summers to live without the protection of a husband, or some other male relation?" The sharp-featured Master Bayldon's thin mouth betrayed no sign of the pleasure he was taking in his part of the proceedings. He raised his eyebrows by way of reiterating the question.

"I have no parents nor living male relatives, sir. And no man has yet asked for my hand in matrimony."

There were murmurings of disbelief at the girl's reply, for there was no doubt that she was a real beauty.

"No man has asked to wed you?" Master Powell folded his fat arms and rested them on his paunch. He felt a frisson of excitement at the thought of his power over the young maiden, and he licked his lips as he added:

"You are asking this court to believe that a woman as...comely as you, has had no suitors?" The other three men on the bench shot him a sideways glance, but he continued:

"There are few in this courtroom today would believe this to be the truth. Is it your habit to lie, Mistress Woods?"

"If it is, I wish she would lie wi' me," called out a black-toothed man in a pair of grimy breeches, and the crowd laughed. A pang of humiliation like a shard of glass pierced the girl's heart. Her life was hanging by a thread through no fault of her own, yet she was being made sport of, the butt of a lecher's levity, and a crowd's entertainment.

Matthew Greer banged on the table, and stern-faced, demanded silence.

"How, may we ask, do you make your living, with no man to support you?" he barked at the girl, when the onlookers fell quiet once more.

"I make and sell wooden artefacts, sir," replied the maid, a tremble in her voice.

"What kind of artefacts? Speak up!"

"P-platters and bowls, sir. And spoons."

"Is this one of your...artefacts, Mistress Woods?" The voice had an insinuating edge to it; from his coat, Master Bayldon produced a small, carved object, and held it up to show the court. There were gasps and low conversation. He held aloft the wooden doll and spat the word: "Effigy!"

"No, sir, no, you are mistaken," replied the girl in great consternation, "it is but a child's doll!"

The noise within the courtroom had risen to such a pitch, it was necessary for Greer to shout for silence. As the sound of the audience subsided, the maid could be seen shaking her head in disbelief.

"From any other than a vessel of Satan, one may indeed accept the fact that this be a doll – but with the evidence I am now about to produce, it will be seen for what it really is! An effigy, fashioned with intent to practice the Black Arts of the Master of Evil!" Powell delivered the words in a declamatory tone, relishing the dramatic effect he produced on the assembled company, who were once more whipped up to heightened commotion.

The young girl sat stupefied. How had they obtained this doll? As yet, it was roughly hewn and unfinished. The last she had seen of it was in her cottage, on the dresser, awaiting completion, a toy for a little girl in a neighbouring hamlet. What had she done to deserve this treatment? It was a living nightmare.

"Let us have the evidence before us!" Tavistock's turn it

was to wield his power. "Irrefutable evidence exists, that this wench is indeed a witch! She has in fact, a familiar, with which she has been seen. We have an eyewitness! Call Jed Brownmoor!"

The court was in a state of high excitement. Jed's mother put her hand up to her mouth, as the boy, with some trepidation, took his oath upon the Holy Bible.

The young maid watched in horror as the boy stood before the court. A witness to witchcraft! No, it could not be! She was no witch, and wished no harm upon a living soul. How could this be?

"Silence! SILENCE IN THIS COURT!! Silence or I will have this court cleared!"

The threat had its desired effect, and a hush fell in expectation of the boy's testimony. The girl's heart beat with a strange, irregular rhythm, her breath was tight in her chest. She listened, wide-eyed and anxious as Greer's voice boomed throughout the Meeting House.

"Tell the court of what you have witnessed. Speak up boy. Go on."

Jed Brownmoor stood rather awkwardly, his eyes cast to the floor, then he raised them towards his mother, who, sombre-faced, nodded her encouragement.

"Well, sir..." The voice came out somewhat indistinctly, as though the boy was talking through frog-spawn.

"Speak clearly, boy!" Tavistock's tone and quick interjection were a clear indication that he was keen that the proceedings be hastened towards conclusion.

"Yes, sir." The boy cleared his throat and began.

"I was comin' out of the woods after stalkin' a deer – not with the intention of doin' it harm, you understand," he added hastily, for he was unsure if he was breaking any law by admitting his action. "I was just practisin' stalkin', like." There were a few giggles from some of the younger members of the audience.

"Silence," said Greer, and silence there was. "Continue."

"As I was comin' out of the forest, like, I caught sight of a girl."

"Which girl?" Powell said irascibly.

Jed Brownmoor's eyes went unwillingly to the lass on the bench. Her large eyes and mane of dark hair were raised and turned in his direction. She met his gaze and the look he saw there caused an unpleasant sickness in the pit of his stomach. He looked down at the floor once more, and with difficulty he muttered: "The lass on that bench, sir."

"The wench Catherine Woods? The Accused?" Bayldon's voice was charged with eagerness.

"Yes, sir." Jed Brownmoor looked into Bayldon's visage, and the sick sensation intensified. What had he got himself into? And worse, the poor lass on the bench? But now he was here, his testimony had begun; there was no going back. He had to tell the truth, he had sworn before God to do so. He looked up at his mother. There hung the silver cross around her neck.

"Well, boy, what was the girl doing that caught your attention so?" snapped Powell, keen for the court to hear Brownmoor's testimony provide the evidence by which he wished the wench to be damned. He salivated at the prospect, and spittle flew from his lips as he shouted: *"What was she doing?"*

The courtroom was hushed, awaiting the boy's reply. Jed Brownmoor almost jumped out of his skin at the force of the question.

"Sh-she was feedin' a wolf, Sir."

The gasp from the listening crowd had the effect that the four men desired. Greer savoured the words, and his mouth curled in wry satisfaction as he said in a low tone: "Feeding a wolf."

Jed Brownmoor nodded. He looked up imploringly at Greer's face. Greer nodded. "You may stand down, Master Brownmoor."

The maid felt a deep, nauseous anxiety creep upon her as

words and phrases from the crowd around her entered her consciousness.

"...a wolf! Some do have a cat..."

"...more powerful magic from a wolf, to be sure..."

"...no doubt then, she's a witch..."

"...the Devil's own spawn..."

Her head swam as Greer's voice again demanded silence, and she heard her name called out across the courtroom:

"Catherine Woods, I put it to you that the beast in question is in fact your familiar, and that you are guilty as charged of the practice of Witchcraft."

"Oh no sir, no, no indeed no! The wolf is but a friend, as are all the animals in the forest – I look kindly upon all God's creatures!" The girl's voice was desperate in its intensity.

"See how the witch is afeared, and even now would have the gall to suffer the Lord's name upon her evil tongue!"

The courtroom rang with the hysteria created therein. Over the noise, Greer's voice was heard anew.

"Silence, I say! Silence!! The time is come for the evidence to be weighed and the judgement pronounced!"

By degrees the courtroom once more became hushed. The four men sat still and grave as they faced the court. Greer then rose for the last time and addressed the village folk, his back straight, his face a stony grimace.

"The indictment: that The Accused, Catherine Woods, is a practitioner of the Black Arts, in league with Satan, and engaged in the heresy of Witchcraft."

The girl shook her head imploringly, her lips parted, her eyes filled with tears of sorrow and disbelief.

"The evidence," continued Greer, now leaving his seat and walking with measured step into the body of the courtroom. He looked directly into the faces of the villagers, his eyes burning into theirs, heightening the sense of his own power.

"Yes, the evidence. This woman, Catherine Woods, has no man as either guide or protector. But then, what need a witch for a protector when she has the power of the Black Arts at her disposal? The wooden artefacts she fashions are not confined to the tools of the kitchen and hearth, but extend to human effigies – I put it to you that the bowls she makes are the vessels of Satan, the spoons for stirring the witches' brews that aid him in his evil works." Some moved uncomfortably in their seats; they had purchased wooden artefacts of just this nature from The Accused – to be sure, in innocence, as useful aids for their households, but nonetheless...vessels of Satan! More than a few who faced Greer crossed themselves as he spoke.

"And then...then there is the question of the wolf."

He turned to look at Bayldon, Powell and Tavistock, who nodded their heads in grave agreement, a contemptuous curl to their lips, but barely concealed delight in their eyes. He returned his stern gaze to the mesmerised village folk.

"So many of you have lost your livestock to the wolf. Does this wench take the opportunity to rid you of this murdering beast? No, she does not. She feeds it, she nurtures it, to aid and abet The Devil in his evil ways. The wolf in fact is her familiar. *For she is indeed a witch!!* AND THE PENALTY FOR WITCHCRAFT IS TO BE BURNED ALIVE UPON A STAKE!"

Terror permeated every fibre of the maid's being. She was speechless in her fright, only whimpering sounds came from her, alien to her own ears. She was barely aware of the crowd upon its feet, the hubbub surrounding her as she felt herself lifted up, the bench underneath her falling with a crash to the ground in the frenzy; faces flashed by as she was carried along, their expressions in turn grim, contemptuous, leering. Old Josiah, Jed and Mrs Brownmoor stood apart behind the swirling mass, aware of their part in this most terrible of events. Their hearts were heavy in their breasts; the sound of the poor girl's own heart was thundering in her ears, before she fell into a merciful, black unconsciousness.

* * *

"Bless you my son," said Tavistock, dropping two florins into the boy's hand. "You did well in procuring the wooden effigy. You provided us with irrefutable evidence that this woman is a witch, and consequently have helped to rid the world of a daughter of Satan. The work of the Lord does not go unrewarded. Here are two more florins, as promised."

Jed Brownmoor looked at the coins and somehow saw not two florins, but thirty pieces of silver.

Tavistock departed to join Bayldon, Powell and Greer at the foot of the stake, which Greer had ordered to be built the day before.

* * *

The cheer that went up from the mob as the dry straw was lit brought the poor lass to consciousness. The smell of smoke below her brought the recollection of her plight into frightful focus. She looked down, and through the waves of smoke that would soon be choking her, she saw a smudge of black – the four men who were responsible for her persecution were watching with satisfaction, anticipating every awful second of the agony she was about to endure. She struggled against her bonds, but the ropes were tight upon her wrists and ankles, and around the wooden stake to which she was tied. The fear of the pain to which she would soon be subjected was greater than any she had ever known in her young life.

All at once came a dreadful sound – the wind rushing across the kindling – a hideous crackle as the strong flame licked the dry straw and leapt upwards, its heat intense – and she could not lift her feet away from its searing burn. Her tortured screams rent the air above the crowd as she foresaw the extent of the excruciating pain she was about to suffer when the flames at last engulfed her.

Then it happened. The watchers, as one, let out a cry of astonishment.

The girl appeared to be shrinking, diminishing by the

second; her arms, legs and head began to grow smaller, thinner, her body to contract in height and width. The ropes which bound her slid from her wrists and ankles. Her clothes fell downwards into the raging inferno, and in a sudden, rapid movement, she turned her back on the crowd and held fast to the stake for dear life.

The gasp from the onlookers was audible even over the sound of the flames. The long, dark hair now covered her entire body. Then came a shriek of amazement as the cat sprang up from the stake and over the flames to the ground below. Its speed was breathtaking.

It vanished from sight within seconds.

* * *

Blind panic had almost caused her Gifts to fail her.

Kit shuddered inwardly at the thought of what might have been, had she been but a few seconds later in her transformation; the events of that day had certainly taken their toll.

She lay quietly in the hollow of a huge oak tree in the centre of the forest, her tabby fur a perfect camouflage in the dappled light. She licked the pads of her hind feet in turn, the healing saliva easing the soreness of the scorched flesh, aided by a gentle breeze that lifted the dry leaves from the forest floor and danced them to a new destination. Her cat's eyes followed their progress for a moment or two, then she returned to the task of bathing the black flesh with the moisture of her pink tongue.

She would remain here until she was ready to do the work for which she was best fitted.

* * *

Tavistock, Bayldon, Powell and Greer felt cheated of their long awaited pleasure. The wench Catherine Woods had seemed the perfect choice for their desire "to do God's work" – a blasphemous cloak for their cruel appetites. Their anger at the turn of events they used to their advantage, vociferously proclaiming that their accusations had been correct, that it was now obvious to all who witnessed the scene that the girl was indeed a witch, snatched from the flames by Beelzebub himself, to continue his evil works.

Old Josiah had lived too long and had seen too much of the Witchfinders and their kind to believe such scurrilous tales. Convinced throughout that the maid was innocent, he thought it more likely that God, rather than Satan, had had a hand, and indeed that a miracle had occurred – though he wisely kept his counsel and told no one of his thoughts on the matter.

* * *

The night was sultry and the windows of the inn lay slightly ajar.

Silently the tabby leapt up to the windowsill of the ground floor, balancing on the slender wooden ledge with delicate poise. She measured her distance with expert ease and landed on the ledge above, outside the room in which lay Tavistock, his black beard rasping on the white pillow as he slept.

"A beard as black as his heart," thought the cat, and dropped quietly onto the floor beside the bed. The moonlight through the window cut a diagonal slice of light across the room, and she made for the triangle of gloom on the far side. Within its shadows, the cat began to grow, assuming the shape and face of the girl who had been known as Catherine Woods.

Upon a wooden table lay a Bible and Tavistock's black hat. From round her own neck whereon lay the brown velvet band, Kit lifted a small bird's feather, of which she had made a quill.

"It's blood you want. It's blood you'll have," said Kit inwardly, and pierced her wrist with the tiny sharpened end of the feather. She felt the blood warm and moist upon her skin, and dipped the tip into the dark, red ink.

Silently into the illuminated triangle she carried both quill and Bible. She opened the cover and wrote on the flyleaf of the Holy Book:

For the Lord your God is a devouring fire

Her slender, womanly figure was silhouetted against the soft glow of the moon outside the window.

Of a sudden, Tavistock stirred in his sleep and turned towards the window, momentarily opening his eyes. A wench! He opened his eyes again, and was about to raise himself from the bed; but this time he saw nothing. A dream. He turned over and faced the gloom, his eyes closing once more, and in a few moments slumber reclaimed him.

In the instant he stirred, Kit had moved with the speed of a cat, and had concealed herself in the darkest corner of the room, her sheet of dark hair further obscuring her from sight. She remained secreted until sure that Tavistock had returned to sleep, then quietly placed the Bible, open at the flyleaf, upon the table. She replaced the feather in the velvet collar, and in a trice was outside upon the window-sill, her silky paws made ready for the leap to the ledge adjacent.

Softly she entered the room in which Bayldon lay.

* * *

Her change from feline form was now effected with greater alacrity. The night's work was far from over.

Kit stood at the end of the bed, Bayldon's Bible lying heavy in her small, slender hands. She looked down at his thin, pinched features, and the pointed jaw sagging onto his bony chest as he snored. She felt utter contempt for this gruesome creature, the eager recipient of filthy lucre, paid to assist Greer in his dreadful career.

Taking the quill again to hand, she dipped it into a vein of her left wrist and wrote upon the flyleaf of the Good Book the quotation:

Cursed be he who takes a bribe to slay an innocent person

* * *

It was but a moment's work for her sleek feline form to enter the chamber in which lay the loathsome Powell. His corpulent stomach rose and fell with each breath, exhaled with a noisy reverberation of his fleshy lips.

Kit fought against a strong desire to leap upon the heaving belly and claw Powell's eyes from his head, sink her claws into the suety face and rip it apart, so it would never again taunt an innocent maid with its hideous leer. How violence does breed violence! She was not here to inflict harm, but to prevent it. She retracted her claws, and in the time it took to silently draw in her breath, she was a woman once more, her wrist oozing droplets of blood, her quill upon the flyleaf of Powell's Bible.

When she had finished writing, the quotation read:

Neither shalt thou bear false witness against thy neighbour

* * *

The architect of the depravity of June the sixth had retired to bed early that night, the better to be prepared the following day for his next planned atrocity.

The element of surprise he employed when accusing his terrified victim, and the consequent drama of the 'trial' in which she suffered publicly so much anguish, he relished as a prelude to the torture to come. Greer had lain awake for some considerable time, enjoying the thought of tomorrow's delights. He could almost smell the wench's fear, the scent of her burning flesh.

He said his prayers and went to sleep.

The cat's front paws set down gingerly on the uneven floorboard. She remained utterly still and silent for a second or two, as if stalking her prey, before the hind feet quietly touched down behind the front, and back arched, she turned her eyes upon the slumbering Greer. A ripple ran the length of black fur along her spine; she shuddered, her body and mind equally repulsed by the sight of him. She watched as he slept deeply. Man of God! A prayer would be blasphemy from those cruel lips.

Determination to bring to an end his contemptible practices caused a shape-change so rapid that Kit almost reeled at the speed of her mutation. She steadied herself and tried to control her breathing; her heart thudded so loudly she was afraid of wakening Greer with the sound. He did not stir, however, his hawkish face creased with aggression, even in sleep. What evil there lurked behind that cadaverous countenance! What sickness within that sinful mind! Hatred and loathing threatened Kit's ability to function – she must not give in to emotion, but think intelligently, control her movements...act like a cat...

Swiftly and silently she made for the wooden table opposite the window. The light from the moon outside fell on Greer's Bible, its gold lettering shimmering on the black leather binding.

She moved back the cover, exposing the first page, on which was written the name of the owner. "Matthew Greer" said the flyleaf, then "Holy Bible". She narrowed her eyes, pursed her lips and shook her head. The man could lay claim to the book, but never to its values.

The blood still pounding in her ears, Kit took up her quill. She turned to look at her tormentor, his eyes closed now, but their gloating look of triumph as she writhed upon the stake would never leave her memory. She almost cried out in pain at the remembrance as she stabbed the quill once more into her wrist.

He never moved. Still he slept on. Kit turned back to her task, the quill heavy with her blood, her eyes brimming with tears of anger. Her hand shook; she steadied it, and holding her breath, she wrote slowly and deliberately in large, deeply scored letters.

The quotation was both a pronouncement and a warning:

THOU SHALT NOT KILL

* * *

Of course it had not been the innkeeper. He was barely literate, and by his appearance had little enough blood inside him to keep him alive, let alone enough to spare for biblical quotations. Besides, he and his granddaughter had been called away to his old sister's house that night, as a neighbour feared she was dying. They had spent the night at her bedside, the neighbour keeping them company. Indeed the old woman did pass away, and the landlord, despite his grief, returned red-eyed and hollow-cheeked in the morning to fend for his clients. He found them to be somewhat perfunctory in their condolences. It was obvious they had other things on their minds.

It surprised the innkeeper that there were but three of the men at breakfast; the man they called Bayldon had departed without so much as a by-your-leave.

The other men had little to say to one another. The landlord supposed they were engrossed in thoughts about the day's business. A surge of grief at his own recent bereavement caused him to excuse himself after serving the repast. The men nodded absently, then one threw coins down onto the table. They all stared at the coins for a moment or two, considering the night's events, each thinking on the biblical quotation he had found upon rising that morning.

From whence had it come? They had all in fact spent the

night entirely alone at the inn. Though they would not vouchsafe each to the other what they had found, it was obvious to them all that some disturbing event had occurred to each one of the party; and clearly by their demeanour, none of them was responsible. Each was struck with the same fear; no other hand was present the previous night; it was inconceivable that Satan or his agents would quote from, or write upon the Holy Bible.

Surely this must be some kind of warning...from the Lord Himself? And was then the transformation of the girl into a cat some kind of miracle? Not a sign of Satan's power as they had proclaimed, but that of the Almighty? He who saw into the hearts and minds of men must surely know their motivation. For the first time in their lives, these thoughts pierced them like poisoned arrows. They sat in growing anxiety, as had their many victims before them.

Powell was the first to move. He made the excuse that he was feeling unwell – perhaps it was the heat which had built up over the past few days. The others, he was afraid, would have to manage without him that day; he would return to his own home until he was recovered. Without waiting for reply, he made his departure.

Afraid of what unearthly retribution would befall him if he should continue his association with Greer and his deeds, Tavistock muttered through his beard that since they were depleted in numbers, the impending capture and trial should be postponed. 'Postponed' was the word he uttered; and though he did not admit as much, in his mind the word he intended was 'repealed'. He rose from the table as he spoke, and bid a hasty farewell.

Greer was now convinced beyond a shadow of a doubt that a mightier force than himself was at work. He trembled in his very soul, and sick with fear, he went to his own room to retrieve his belongings. It was with tremulous hand and great trepidation that he opened the cover of his Bible once more. Perhaps...

No! The words were still upon the page, so deeply scored there was no doubt of the author's intention. His days as a Witchfinder were over.

Not one of the four men ever met again after that day. Where they went, or what they did thereafter remained a mystery.

The maid who was to be declared a witch on June the eighth mercifully never knew it; never knew how close she had come to ending her young life that very day upon the stake. She went about her business as usual, light of heart, for she was to marry her sweetheart in the month of July; she was sure that God smiled upon their match, and had had a hand in her good fortune.

Jed Brownmoor took his vows and became a priest. He never spent the two florins he had been given at the witch-burning, but kept them in a wooden box to remind him of why he had entered his vocation. He lived a long and useful life, a kindly and enlightened messenger of the word of God.

The last recorded witch-burning was in Dorloch in 1722; but the last ever witch-burning was in Witlock on June the sixth, 1723.

"Tell me about my father," the young Kit would say, as she helped her mother prepare the dough at the kitchen table. *"Tell me about your meeting."*

Her mother's eyes would twinkle, and she would smile as she retold the story of which the little girl never tired. She always tried to find new ways of presenting the tale, and Kit would listen avidly for any snippet of information which had escaped the telling on previous occasions.

"Oh, but he was a handsome one, was your father," said her mother. *"And talented too, he was. An actor in the company that performed Master Shakespeare's plays at the Globe Theatre. He could make you laugh, or make you cry – and he could terrify you too, if 'twere called for. He could play any part required of him – yes, even a girl's part, for he was so good-looking he could pass as a pretty wench upon the stage. And did on many an occasion."*

"What did he say when you met for the first time?"

Kit never tired of hearing the words, or seeing the years fall from her mother's face as she recalled in her own mind's eye the scene of that fateful meeting.

"I was passing the theatre door as he came out after the performance – he'd been playing Oberon that evening. Our eyes met, and he stopped right there in the street. He drew in his breath slowly, then said to me: 'Fair maid – nay, fairest maid – art thou in want of a husband?'

"Well, to be sure, it wasn't a question I had ever asked of myself – but I had the presence of mind to reply: 'I am none too sure, Sire, that I am in want of anything at present; but should I require a husband, I am sure that I shall come by one, for it seems to me that the world is not lacking in gentlemen in want of a wife.'

"'Indeed it is not,' said he fervently, 'for I am one of them.' Then he spoke in a declamatory fashion, as though performing the work of Will Shakespeare himself: 'So before thou shouldst come by any other, I wish here and now, good lady, to put my humble self at thy disposal – Nay! (he said

falling to his knees and bowing his head) - at thy feet –'

"'Kindly rise, Sire,' said I, as by now a large crowd had gathered, thinking this was a theatrical performance, 'since thou art in danger of gaining a hole in thy breeches, rather than a wife for thy house,' and the crowd roared with laughter, and he looked up and smiled impishly at me, and I looked down and smiled (encouragingly!) at him. Then he rose and doffed his hat with a flourish, and I curtsied, and the onlookers applauded – and needless to say, I had come by a husband and he a wife, for we liked each other so well, that from that moment on, we scarce spent a moment apart. We did of course marry, and lived happily ever after."

Then sometimes her mother would sigh, and Kit's heart would contract in pity for the sweet sadness her mother felt as she remembered the great love of her life – and the anguish of his passing.

For Kit's father had died of a cruel sickness which came upon him of a sudden. The fever took him, and grief almost took her mother with him. But as she had the two year-old Kit to care for, Bess had had to dry her tears, live on, and tend her offspring.

One day, in her thirteenth year, Kit asked her mother the question: "Did my father know you could change yourself into a cat?"

Bess widened her eyes in surprise.

"Lord bless you, no! For it was the Condition of my Bestowing that I never reveal to a human soul the nature of my abilities, lest the power be withdrawn, never to be used again."

"Did he never guess? He never suspected, nor saw you transform? Not even once?"

"Never, Kit. In order for me to pass the Gifts on to you, I had to keep the secret. It was the only thing I ever kept from him."

"I'm sure he has forgiven you," said Kit with a smile.

Bess smiled back. "I'm sure he has. He was a good man,

kind and caring. He would have approved the use of my Gifts for the good of humanity."

"Tell me of some of your good deeds, Mother."

"Good deeds are to be done, not talked about, dearest. One day you shall do your own good deeds, for I shall bestow the Gifts to you. The Condition of your Bestowing will be only that you use them wisely – and for Truth, Justice, and the Benefit of the Deserving. And I know in my heart that you will."

Bess stroked Kit's cheek.

"But all in good time, Kit. All in good time."

1815

Beech House was neither huge nor imposing, but of modest proportion and great charm.

The beech trees in the garden, from which the house derived its name, were of varying heights and colours; but the favourite tree of all who had dwelt there throughout the ages was the huge copper beech, with its red-brown foliage and sturdy trunk, towering above the rest, standing proudly in the centre of the garden like a huge goddess with a mass of copper hair. Many a scene of joy, sadness, laughter or grief had taken place under the shade of its magnificent branches; many young lovers had pledged or mourned their love under its protective arms.

But the scene taking place there one sunny afternoon in May 1815, was of a somewhat different nature.

"So, my girl," said Ludlow Hynde, grabbing one of the small, lace-gloved hands which lay delicately in the lap of the young woman sitting next to him, "not long, eh? Only a month now until you can proudly sport the name of Mrs Ludlow Hynde, Mistress of Marleigh Manor. And who knows?" – he squeezed her hand until she almost felt her bones turn to dust under the force of the pressure – "maybe soon after, the doting mother of the young Master Ludlow Hynde."

Bending his huge frame towards her, a grin upon his fleshy features, he winked a slow, knowing wink. She caught the smell of brandy upon his breath, and it was all she could do not to wrinkle her pretty face in disgust. She merely pursed her lips and looked down at the ground, a gesture which her fiancé took to be the feigned embarrassment requisite of a genteel young lady not yet embarked upon the state of matrimony.

He took his leave by standing up abruptly and calling over his shoulder as he left, that he would call again next week on his way to London, and thereby bade his farewell.

If Emily Boswell had ever felt more wretched in her life, she could not remember it. The thought of her forthcoming marriage to the boorish Hynde was frightful enough; his allusion to the fruits of marital congress was downright shocking to a young woman of her sensibilities, and she blushed violently at the memory of the conversation, and did her utmost to expunge it from her thoughts.

Sitting on the wooden seat under the copper beech, she felt in turn nausea and desperation at her plight, and inwardly railed at the state of affairs which had brought about this intolerable situation.

Her father, Marcus Boswell, since becoming a widower some years earlier, had found himself responsible for the upbringing of two young daughters: the elder, Emily, being named after her mother, the younger, Elizabeth, six years her junior.

A month or so before Emily's eighteenth birthday, Mr Boswell had received intelligence that due to freak weather conditions in West Africa, the value of his stocks and shares had diminished so alarmingly that he was on the brink of ruin. As Mr Boswell (already in poor health) was reaching the age of retirement, and would therefore be unable to support himself and his daughters by pursuing an occupation, things were looking decidedly grim; the house he and his family had loved so dearly would have to be sold. But where they would go and what would become of them thereafter, when the money came to an end, became a constant source of anxiety for the poor man.

Until that is, fate took a hand. Ludlow Hynde, a rich landowner, took a great fancy to Miss Emily Boswell and assured her family that upon his marriage to this worthy young woman, all Mr Boswell's financial worries would be at an end. As Mrs Ludlow Hynde, Emily would of course have an annual settlement at her disposal to do with as she pleased. Emily herself knew that this settlement would be just sufficient to support her father and sister and allow them to remain at Beech House, the home they knew and loved. This was Providence, to be sure! Mr Boswell no longer need fear that his children would be destitute in the event of his demise; with one daughter Mistress of Marleigh Manor, and the other now to be well provided for in Beech House, he was relieved and delighted that his problems were at last to be resolved as a result of his daughter's fortuitous match.

As for the daughter in question, there seemed to be no choice about the arrangement. To decline this offer of marriage would mean the loss of Beech House, and penury for her father, her sister and herself. So it was with inward reluctance and outward grace that she accepted Mr Ludlow Hynde's proposal, and the date had been set for June, which was then three months hence.

Miss Boswell's courtship had hardly been the stuff of romantic novels. During March, Mr Hynde's carriage had clattered up to Beech House six times. On each occasion, Mr Boswell tactfully retired from the drawing room where the family received the landowner, and called for Elizabeth to accompany him into the garden, the better for Emily and her suitor to become acquainted.

This arrangement suited Mr Hynde far more than it did Miss Boswell; for she was from the first uncomfortable in his presence, feeling that his physical proximity upon their initial meeting was more than a little too close, as his choice of seating was next to her upon the settle, rather than on the armchair which she had indicated with a graceful gesture of the hand, and a pleasant, if formal demeanour. As she had feared, their second encounter brought further uninvited intimacy, for he had taken her hands in his with a startling ferocity, and had by force of pressure kept them there throughout the entire conversation.

In fact, the word 'conversation' was not entirely appropriate for the occasion, as it consisted of a monologue from Mr Ludlow Hynde, the content of which was completely centred upon himself, his wealth and his land. His great achievement in holding onto the two latter in such precarious financial times took up the third of their meetings; by the fourth and fifth, Mr Hynde, convinced that he must by now have made Miss Boswell fully aware of her good fortune in his taking such an interest in her, decided that the question of the date of the marriage be settled by the end of their next encounter. On the occasion of their sixth meeting he proposed it in such a way as to suggest that he had indeed found her suitable for the post of Mistress of Marleigh, and that the date for the nuptials should be set for three months hence on June 20th.

That he found her 'suitable', Emily supposed, was largely due to the fact that she had little to say during their communication (in truth she barely had a chance to get a word in edgewise) for it was apparent that Mr Ludlow Hynde was seeking a wife who would afford him silent compliance in everything he wished. This was not Emily's idea of a marriage partnership, but she reasoned that it should not be too difficult to remain a silent partner, as she found she would have very little to say to a man like Hynde at the best of times. As to the rest...well, Emily shuddered at the prospect. Then she remembered the look of relief on her father's face at her betrothal, and let out a long sigh of resignation. The die was cast.

Thus it was that she found herself on this lovely May day in the position of saving the family home and becoming the future Mrs Ludlow Hynde.

* * *

Elizabeth followed her father into the drawing room, carrying a tabby cat in her arms. She put it down on the hearth-rug and stroked it gently. The cat leaned against the hem of her dress and gazed up at her, purring.

"Oh, Father, please? Can we keep her? She's so lovely. See how affectionate she is, and how she looks at you with those big, green eyes."

"She is rather sweet, Father, is she not? Such a beautiful

sound, a cat's purr." Emily leaned down from her armchair, putting her embroidery aside, and stroked the cat's silky fur. "Look, she has a collar – she must belong to someone. It has her name on it. "*Kit*".

The cat purred loudly at the sound of the name and Elizabeth laughed.

"Please, Father?"

"Well, until someone claims her, or she wanders off, I suppose you could look after her a while," smiled Mr Boswell, and Elizabeth swept up the cat delightedly and bore her off to the kitchen to beg some milk from Effie the maid, who was preparing the luncheon.

Emily and her father smiled at one another.

"It is to be hoped that Elizabeth will be kept amused for the better part of the afternoon; a most timely arrival from our feline friend," said Mr Boswell, "for Elizabeth finds sitting still and receiving visitors rather tedious."

"There is no doubt that she finds Miss Abbott extremely tedious," replied Emily, taking up her sewing once more. "Poor Miss Abbott. She has very little to talk about, having few friends, and no relations save for her nephew, whom no one as yet has ever seen."

"With regard to the latter observation," said her father, "the situation is soon to be rectified, for I am informed that Miss Abbott's nephew is visiting her at present; indeed the entire neighbourhood seems to be talking of little else. He is penniless, it is said, though he is a published poet. Poetry never was a lucrative profession – perhaps he should have become a lawyer instead. There are some, though, who doubted the existence of the young man at all, so long has Miss Abbott been chattering about him without his ever having made an appearance."

"So we are to be honoured with the presence of a poet in our midst," said Emily, finishing off her embroidery and setting it down on the table beside her.

"At two-thirty this afternoon, to be precise," replied her

father.

"Am I to understand Miss Abbott's nephew is accompanying her and taking tea with us this very afternoon?"

"You are correct, my dear. I took the liberty of inviting both of them – it seemed a kindness, for Miss Abbott is obviously very keen to show off the young man."

"Indeed, it was kind of you, Father," said Emily, rising and kissing her father's cheek. "I will change after luncheon and we will receive here in the drawing-room. I do hope the young man likes cake as much as his aunt, for Effie has been in the kitchen all morning, baking a choice of several kinds."

Mr Boswell tapped out his pipe and leaned back in his chair.

"Effie does not want to be outdone. She is determined that hers are going to be the best and most memorable cakes this poet has ever tasted."

Emily laughed.

"This poet has caused such a stir of interest that I hope sincerely he will live up to his reputation – and Effie's cakes."

* * *

Elizabeth and her new companion spent a most agreeable time in the garden, until the effects of the warm sunshine caused the little girl to become drowsy, and she fell asleep with her arm around the cat, lying against the copper beech in the garden.

Kit thought this a good opportunity to eavesdrop on events taking place in the drawing-room, so she eased herself gently from under Elizabeth's arm, and left her sleeping soundly in the shade of the tree. She padded softly over the grass, and sprang lightly up onto the sill of an open window, where she could see and hear all that took place in the drawing-room of Beech House.

* * *

Emily rearranged a stray lock of hair, and smoothed down the front of her blue muslin dress, as she heard Miss Abbott's high-pitched, breathless voice outside the drawing-room door.

"Dear oh dear, I do hope we are not late – we have had such a terribly busy morning in town, have we not, Edward dearest?"

The door opened and Miss Abbott bustled through as Emily rose to greet her.

"Emily, my dear! How lovely to see you again! I do hope you are well," and without waiting for a reply, she stepped aside, and with a flourish of her hand gestured to the young man entering the room behind her. "My nephew Mr Edward Dalton, the poet, you know. I think I have spoken of him to you, have I not?"

As Emily set eyes upon him, she felt her heart spring up into her throat, and then return to its rightful place, pulsing more strongly than she had ever known. Mr Dalton's blue eyes met hers, and he smiled. It was a polite and friendly smile, disguising the tumult inside him as he looked upon Emily's lovely face; the soft brown eyes, the blonde curls – such an unusual combination, such uncommon beauty.

Emily found herself going through the motions of polite enquiries upon the health and well-being of the visitors; seeing to their being comfortably seated; ensuring her father was also well attended to; calling upon Effie to serve the afternoon tea and some of her excellent cakes...and all the while, she was inwardly in turmoil, trying her utmost to appear serene and composed; inside, her whole being seemed to be consumed with thoughts of this devastatingly handsome young man, his thick, black hair, his even, white teeth, those piercing blue eyes...and a poet too! A man with a soul, a love of beauty, an appreciation of life in all its richness and diversity. And she was to marry Ludlow Hynde! A picture of Hynde leapt into her mind; his corpulent body, his fleshy leer, his balding head with the remaining hair in too-tight, tiny curls about the folds of fat upon his neck, his brandy breath, his boorish ways...

"...truly delicious!" Miss Abbott was declaring emphatically, waving one of Effie's creations in the air as she spoke through a mouthful of cake. "Effie has surpassed herself, has she not?"

A glance passed between Emily and Mr Dalton; his eyes were twinkling with amusement at his aunt's over-enthusiasm, and Emily returned the look, and smiled benignly at Miss Abbott's gesticulations, even though they resulted in large amounts of cake crumbs finding their way onto her blue muslin. Emily was far too well mannered to brush them off and embarrass Miss Abbott by acknowledging their presence, so she sat still and continued to make polite conversation, trying her best not to look overly much in Mr Dalton's direction, though the desire was intense. How she would love to converse with Mr Edward Dalton! How she would like the assembled company to disappear and leave her alone in the room with him...what *was* she thinking? She, about to be married, promised to another. Such thoughts were shocking, especially to herself.

Then she heard her father's voice, its tone designed to change the subject of Effies's cakes, upon which Miss Abbott had dwelt rather too long, "Emily dear, why not show Mr Dalton the garden? I'm sure he would appreciate a little fresh air on a day such as this."

"Indeed, that is an excellent idea, Father," Emily found herself saying, and she rose, asking Miss Abbott, "would you care to join us, Miss Abbott? The garden is at its loveliest at the moment."

Miss Abbott declined the invitation, saying she couldn't possibly leave Effie's cakes unfinished, lest it offended her after all her hard work, so she would leave the garden to the young people and would remain indoors to keep Mr Boswell company.

Miss Abbott never knew it, but she had never before made two young people so utterly delighted.

* * *

When Elizabeth awoke, she was disappointed to find that her new feline friend had disappeared, but since hunger was, at the time, stronger than disappointment, she made her way to the kitchen, taking care not to pass the drawing-room, as she did not wish to be seen by any visitors who might become desirous of her presence amongst them.

She entered the kitchen and found Effie preparing vegetables for the evening dinner. Effie looked up as Elizabeth peered around the door.

"Hello, Miss Elizabeth. Is it more tea as is required in the drawing-room?"

"I don't know, Effie, but I'm requiring tea. And some of that cake you made this morning too, for I'm famished."

"Sit down there at the table then, and I'll fetch you some. I made extra today, as I knowed Miss Abbott was comin'."

They both laughed. Effie set a slice of cake down in front of Elizabeth, and put on the kettle.

"Once that young 'un is in the kitchen," thought Effie fondly, "she'll be here until the cake runs out."

* * *

Neither Emily nor Mr Dalton could ever remember a more delightful afternoon. The sun shone, the birds sang, and as they walked and talked together, Mr Dalton admired the flora and spoke knowledgeably about cultivation. The talk naturally turned to Mr Dalton's poetry. (Emily ensured that this topic was introduced early in their conversation, lest they suddenly be arrested by being called back into the house, or by coming unawares upon Elizabeth, who would doubtless rather speak about pussycats than poetry.) Mr Dalton was modest about his accomplishment, but nevertheless promised to give Emily a signed copy of his book, and her delight pleased him so much that he almost allowed himself to feel that she looked more than a little kindly upon him.

Then they discussed poets and poetry they both admired, and Mr Dalton was exceedingly gratified to discover that they both shared a love of the sonnets of Shakespeare, Emily quoting freely and speaking eloquently about perception and metre and the music of the words. Mr Dalton's voice was soft and mellifluous, and his intellect was evident in his every sentence. He chose his words with care, and delivered them with sincerity, and Emily inwardly felt that he was a poet by nature, living his profession in his every word, movement and inflection of his voice.

Mr Dalton privately thought Emily to be the most beautiful, delightful, intelligent and cultured girl he was ever likely to meet.

In short, by the end of their sojourn in the garden, as they sat under the shade of the copper beech, they were, Kit noted with satisfaction from a branch high above their heads, very much in love.

* * *

A few days after the visit of Miss Abbott and Mr Dalton, Emily and Elizabeth went shopping for dress material in the nearby town of Maltham. Upon their journey home, the heavens opened, and both girls returned to Beech House tired and soaked through. A wind had got up, and as a result of the drenching and the inclement weather, Emily and Elizabeth caught head colds, and were forced to remain indoors until their health improved.

As far as Elizabeth was concerned then, the invitation to the soirée to be held at Miss Abbott's house the day after, seemed to be perfectly timed; for she was legitimately detained at Beech House through ill health and therefore could not possibly attend such an occasion.

Her sister, however, was not of the same mind. That she had the opportunity to meet Edward Dalton again at his aunt's house, and that she was physically unable to do so, was to Emily nothing short of a tragedy. What a dreadful misfortune was this accursed cold, come upon her at the worst possible moment of her life! What a frightful turn of events! To miss the opportunity of speaking to Edward Dalton; to forgo the pleasure of the sight of him, the sound of his voice – perhaps even the performance of his very own poetry, was too, too cruel. It was with a heavy heart that she took up her pen and replied to Miss Abbott:

It is with the very deepest regret that due to having recently contracted a heavy cold, I must decline the very kind invitation to your soirée.

I am sure, as ever, that it will be a most delightful evening (here Emily sighed at the thought of just how delightful it could have been) and I look forward to hearing all about it upon your next visit.

Please extend my best regards to your nephew Mr Dalton, and of course I send my best wishes to you, dear Miss Abbott.

Yours very sincerely

Emily Boswell.

Elizabeth penned a note in similar vein, which Effie delivered with that of her sister.

Miss Abbott was very sorry to read the letters declining her invitation, and while anxiously enquiring of Effie how the young ladies were faring today, passed them to her nephew to read. It would have been very hard to decide who was the more disappointed that Emily could not attend; Emily herself, or Mr Edward Dalton.

Miss Abbott, deeply engaged in conversation with Effie, did not notice that the Boswell's tabby cat had trotted behind the maid, and found its way to the windowsill of her nephew's room; nor did she see Mr Dalton himself secreting Emily's letter in his pocket, later to entrust it to the drawer in the escritoire in his room.

* * *

Emily sat at her writing desk, her head swimming. She had scarcely been able to think about anyone or anything but Mr Edward Dalton since first they had set eyes upon each other. She felt she must tell someone of her feelings or she would surely die of excitement.

Her chosen confidante was, as ever, her dear friend Lucy Anderton, whom she had known since her schooldays, and trusted implicitly.

So that night, in the light of her lamp, she poured forth her thoughts and sentiments onto the crisp, white notepaper, alone, save for the company of her little feline companion, who sat curled up close by, purring softly in the lamplight, a musical accompaniment to the sound of her pen, which flew over the page in a flurry of emotion.

"Dear Lucy, (she wrote)

"I cannot begin to tell you how I feel as I pen this note to you! I have never before felt the way I do tonight – there are not words eloquent enough to describe the mixture of great joy and agonising pain to which I am subject at this moment. For I am in love! Yes, this must be, since I think of him every second since first we met. His wonderful smile, his so-handsome face, his great soulful eyes of the deepest, deepest blue; his intellect, integrity and gentlemanly demeanour – oh, my heart almost bursts and tears well in my throat as I think on him.

"Of whom do I speak, dearest Lucy? None but the poet Edward Dalton, who walked into my life and changed it forever! The sweet and tender feelings he has aroused have lain dormant within me all these years, and yet they will now remain aflame my whole life long, for I know I could love no other.

"And yet I must marry the boorish Hynde to save my father and sister from penury! Every moment I spend with this vulgar creature is repellent to me. To think I must promise to love, honour and obey him, and spend the rest of my life in his dreadful company! The pain and agony are too great to bear, for with all my heart I love Edward, and I always will..."

Footsteps outside the door caused Emily to stop, and hastily secrete the letter in the writing desk drawer, as Elizabeth entered the room after a perfunctory knock, looking as pale as her white linen nightgown. She complained of feeling nauseous, and Emily, all concern, led her back to her room, and ministered unto her quietly and efficiently, so as not to rouse the remainder of the household.

Upon Elizabeth's request to remain with her, Emily promised that she would, and lay down beside her little sister, until eventually the nausea subsided and they both fell asleep. Elizabeth's dreams were sweet; but Emily's, which featured a certain Mr Edward Dalton, were sweeter still.

* * *

The next day, however, Emily awoke with a headache, brought on she assumed, from not sleeping in her own bed the night before; so her plan to finish her letter to Lucy was put in abeyance until she was feeling better. She spent a good part of the day on the chaise longue in the drawing-room, hoping that she would soon be relieved of the pain, but as was sometimes the case, it persisted, and she was unable to concentrate, and found reading difficult. Elizabeth returned the kindness of the previous night, and brought her sister tea and sympathy. But the pain in Emily's head was nothing to that in her heart as she thought of Edward Dalton, and her own forthcoming marriage.

* * *

In a pool of sunshine, the tabby cat lay on the pavement, sunning herself and watching the townsfolk go by. On the wall against which she lay, was a brass plaque which read *Messrs Bumbridge, Rattle and Wick, Attorneys At Law*.

The heat was quite intense, and through the open window above her, voices could be heard.

"A most pleasant duty, to be sure," said Mr Wick, perusing a letter, which he handed to Mr Bumbridge. Mr Bumbridge cast his eye over the contents and passed the document to the Junior Partner, Mr Rattle.

"It is not every day that the family solicitor has the pleasure of informing a young man that he is the beneficiary of fifty thousand pounds! You shall be the bearer of the glad tidings, Rattle, dear fellow. Mr Dalton is in fact residing with his aunt at present – er, a Miss Abbott. Here's the address, dear boy. The earliest we could spare you is this afternoon, for we must finish work on the Wigmore Portfolio as it is a somewhat more urgent matter."

Young Mr Rattle agreed, and said he would inform Mr Dalton later on that afternoon, and that he wished that *he* had an uncle in South Africa whose demise left him fifty thousand pounds the richer.

As the men chuckled, the cat rose from her spot by the wall, and padded purposefully off in the direction of Beech House.

* * *

Since Mr Boswell was sitting under the copper beech in the garden, and Elizabeth was keeping Emily company in the drawing room, reading aloud to her from a recently published novel, Kit was able to enter Emily's room unseen.

She took care to remain in feline form until she had ascertained she would be undisturbed, then upon gaining access to Emily's writing table, she effected a rapid change to her womanly shape, the better to purloin Emily's unfinished letter to Lucy. She folded the letter small, and slipped it underneath the velvet band upon her neck, smiling at the thought that stealing such a personal declaration would under normal circumstances be considered to be morally reprehensible. But the intention behind the action was of the purest nature. What a strange, contradictory world was that of the human race!

Hearing Elizabeth's footstep on the stairs, Kit resumed her tabby form, sprang lightly through the open window, down yet again to the sill beneath, and bounded off towards the house of Miss Abbott.

* * *

Though Miss Miller's maid Hester was not in Effie's league as a baker of exquisite fancies, Miss Abbott found her efforts tolerable enough, and had managed to partake of several slices of ginger parkin as she extolled to her hostess the virtues of 'having a man about the house'.

Miss Miller nodded politely and resigned herself to another hour or so of Miss Abbott's eulogy of Mr Edward Dalton, who at the moment, his aunt explained importantly, was at home, engaged upon the composition of his newest poem, having been solicited by his publisher to embark upon another volume.

Miss Miller contented herself in occasionally allowing her thoughts to wander to various divine hats she had spotted during her last trip to Maltham as her companion rattled on; Miss Abbott, of course, was in her element, and the cake crumbs flew accordingly.

* * *

Edward Dalton was taking advantage of his aunt's absence

and the consequent golden silence it afforded, and was engaged in considering the music of his second stanza, when, whilst glancing through the window, his attention was caught by the sight of a young woman, from whom came a cry of distress, as she fell with a thud to the ground outside the garden gate.

In a trice, the young man sprang to his feet, and before the count of ten he had run down the stairs, out of the house, and through the garden gate. He lifted the young woman up and carried her to the chaise in the drawing room, where he set her down in a recumbent position, placing a cushion gently under her head.

She seemed to have fainted, but was coming round, her eyes beginning to focus slowly upon the anxious face of her good Samaritan. As she became conscious of her surroundings and her benefactor, the girl let out a gasp and tried to sit up, but Mr Dalton would not hear of her moving until she had rested awhile and partaken of some food and drink – for it was apparent that she was weak from hunger, and only rest and sustenance would properly revive her. She smiled weakly, her heartfelt thanks apparent in the expression in her eyes, and Edward hastened to the kitchen to fetch bread, cheese and cake. The maid was not present, due to it being her afternoon off, when she usually went to visit her sister in Maltham, so Edward busied himself making tea and preparing a tray.

The gypsy girl, he surmised, (for it was evident from her apparel that she was of Romany origin) was evidently feeling the effects of the heat, and had doubtless come some considerable distance on foot, since there was no evidence of a horse or caravan nearby. Perhaps she was on her way to her encampment when she began to feel faint. How fortunate he had remained here this afternoon! – for today there was no one else here to assist the young woman but himself. How would she have fared if he had not stayed in his room to write this afternoon?

While thus engaged in thought and deed, he was unaware

that the gypsy was no longer prostrate upon the chaise, but was running up the stairs on four silent paws to his room, and upon transformation to human form once more, was depositing a letter upon his writing desk. It was folded many times, as it had been retrieved from under the velvet choker around her neck. She smoothed out the letter, opened the drawer of the writing desk and took out the previous letter which Emily had written, declining the invitation to Miss Abbott's soirée. She placed both letters adjacent to each other, then hastily took up Edward's pen, writing upon a clean sheet of his notepaper the following stanzas:

> *Compare the hand!*
> *For she who writes these both*
> *Doth only await*
> *That thou shallst plight thy troth.*
>
> *And tarry not!*
> *For it shall surely be*
> *That soon the winds will change*
> *And fortune smile on thee.*

With the greatest alacrity, the gypsy turned once more to silent feline form, and descended the stairs, unheard and unnoticed. She trotted into the drawing-room and sprang up onto the chaise, where within a second, she became once more a weary gypsy traveller.

Before long, Edward entered bearing a tray, which he set down on a table next to the chaise.

"Here now," he said kindly, "take some food and drink this tea. I'm sure you'll feel better with a little nourishment."

The gypsy smiled – a lovely smile, Edward thought, which lit up her tired face and lent a brightness to her green eyes.

"Sir, you are most kind. I cannot thank 'ee enough."

Edward smiled and waved away her thanks.

The gypsy continued: "I was, I admit, faint for lack of

food, for there is nowhere to buy a morsel between the towns hereabouts." She sat up slowly, then gratefully began to partake of the contents of the tray as they engaged in further conversation.

"Have you come far?" enquired Edward.

"Yes, sir," she replied, "I've walked from Kirkfield Town where my horse became lame, and had to be put down." Sadness flickered across her face, and a couple of teardrops fell onto her skirt. She wiped her eyes with the back of her hand. "He was a good horse. We travelled many a mile together. But such is life," she said, regaining control of herself, and smiling at Edward, who nodded sympathetically. "I'm on my way to meet my family, just the other side of Maltham," continued the young woman. "They're camped there 'till this evenin'. I've been a-sellin' pegs at Kirkham Town. An' I've done quite well," she said proudly, taking a bag of coins from the pocket of her dress, "so I may repay you for your kindness, sir."

"Oh, I wouldn't hear of it!" said Edward, aghast, "for if we cannot do one another a good turn in this world, it is no world to live in, to be sure."

"You have been most hospitable, sir, and I shall never forget it." She finished her food and sipped the remainder of her tea. "Perhaps then, you would let me return your kindness in another way, by allowin' me to read your palm for you?"

"You mean, tell my fortune?" smiled Edward.

"Yes, sir. I'm known for my accurate predictions. My family say I have the gift, bein' a seventh daughter of a seventh daughter."

"Well, indeed I should be most grateful," replied Edward, proffering his hands, though his action was prompted more by a desire to please the gypsy rather than to hear his fortune, for in truth, he doubted the possibility that the future could be told at all. However, the happiness on the face of the young Romany was reason enough for him to sit still, palms upturned, and listen to her attentively, as she studied the lines of his hands.

As she did so, her eyes widened momentarily in surprise, and despite his intellectual scepticism of predictions of the future, he could not help but feel a twinge of interest at the gesture, and wondered what had caused it. He did not have long to wait, for the young woman looked up into his eyes, and beaming a smile of delight, said, "Oh, sir! You cannot know how gratified I am to see that you have ahead of you such pleasure and contentment as you never would have dreamed of! For I see words – words from three sources, which will change the direction of your life, and bring you great joy."

Edward smiled his gratitude, but before he was able to formulate a suitable reply, a bell sounded, signalling a caller at the door. He rose and excused himself to attend to the visitor.

The gypsy was privy only to the first words she heard from the gentleman caller, who introduced himself as Mr Frederick Rattle of Messrs Bumbridge, Rattle and Wick, Attorneys at Law, before breathing a sigh of satisfaction, then leaping, tail held high, through the open window to the garden beyond.

* * *

If Mr Dalton was surprised and delighted at the outcome of his meeting with Mr Rattle, and the accompanying letter proving his good fortune, his feelings were as nothing compared to the indescribable elation he felt at the realisation that the handwriting on Emily's letter of declination to his aunt's soirée, and that of the many times folded letter which he found upon his desk, was in fact identical. The content of the letter made his heart leap with joy – that she loved him so was to him so utterly amazing and wonderful, that the thought of how all this had come about, and how the letter and the strange poem had arrived upon his desk, scarcely managed to find room in his mind, until he came becalmed, and began to think more rationally. With fifty thousand pounds and the love of his dearest Emily, he was, as the stranger's poem had prompted, now able to ask for Emily's hand in marriage, and bring her, and her family, the happiness they deserved.

How had such a personal declaration of love arrived upon his desk? This incomplete letter which had completed his own happiness – did Emily herself know of its whereabouts? How came it there? Who wrote that extraordinary poem, so very apt in content, so very urgent in its expression? Then there were the words the gypsy had used, playing over and over in his brain; words from three sources...three sources. Words from the writer of the poem; words from the solicitor; words from dearest Emily. The gypsy had been right.

The gypsy who, to his great surprise on re-entering the drawing-room, had disappeared, seemingly into thin air. Such strange occurrences! Perhaps the young woman, hearing that a visitor had arrived, had tactfully withdrawn, not wishing to further encroach upon his time. But then, she must have left through the open window! Very odd! However, many strange things had happened that day since her arrival. Maybe all of this *was* attributable to the Romany girl. But how? Edward could not fathom for all his intelligence, the answers to these questions.

He must not either, spend time in trying to do so, for as the words of the stranger's poem made clear, he must "*Tarry not!*"

* * *

Ludlow Hynde appeared more annoyed than heartbroken at his fiancée's end to their engagement, and (perhaps understandably) was one of the few who did not wave off the happy couple as they left Beech House in their carriage, to honeymoon in Italy.

In years to come, they would wonder at the extraordinary events which resulted in their marriage, but never ceased to give thanks that they did; for no two people lived more happily together throughout their lives than did Emily and her husband Edward.

Elizabeth, though delighted for her sister, was heard to say that she missed her very much, but that she would perhaps miss her a little less if Kit were around to console her; for since witnessing the wedding celebrations from high in a branch of the copper beech in the garden, she seemed to have disappeared, as no one had seen her these three months past.

"Never mind, Elizabeth dear," said Mr Boswell as they walked arm in arm into Beech House, "I'm sure we will find you another cat quite soon."

"Oh no!" cried Elizabeth. "I wouldn't want any other cat! There will never, ever, *ever* be another cat like Kit."

A picture of herself and Bess picnicking in a meadow, under the shade of an ash tree, sprang into Kit's mind. She remembered how their conversation had started, for Bess was recovering from an illness, and had laughingly said that it must have used up three of her lives.

"It's true, then? You really do have nine lives?" Kit said in wonderment, hoping that her mother was wrong about the illness, and that she really had her whole nine lives still left intact.

"So people say, Kit dear. But you know," she said, her eyes twinkling, "I must have had at least twenty-nine lives thus far, for have I not lived through two centuries? – and Lord knows how many adventures, all of which could have resulted in my early demise – but the secret of a cat's longevity, my sweet, is the use of one of the greatest of all the feline gifts – that of being in the right place at the right time. Some do call it luck – but I know it is an instinct, and one which has served me well these ages past. Aye, and others too. Trust your inner knowledge, Kit, and ask not from whence it comes. Just be thankful that it does."

* * *

Kit had had many an occasion to trust her inner knowledge and to be very thankful for it too; it never ceased to amaze her just how many gifts she had been granted, and she honed her skills until they were perfect, remembering her mother's advice to practice all her gifts, and never allow them to fall into disuse; for once lost, Bess had said, they would be exceedingly difficult, if not impossible, to regain.

Kit cast her mind back to one of the most difficult skills she had had to develop; that of changing from cat to human and vice-versa, with the added encumbrance of human clothing.

At first, she found that upon changing to feline form, she had to fight her way through voluminous petticoats to free herself from the female attire, which also resulted in the untidy problem of piles of clothing upon the floor. This of course would not do; to attract the attention of human beings in such a fashion, whilst engaged upon some mission, would result in discovery at some point in time.

To try to re-attire herself correctly, whilst changing back to human form, often resulted in clothes appearing to have a mind of their own, and turn themselves inside out, or back to front, as she transformed too rapidly for proper co-ordination. Indeed, many of her attempts were so risible, that oftentimes Kit knew not whether to laugh or cry at the fruits of her labours.

So the first few missions she undertook were at night, under cover of darkness. But whatever clothing she wore, her velvet collar never left her neck. It was an unusual velvet, in that it stretched and contracted to the size of her neck, whether she was cat or human, and to live one moment without it, she thought, would feel akin to missing a limb of the body, so much was it part of her.

As time progressed, Kit began to understand the nature of the problem of clothing, and how to deal with it. Instead of perceiving her vestments as matter existing outside of herself, she began to perceive any outer attire as being an extension of her own body, and as a result, was able to assimilate those extraneous coverings into her own body matter by the sheer power of concentration, before continuing her mutation to feline form. The molecular composition of the clothing changed as she exercised these powers, and the clothes seemed to melt from view, remaining a mental picture in her brain, to be retrieved and restored once more to their original state and position when she exercised the powers required to return to human form.

There were a few disasters along the way, such as the time when her concentration was interrupted and she became confused, resulting in a creature with the head of a feline, the torso of a woman and the lower body of a cat, wearing lacy bloomers, out of which stuck, incongruously, a tail. It was fortunate that the only witness to this fiasco was Kit herself, who was rehearsing in front of a mirror in her room; but the mistake served its purpose, to remind her that her skills needed to be completely perfected if she was to successfully achieve her missions, whilst keeping her identity and her secrets undiscovered.

She learned through many, many hours of practice that the secret of her skills was correct thought processes in conjunction with her bodily composition; mind over matter. Perfect mutation could be achieved only when the co-ordination of mind and body were perfectly synchronised.

Like a musician practising a passage slowly and carefully at first, and then with gradual and manageable increase of tempo, Kit developed her abilities, striving first for accuracy, eventually for speed.

Her delight at her success in her first perfect and rapid transformation was only marred by the thought that she wished her mother had been there to witness it. How pleased Bess would have been! How proud she would have felt at her daughter's success!

Kit spoke the words aloud:

"This one is for you, mother," and in a split second she repeated her performance, perfect in every detail.

1900

"Ay say, Ay say, Ay say; wot is the difference between a elephant and a Peeler?"

"Ay don't know. Wot is the difference between a elephant and a Peeler?"

"If you don't know that, ay'm not sendin' you to fetch a policeman."

To the sound of a glissando and a fanfare on the slide trombone, Lambton and Lowe executed their perfectly synchronised exits on one leg apiece and hopped into the wings at the side of the stage.

Winnie the Wigan Warbler was just arriving, somewhat breathless from the dressing room, ready to start her act, and was hurriedly putting the finishing touches to her wardrobe as she heard Fred, the Master of Ceremonies, beginning his long-winded and highly alliterative introduction to her performance.

"Well?" she whispered to Albert Lambton, as she yanked in unladylike fashion at the bodice of her rather too décolleté crimson taffeta dress, "what about the audience, then?"

"Two," replied Albert in a hoarse stage whisper.

"Mmm. Two 'undred. Not bad. An improvement on last night, then."

"No. Two."

"Two?"

"And one of them's the theatre cat."

"Well, I'll be...oh, oh, I'm on."

She swept onto the stage to the sound of her opening bars, and began to sing in a raucous mezzo voice the first line of her song:

"Parting forever, they tenderly kissed goodbye..."

Eddie Lowe scrumpled up his face and put his arms over his head.

"Oh Lord," he said, "she's done it again."

"What?" whispered Albert.

"Sung it in A Flat," said Eddie impatiently.

"What's wrong with that then?" retorted Albert, who carried a torch for the lovely Winifred.

Eddie sighed.

"The pianist's playing in G."

* * *

Three nights into the run of *Marston's Music Hall Magic*, things were looking decidedly grim.

Fred Marston had received a warning from Mr Tomlinson, the theatre manager, that unless both the performances and the takings began to dramatically improve, Marston and his mélange of Manchester maladroits would be given their marching orders. This was somewhat insulting to them, as most of the troupe hailed from Bolton. He slammed the door on his way out (making a more dramatic exit than had been seen for many a year upon his stage) and left the troupe low in spirits and high in anxiety.

"What are we going to do?" wailed Sophie the Salford Songbird, pacing the floor and wringing her pale, slender hands. "We can't change our performances at such short notice! It's taken young Henry *months* to manage the accompaniment to *The Soldier at The Fair*. I can't ask him to learn something else for tomorrow night. It really is too bad!"

"And I most certainly can't learn another Shakespeare monologue overnight," said Munro Pickering crossly. "I don't know what's the matter with the audiences in London. My 'Tomorrow, and tomorrow and tomorrow creeps in this petty place from day to day' goes down a treat in Blackburn. They've no soul, these cockneys."

"They've no sense o' humour, either," complained Eddie Lowe. "When we 'op off the stage one-legged in Lytham St Annes, they laugh fit to bust their guts."

"Oh, they don't have *guts* in Lytham St Annes," said

Sophie, wrinkling her brow and pursing her lips with distaste. "They're *far* too refined."

"You'd think at least my act would go down all right," sighed Marvel the Magician. "At least magic is universal. Folks are amazed by tricks the world over, aren't they? I mean, who wouldn't be surprised by a rabbit coming out of a hat?"

The others privately thought that since every known magician produced a rabbit out of a hat, the entire population of the world would hardly be surprised, but since Marvel was a kindly and helpful chap, no one liked to challenge his view, and they fell silent. The only sound to be heard was the purr of the theatre cat, as it lay upon Winnie's knee. She stroked the tabby's smooth fur, then broke the silence.

"Well, what do you think, Fred?"

Fred Marston scratched his head and then sighed a long, weary sigh.

"Well," he began, and as ever they all hung upon his every word, "...I'm stumped."

* * *

'MARLBOROUGH THEATRE' read the advertisement in the newspaper, 'CLEANING STAFF REQUIRED.'

Winnie curled her lips in annoyance. "Cleanin' staff!" she spat contemptuously. "Readin' that advertisement you'd think Tomlinson were goin' to employ a whole workforce rather than one old woman wi' a mop an' bucket. That old cheapskate would 'ave his granny doin' the job for nowt rather than dip into 'is profits." She crumpled up the newspaper and threw it into the corner of the dressing room in disgust, narrowly missing Kit, who was curled up on a nearby chair, her nose resting on the tip of her tail.

"If you don't start singin' in tune, lass, it might be you who wields that mop an' bucket," said Eddie, then immediately regretted it as he ducked beneath a flurry of blows from the irate Winnie, who reminded him that he'd better watch his lip if he wanted to be able to use it in tonight's performance. The others laughed, and having made her point, Winnie returned to the task of beautifying herself for the matinée.

Albert watched in awe as she preened and painted. The crimson taffeta was getting a little tighter (due no doubt to Winnie's fondness for cakes and ale), but Albert found no fault. He was exceedingly fond of the winsome Winnie.

"It's not surprisin', folks desertin' this theatre. The cleaner left two days ago in a huff, 'coz old Tomlinson wouldn't give 'er time off to look after 'er 'usband, who's poorly," said Marvel, shaking his head.

"Well, *I'm* not desertin'," said Winnie, applying the finishing touches to her make-up. "Not 'til I'm paid. Then I'll be out of 'ere faster than a ferret up a trouser leg." She swept up Kit as she rose from the mirror and kissed the tabby on the head.

"You're no deserter, are you Kitty?" she said rubbing the tip of her nose against the cat's velvety one. "You're always around to give us a bit o' moral support. At least we can rely on you."

Kit purred in agreement.

* * *

The following morning there came a knock on the door of Mr Tomlinson's office. It was not a timid knock, nor a perfunctory one, rather the decisive 'rat-tat-tat' of someone who meant business.

Mr Tomlinson opened the door and his tall, thin, frame towered over a slim woman, dressed in worn but respectable clothing, straight in posture and bright of eye.

"Mornin' sir. I've come abaht the position," she said in a brisk and businesslike manner.

Tomlinson raised his eyebrows, then nodded as he realised her meaning.

"Ah," he said, "the position of cleaning staff. Yes. Come along in Miss – er?"

"Mrs. Mrs McKittrick."

"Mrs McKittrick." He indicated a chair set in front of his desk, and the woman sat down and smoothed the skirt of her coat. Tomlinson took his seat behind the desk and leaned forward, peering at Mrs McKittrick through his spectacles which were perched on the end of his nose.

"I take it you have experience in this line of work?" he asked. "And of course a letter of reference?"

"Yes to bofe questions, sir," she said in a cockney accent Tomlinson recognised as being distinctly East End. She handed him the reference, which she produced from the pocket of her somewhat threadbare brown coat, and he read it, nodding occasionally, and then looked up and said:

"This seems most satisfactory. However, I must ask you if you have any dependants who may from time to time be the cause of your being detained from work. It is of course necessary, that being a public venue, this theatre must comply daily to a high standard of hygiene. I must be able to rely on a consistent and conscientious person to undertake the responsibilities of the position. Absenteeism is simply not an option, you understand."

"I do, sir. I understands completely. An' I 'ave no dependants. I'm a widder. No kids. I takes a real pride in me work, an' I've never been absent, nor late, not for one day, in any of the positions wot I 'ave undertook thus far." She pursed her lips into a tight smile, and nodded curtly by way of assertion, and Tomlinson peered at her closely for a moment before sitting back, clasping his hands and stating:

"The position is yours, Mrs McKittrick. The terms are as stated in the advertisement, so you may start with immediate effect and prepare the theatre for today's matinée. You will find all the necessary materials in the store cupboard next door. Now, if you'll excuse me, I have work to do."

He rose, they shook hands, Mrs McKittrick thanked him

brusquely and left the room, closing the door quietly behind her.

"Mm," thought Tomlinson. "I hope she's as good as she appears to be."

* * *

After the matinée that afternoon, the troupe was poring over the newspaper, reading the notices from the night before.

"What does 'ex-cru-ti-a-ting' mean?" asked Henry the pianist, whose grasp of the English language was on a par with his somewhat limited musical ability.

"I think it's something rude," sighed Sophie.

"It usually is," said Fred. "But I never cease to be amazed at the number of ways they can be rude to you in these London papers. You 'ave to 'and it to 'em, they're very inventive."

"Well they've invented our audiences right out o' t' theatre," said Winnie venomously. "An' if we don't get some folks in them seats pretty quick, we'll be fightin' wi' t' pigeons for t' crumbs in that there Trafalgar Square. I s'all be fadin' away to nothin' soon."

"We 'ad a good-ish 'ouse this afternoon," said Marvel encouragingly. "There were about six."

"Yeah. There were five an' the new cleaner in t' front row," said Winnie, "an' I wouldn't be surprised if the five weren't courtesy of Burke an' Hare. I've seen more life in a tramp's vest."

"Well, I thought you were all champion today," said Fred to his players, and they looked a little cheerier.

"An' so were you, Fred," replied Sophie generously. "There's not a Master of Ceremonies anywhere in England as can match you for nice long introductions."

"Wi' nice, long words," added Henry.

"Well p'raps things'll start to look up tonight," said Marvel brightly. "We've been through bad times before, an' we've come through 'em when we all pull together."

"Aye, that's true," said Winnie. "We 'ave. All we need's a bit o' faith, an' a bit o' luck. An' a few 'alf quarterns wouldn't come amiss, neither."

* * *

A few half quarterns later, the troupe returned to the theatre, to ready themselves for the evening performance, which Tomlinson had warned them would be their last if the audience numbers weren't up on those of the previous night. Despite the effects of the ale upon their spirits, Fred and his band of players were privately not so optimistic as their banter in the Marlborough Tavern made them out to be, so it was with stunned amazement that they stood in front of the posters outside the theatre which read:

MARSTON'S MUSIC HALL MAGIC
Retained by Public Demand.
Exciting new show.
Only a few tickets left.
Get yours now!!!

The clerk in the booking office confirmed the fact that ticket sales had taken a surprising turn for the better (since the erection of the new poster); it was just such a pity that old Tomlinson wasn't here to see it. It was his day off, and he was going to another theatre that evening, taking his wife to see the great Marie Lloyd.

The group headed towards the dressing rooms, wondering how this startling turn of events had come about, and were met by the new cleaning woman, Mrs McKittrick, who was putting away her equipment in the store cupboard next to Tomlinson's office.

"Evenin'," she said brightly.

"Evenin' lass," replied Fred, and Albert and Eddie touched their hats to her, as Winnie, Sophie, Henry and Marvel brought up the rear, and said hello.

The troupe wandered into a dressing room, still ruminating on the poster, which they were sure had not been there when they left after the matinée. So busy were they discussing the implications of the occurrence, that at first, they did not notice a familiar sound which had been absent for some considerable time – that of the hum of voices and the tread of feet as hundreds of people poured into the auditorium.

"Shh! What's that noise?" interrupted Winnie as the level of sound began to intrude upon their conversation.

They all stopped and listened.

Then a grin spread over all their faces.

"Sounds like music to my ears," said Fred.

"An' mine!" the others chorused.

"What did I tell you?" said Winnie, "a bit o' faith, a bit o' luck –"

Albert grabbed her by the waist and lifted her joyously and with the greatest of difficulty a full two inches from the ground.

"An' 'ere was me thinkin' it was the effects of the old 'alf quartern."

* * *

If the events of the afternoon had surprised the players, then the performances that night of 21 October, were a source of sheer amazement.

It all started with a boiled sweet which Mrs McKittrick offered to Henry the pianist as he waited in the wings, nervously clutching his copy of *Out in The Moonlight*.

He knew he shouldn't have accepted her offer, as he had oftentimes said to the others, that although he absolutely couldn't resist them, they often caused him to cough and splutter. Had he not been saying that very thing to his fellow players the day that Tomlinson issued his ultimatum?

Everything was fine at first as he sucked on his pear-flavoured sweet and listened in awe to Fred using long words such as 'chanteuse' and 'vocalising'.

Then it happened. He started to cough. And then cough some more. Then...oh dear, he couldn't go on like this – it would be impossible to play the piano in this condition. He began to panic. What was he to do? He backed further into the wings so as to avoid being heard in the auditorium.

Winnie's crimson taffeta was starting to advance into the wings on the opposite side of the stage, Winnie inside it, looking like Boadicea about to take on the Roman army. Henry broke into a cold sweat of fear. A huge audience at last, and Winnie without an accompanist! He dreaded to think what she would do to him. She was always threatening to turn him into mince and put him in a pie...

Suddenly, he felt the music being removed from his hand, and a voice in his ear whispered: "Don't worry, ducks. 'Ere, drink this water an' get yerself right."

As Henry coughed out his sweet and gratefully began to sip, he suddenly became aware of Mrs McKittrick tipping him a long, slow wink, and before he knew it, the introductory bars of *Out in The Moonlight* were being played with a dramatic flourish as Winnie appeared on stage in full sail and full voice. To Henry's surprise, she seemed to be singing in tune. He, and the other members of the troupe who were watching from the wings on the opposite side of the stage, stood gawping in amazement.

Mrs McKittrick was accompanying her.

Recovered now from his coughing fit, Henry craned forward and squinted as the cleaning lady's fingers flew over the keys. She was playing in A Flat Major, despite the fact that the music was written in G. Astonishing!

By now, Winnie was in her element. She was completely unfazed by the fact that her accompanist had apparently changed gender. She began to conduct the audience, inviting them to join in the chorus, which to everyone's delight, they did. A few at first, then more, until the auditorium was ringing with the sound of happy voices. Fred and the troupe were delighted at the way things were going.

But oh-oh! What was this? Winnie, encouraged by her success, was singing rather more loudly – and in a higher key. Henry could see Eddie Lowe's familiar gesture, his arms over his head, glee turning to despair as Winnie climbed into the key of A, leaving the audience, somewhat bemused, still in A Flat.

But Mrs McKittrick was not to be discomfited. Rather than have Winnie appear tone-deaf, up she went into A Major to join her, and thinking they'd missed hearing the introduction to the key change, the audience followed. Everyone was singing lustily in A, together once more. Eddie's arms came down again. The troupe, standing in the wings, holding their breath, relaxed.

Winnie was having a high old time. Quite literally. By now she was in B Flat; Mrs McKittrick masterfully transposed; the audience obediently followed. The excitement of it all sent Winnie into further flights of over-confidence. By the next line she was in the key of B, joined by her intrepid accompanist. The audience barely had time to access B Major before Winnie was in C, Mrs McKittrick close on her heels. The melody line was becoming increasingly difficult for the audience to sing, especially for the men, some of whom had discovered their falsetto voices for the first time in their lives.

By the following line, Winnie had raced through two more keys, Mrs McKittrick in hot pursuit, and the troupe in the wings was almost having a communal fit of apoplexy. But as the keys became ludicrously higher and the audience was squeaking a (by now) barely recognisable rendition of the melody, the sound of laughter began to be audible in various parts of the auditorium. Winnie took the tune to hitherto unknown heights, sounding like a mouse under the effects of helium. Mrs McKittrick went with her, and fell off the end of the keyboard in the attempt to chase higher notes than actually existed on it, and by this time the audience were hysterical with laughter, wiping their eyes, stamping their feet, whistling and calling "Encore!"

Never had they enjoyed community singing so much.

"Well, I take back all I said about cockneys," grinned Eddie. "They really do 'ave a sense o' 'umour."

* * *

When Winnie and Mrs McKittrick had taken their (quite considerable) number of bows and finally left the stage, Henry had joined the rest of the troupe who excitedly congratulated the two ladies on an astounding performance. They were all very surprised at the cleaning lady's remarkable musical ability, but she waved away their thanks and simply said: "I always likes to 'elp out if I can," and at the troupe's request, sat on a chair in the wings to watch the remainder of the performance.

Following Winnie on the programme was Marvel, who was considerably more nervous than usual. As it happened, he had good reason to be.

When he first included his 'disappearing lady' trick, the box with the false back seemed the ideal equipment for his illusion. The idea was that the lady to be 'disappeared' took her place inside the box in full view of the audience, Marvel closed the door, and while he was tapping his wand on the side of the box and saying his 'magic' incantations, his assistant would open the panel behind her, climb into the second chamber, and close the panel door once more. Marvel would then open the door to the box and reveal to the audience that the lady had disappeared. He would then close the door again and quickly turn the box upon its castors until the front door faced the audience. After more elaborate magical utterances, he would tap on the door, open the box and reveal the lady 're-appeared' in the front chamber.

Now this would not have been a problem were it not for the lady in question, who just happened to be Winnie. Sophie had initially been asked to aid and abet Marvel, but since she suffered from claustrophobia, she had to decline the offer. Albert and Eddie gamely put themselves forward for disappearance, but as Fred tactfully pointed out, audiences tended to like to see attractive young ladies assisting magicians, rather than decrepit old gentlemen. The chaps took his humorous remark in good part and suggested that despite Winnie opening the show, she could perhaps also appear in the following act and assist Marvel in his 'incredible illusion'.

Winnie agreed to help out, and up until August (it now being October) had managed to get herself ensconced in the required chamber at the required times.

However, between August and October, Winnie had had something of a struggle to effect these changes, since she had taken advantage of the troupe's appearances in Devon to consume copious amounts of scones, jam and clotted cream. As a result, what was at first a fairly tight squeeze became a task of Herculean proportion as she tried to accommodate her burgeoning figure to the small spaces between the panels of Marvel's box.

Since it therefore took longer to perform this miracle, Marvel's magic incantations had correspondingly lengthened, until thinking the magician had swallowed a Latin dictionary, the audiences began to get bored and restless, some even having the cheek to suggest that the lady must be having trouble finding her way through the false panel at the back of the box.

On the last rehearsal, Winnie had become wedged in so tightly that Marvel feared they may require the services of a joiner to free her, and Winnie complained her bosom would never be the same again.

This statement concerned Albert so much he thought the worry might rob him of the few hairs he had remaining on his head, so he suggested that perhaps young Henry should don a frock and replace Winnie immediately.

Henry, despite his usually cheerful and willing nature, was

none to keen, especially on the idea of having to wear a wig and make-up, but Fred gave his "we must all pull together, lad" speech, and Henry reluctantly agreed to save Winnie's bosom, and the audience from rioting.

So it was that Marvel stood anxiously, and Henry stood miserably, in the wings, wearing a frock several sizes too large for him, a couple of grapefruit arranged in the appropriate parts of the bodice, and his face painted very girlishly and rather garishly.

Eddie suggested that he'd better not leave the theatre in that get-up lest Jack the Ripper catch sight of him, a remark which did nothing to alleviate Henry's anxiety.

"They'll know I'm not a woman," whispered Henry agitatedly. "Supposin' me grapefruit fall out. I'll be a laughin' stock."

"Well if they do, we'll try melons tomorrow," whispered Albert back to him. "Come on lad, it'll not be that bad."

"It will," said Henry. "I might get whistled at."

"You won't," replied Albert. "You're not that beautiful. Grit your teeth and think of England."

Henry looked as if he might burst into tears. Then a voice spoke up from the chair in the darkness.

"Sit down 'ere, 'Enry."

Henry suddenly felt himself descending onto a wooden seat, and before he or anyone knew what was happening, Mrs McKittrick was on stage curtseying to the audience as Marvel, as surprised as the rest of the players, found himself introducing his 'lovely new assistant'.

As she entered the box, Mrs McKittrick whispered to Marvel, "I'm real quick, ducks. Two taps'll do it."

Marvel, still somewhat astounded at this unexpected occurrence, closed the door after her, tapped twice, and before he could utter his incantation, the door flew open and the audience let out a cry of surprise.

For there in the box sat a tabby cat.

No one was more astounded than Marvel. How had the

theatre cat got into the box? And where was Mrs McKittrick? Stunned, he shut the door, but no sooner had he done so than it flew open once more, and there stood Mrs McKittrick smiling benignly at the audience. She stepped forward onto the stage and bowed.

"Bravo! Encore!" There were calls and whistles and applause such as Marvel had never heard. But he was not awfully sure he was pleased to hear it. How could the illusion be repeated? The cat would hardly allow itself to be kept in that box simply to please an audience. It was likely to wander off anyway, next time it appeared. Mrs McKittrick was right though. She was "real quick".

As these thoughts raced through his head, he heard Mrs McKittrick's voice whispering to him: "Do it again, ducks. They wants an encore."

She stepped inside the box once more, and Marvel, his heart in his mouth, raised his wand and tapped the box. Instantaneously the door flew open and there was the tabby, standing upright on its back legs, its hind paws in Mrs McKittrick's shoes.

The audience went wild with delight. Marvel stood rooted to the spot. Then he heard Fred's voice from the wings in a hoarse whisper: "Shut the door, lad before it escapes!"

Marvel obeyed and slammed closed the door of the box. No sooner had he done so, than it flew open again, and there stood Mrs McKittrick, smoothing down her frock. By now the audience was on its feet, cheering and stamping. Mrs McKittrick stepped down out of the box and took the stunned Marvel by the hand.

"Bow," she said to him as the applause grew stronger. "On the count o' three. One, two..."

They bowed. The audience whooped and whistled. Mrs McKittrick led Marvel off the stage and into the wings, where the troupe patted them on the back and congratulated them on a hugely impressive performance.

"Just a sec," said Mrs McKittrick, and walked back onto

the stage, to the delight of the audience, where she pushed the magic box on its castors into the wings on the other side of the stage. A moment or so later, she returned to the stage and the cheering audience, beckoning Marvel to join her from where he stood with the others. He did so, and they bowed once again, the applause almost deafening them. They returned to the troupe in the wings, their excited voices chattering over the sound of the crowd in the auditorium.

"How did you do that so quick?" asked Winnie in awe. "You'd barely time to open the back panel!"

"Nimble feet, nimble fingers, dearie. I've spent me life goin' in an' out o' cupboards."

"And the cat!" said Sophie, shaking her head in disbelief. "How did you get the cat to –"

"Oh, me, I've got a way wif cats," replied Mrs McKittrick. "That there tabby is very biddable. I've jus' give 'er some fish in the wings over there, an' she's 'appy as a sandboy. She'll be off mousin' somewhere by now, I expect. Good luck to 'er, I say. Come on, Mr Pickerin', it's your turn now."

* * *

As the theatre cat, Kit enjoyed a few perks; lots of attention from the artistes (and occasionally even the manager); a warm, dry home (with lots of titbits to be found) and of course, she was able to see the performances free of charge.

Thus it was that prior to this extraordinary evening, she had shared the auditorium one matinée with five members of the public, who, having little else to do (and possibly because it was raining heavily outside) decided to give *Marston's Music Hall Magic* a chance to prove their worth. They had presumably not read the reviews in last night's paper, or they surely wouldn't have parted with their hard-earned cash, but there they were anyway, and the performances had rolled on (at first with little response on the part of the audience, it must be said) until it was time for Munro Pickering's Shakespearean monologue.

Now Munro, somewhat shaken by Mr Tomlinson's vociferous ultimatum, had partaken, that day, prior to the afternoon performance, a quantity of brandy to calm his nerves, something he was, it has to be admitted, not usually wont to do, his mother and father being members of the local Temperance organisation; so it was with difficulty he rambled through his speech that matinée, the brandy hazing his brain and slurring his speech.

Mr Pickering's broad Lancashire accent was, to say the least, at variance with the pronunciation of the Queen's English as usually employed by a performer of the Great Bard, and the London audiences were decidedly taken aback at his rendition of his chosen speech from *Macbeth*. His undoubted enthusiasm for the words of Shakespeare was unfortunately not matched by his understanding of them. In fact, Munro had a disconcerting habit of accentuating words and syllables which entirely altered Mr Shakespeare's original meaning. He wasn't averse either, to rearranging the punctuation if he felt (incorrectly) that he could effectively maximise the drama of the text.

"Tewmorror, (pause) and tewmorror, (longer pause) "and tewmorror, he intoned. "Creeps in this petty plairce, from dair to dair, 'til the last syll*a*ble of *recorded* time."

This left the audience perplexed, pondering on what sort of time *un*recorded time was, and thereby missing the content of the following lines whilst they did so.

As Munro executed (indeed murdered) his speech, Kit watched in astonishment, and wondered what her father, who had 'trod the boards' at the Globe Theatre, would have made of all this.

Suddenly there was a longer silence. It was apparent that Munro had forgotten his lines, the brandy by now having affected his memory too.

Then he continued.

"It droppeth as the gentle rairn from 'Eaven, upon the plairce beneath."

"Oh for goodness sake," hissed Fred in the wings. "'E's in the wrong ruddy play."

The audience noticed it too.

"My good man," said a voice from the auditorium, "since when did Portia appear in *Macbeth*? Surely that quotation is from *The Merchant of Venice*?"

There was a titter amongst the watchers. Munro rocked gently on his unsteady feet and tried to focus upon whence the voice had come. He peered into the auditorium and tried to grasp from his befuddled brain, at any bits of Shakespeare which floated by in the alcoholic haze. He drew himself up to his full height of five feet two inches, took a deep breath, and raised his fist in the air.

"Cry 'avoc!" he yelled in declamatory (and somewhat defiant) fashion. "An' let slip the dogs o' war!"

"My good man," replied the same voice from the darkness, and the laughter from the others in the audience evidently gave the stranger confidence, for he continued: "I don't remember there being a tremendous number of dogs in *Macbeth*."

Guffaws followed this speech and Munro began to be visibly rattled. A heckler, eh? He was having none of that.

"My good man," he replied slowly and pompously, "I 'appen to be exceedingly fond o' dogs, and I shall insert them – in very large quantities should I so desire, wherever I ruddy well wish."

As he spoke, he narrowed his eyes, wagged his finger threateningly at the heckler, then passed out and fell head first into the orchestra pit.

"Oh no!" wailed the troupe as one.

"It's time to take action," thought Kit.

* * *

Kit felt that what Mr Pickering needed was material which

was more suited to his (very) individual style; something which he understood, the content of which would be more familiar to his own experience.

So after the troupe had returned to their lodgings and the theatre was dark and quiet, Kit transformed herself once more to human form, and at midnight, by the light of a candle, Mrs McKittrick could be seen scribbling furiously away, piling sheet upon sheet as she gathered momentum, until finally, she penned a message which she pinned to her poem. It read:

Dear Mr Pickering,

I have long been an admirer of your sonorous and colourful voice, and have written a narrative poem especially for you.
I hope you will feel that it does justice to your undoubted and individual talents. I would indeed be highly honoured if you could see your way to including it in one of your performances.
In hopeful anticipation,
yours very sincerely,

An Anonymous Well-wisher

Kit sealed the poem and the note inside an envelope and addressed it to 'Munro Pickering Esquire'. Then she dropped it on the floor and trod on it a bit, to make it look as if it had been pushed under the theatre door from outside; then satisfied with her night's work, she put the envelope in the pocket of Mrs McKittrick's apron, and in a trice was the theatre cat again, curled up in the chair in the theatre wings.

* * *

The following morning, when the troupe arrived, Mrs McKittrick was humming a tune and sweeping merrily away.

She stopped as they entered and wished them good day.

"Oh, by the way, guv," she said to Munro, foraging in the pocket of her apron, "this 'ere came for you. It was on the floor when I arrived this mornin'."

"Oh! Thank you most kindly, Mrs Mac," replied Munro, removing his hat and taking the letter from her outstretched hand.

"Yes, it's addressed to me all right. I wonder who it's from?"

"Dunno, guv," said Mrs McKittrick, shrugging her shoulders and resuming her sweeping. "There's only one way to find aht, ain't there? Open it up an' see."

* * *

So it was, that as Mrs McKittrick and the players watched from the wings on the night of October 21st, they witnessed the first performance of the narrative poem which was to make Munro Pickering famous.

"I would like to perform for you tonight," Munro told the audience proudly, "a poem, written especially for me, entitled *The Ballad o' t' Brathwaites o' Bury*."

He cleared his throat, took a deep breath and in sonorous and colourful Lancastrian tones, delivered the poem with wonderful characterisation, drama, humour, and an immaculate sense of phrasing and timing.

"The Braithwaites they lived up in Bury
They 'adn't no bairns o' their own,
So they made do wi' dog, cat an' budgie
To stop 'em from feelin' alone.

To Nora, the cat were the favourite,
For Tess were 'er baby, 'tis true;
While Sam favoured Billy, the bulldog
Wi' 'is face like a pot o' cold stew.

The budgie, Bert, sang an' he chirruped;
(Came out wi' a choice word or three),
'Til Tess, very vexed at his language
Decided to 'ave 'im fer tea.

Owd Sam, 'ome from work that dark Monday,
Saw feathers an' bones on the floor;
So 'e lifted 'is foot an' 'e booted
Poor Tessie right out through the door.

So Nora, distraught an' in tears
Felt now that the future were bleak
Afeared that 'er baby 'ad left 'er,
She took to 'er bed fer a week.

In t' meantime, owd Sam an' t' dog, Billy
'Ad ter fend fer 'emselves every day;
Sam's cookin' were so ruddy awful
By t' weekend, t' dog faded away.

Now Sam, 'e were fond of a tipple
('E drank too much brass, Nora said)
But now 'e'd a reason fer drinkin':
'Is poor little doggie were dead.

'Is wallet 'e kept in 'is greatcoat;
'Is brass, Nora said, seldom viewed –
'E kept all 'is money well 'idden
In a pocket-book, dog-eared an' chewed.

When Sam set 'is eyes on this wallet,
Wi' memories it were imbued
O' Billy, his dear, ugly face; in 'is mouth
The pocket-book, dog-eared an' chewed.

So Sam staggered out o' 'The Nag's 'Ead',
Stayed drunk on the pavement all night;
'Twas only t' next day 'e discovered
'Is pocket-book gone! What a fright!

'Ow was 'e to break t' news to Nora?
They 'adn't a penny, fer sure;
An' when she 'ad 'eard 'e'd been drinkin',
She'd boot *'im* right out through the door.

So lookin' abashed an' all 'ang-dog,
'E tottered back to 'is abode
A-clutchin' some battered owd dahlias
'E'd snaffled from t' boneyard up t' road.

'E entered the bedroom; 't were gloomy –
The bedclothes wuz all of a mess;
An' Nora sat up, an' 'er eyes wuz all red
From cryin', 'coz she'd lost 'er Tess.

"I've brung yer these, Nora," said Sammy,
A-shovin' the flowers in 'er face;
"Why, what've yer done?" replied Nora,
"Yer do look a ruddy disgrace."

Before a reply Sam could muster,
There came a soft footstep instead;
An' to Nora's greatest surprise an' delight
'Er Tessie jumped onto the bed.

As Nora an' Tessie they cuddled an' purred,
Sam's jaw dropped, 'is eyes on 'em glued;
Fer there in the cat's mouth, the notes still inside,
Were 'is pocket-book, dog-eared an' chewed.

"That cat's saved me skin," thought Sam, "there's no

doubt –
An' I laid its life on the line!
I'll buy it a ruddy big fish an' some lamb –
But Nora can cook it this time."

An' so Sam an' Nora wuz 'appy once more,
An' Tess got 'er fish an' 'er lamb;
Eventually Sam got another dog, too:
A female, a bulldog called Pam.

O' Sam's drunken night on the pavement, an' loss
Of 'is wallet, 'is wife never knew;
She thought 'e 'ad found 'er dear Tess, an' was glad
They'd begun their old friendship anew.

An' Sam to this day simply cannot explain,
An' still on the mystery does brood
O' where an' 'ow Tess 'ad so cleverly retrieved
'Is pocket-book, dog-eared an' chewed."

The appreciative laughter throughout the theatre, the roar of applause and the standing ovation at the final cadence were enough to convince Munro Pickering that his days of reciting Shakespeare were finally at an end.

* * *

Thus it was that the fortunes of the members of *Marston's Music Hall Magic* began to take a turn for the better.

The audiences were much more disposed to laugh at the antics of Albert and Eddie, having been put in the mood for humour by Winnie, and Munro Pickering. Even Henry's abysmal piano playing was taken as part of the fun, and the following day, on the 22 October, Tomlinson, amazed at the sudden upturn in the box-office takings, decided to keep the troupe on. They were all delighted, and Mrs McKittrick said she (and the cat) would help them out to the end of their run, which was a fortnight hence.

Tomlinson agreed to get another cleaner to help out Mrs McKittrick in the meantime, so that she could get some time off, since she was now appearing in the theatre as well as cleaning it. He also agreed, at the behest of Fred and the troupe, to pay Mrs McKittrick her full cleaner's wage, plus a little extra, since she was largely responsible anyway for the improvement in all their fortunes.

So each night, things got better and better. The players, flushed with success (and better notices too), imbued their performances with vigour and creativity, adding little things here and there (some indeed suggested by the redoubtable Mrs McKittrick), which made them more interesting, altogether tighter, and more professional. And the audiences continued to attend and to enjoy.

There was only one act everyone inwardly felt could be improved, and that was Henry and Sophie performing *The Soldier at The Fair.*

Actually, there was absolutely nothing wrong at all with Sophie's singing. Indeed it was very pretty, her voice clear, bell-like and tuneful, her rendition sweet and faultless.

No, the problem decidedly lay with the conscientious, but seemingly unmusical Henry, whose mechanical and pedestrian execution of the accompaniment killed the performance stone dead.

Matters were not helped by the fact that once his right foot made contact with the sustaining pedal, the liaison became dangerously intense, so that the foot and the pedal were loathe to part company, and the resulting cacophony of muddied harmonies made it exceedingly difficult for Sophie to tell whether they were both in the same song, let alone the same verse.

Fred politely suggested that Henry should perhaps leave the pedalling out, and just concentrate on his fingers, rather than his feet, a suggestion which Henry accepted somewhat reluctantly. He did, after all, rather like to look like a 'real' pianist. The effect of consigning the pedal to history was to make *The Soldier at The Fair* sound like a military march-past, and the poignancy of the lyrics was entirely lost in the over-accentuation of the first beat of each bar, as Henry tried to keep rigidly to the pulse. The overall effect was of a strong man in a bad temper, hammering the living daylights out of an anvil.

So Sophie's affecting rendition disappeared under the enthusiastic clunk of Henry's ham-fisted chord-bashing, and there was little anyone could do to improve matters, since no one would think of upsetting the lad, whose dedication to his part of the proceedings was downright touching.

Kit sat on Sophie's knee, Sophie stroking her fur delicately, and listened to the conversation of Fred and his troupe, as they waited for Henry to come back from an errand to buy Winnie some violet creams.

"'E's *such* a sweet boy," sighed Sophie. "

"It's just such a shame his playin' doesn't match 'is personality," said Eddie.

Arthur nodded. "Listenin' to 'im playin's like bein' 'it on the 'ead by a fryin' pan thirty times a minute."

"Well, I promised 'is mam I'd tek 'im on," said Fred. "I owed 'er a favour, so we've got young 'Enry, an' there's an end to it."

"We'll just 'ave ter do us best, an' 'ope 'e'll get better as time goes on."

"It'd tek some kind of a miracle," said Eddie.

"Then I'll just have to see what I can do," thought Kit.

* * *

It was Henry's wont to turn up well ahead of time, before the others arrived, and practice assiduously.

It was heart-rending to watch the young fellow as he carefully took his yellowing copy of *The Soldier at The Fair* out of his leather music case, handling it as if it were made of gossamer, and carefully and lovingly place it upon the music stand. Then he would sit down upon the stool, moving it quietly into position, make himself comfortable, and drop his arms down by his side, relaxing them as he had seen many a fine pianist do, before they began to play.

For all the world, to see this prelude to his performance, one would have thought that when he touched the keys, the magic in his soul would draw from the ivories the sweetest sounds upon God's earth.

But the ensuing din that emanated from the instrument, the soulless thunderings reverberating inside the rosewood casing soon dispelled any such expectation in the listener. How strange that such care and dedication should produce so dire a result!

At the end of one such practice session, Mrs McKittrick, wielding her broom, wandered out upon the stage.

"Ooh, sorry ter bovver yer, guv," she said hastily, and made as if to take her sweeping elsewhere.

"Oh, it's quite all right," replied Henry, gallantly, "I've finished, anyway."

Mrs McKittrick smiled. Henry smiled.

"'Ere, guv, can I ahsk yer somefink?" she said suddenly.

"Ask away," said Henry brightly.

"D'yer fink," – here she bit her lip, then continued as if gaining a little confidence – "do yer fink yer could play that there song again, an' let me sing it wiv yer?"

Henry was flattered.

"Of course I could, Mrs Mac. Come on over."

Mrs McKittrick leant her broom against the wall of the proscenium arch and hastened over to the piano.

"I've always fancied singin' this song on a real stage, in a real theatre, like a real Music 'All lady. Yer'd be doin' me a real favour if yer wuz ter accompany me. It'd kind o' make me dream come true, if yer know what I mean."

"Oh, I do," said Henry, "an' I'd be glad to 'elp you make

your dream come true, Mrs Mac."

He sat down at the keyboard, and Mrs McKittrick took her place centre stage, cutting an extraordinary figure in her plain frock and apron, yet by the way she held herself, every inch a Music Hall diva.

Henry thumped out the introduction and Mrs McKittrick began to sing. Her voice was truly beautiful, and Henry felt proud to be part of such a lovely performance as he hammered and banged away at the keys.

At the end of the song, Mrs McKittrick and Henry applauded one another.

Then Mrs McKittrick went over to the piano and said: "'Ere, 'Enry. Why don't we do it again? Let's do it a bit different this time. Say this time yer play this bit 'ere" – she pointed to the music – "a little bit quiet, like...an' then 'ere, if yer could, like, wait a little second or two on that there chord," (Henry took out a pencil from his music case, and feeling rather important, pencilled in the instructions on the score), "an' then on the bit wot goes 'loved him dearly', sort o' stop, like, a tiny bit before yer carry on ter the next bar – fer a bit o' dramatic effect, like, (Henry nodded) an' then jus' before the last chorus, do a nice little flourish on that chord there, (Henry wrote 'flurrish' over the chord) an' then orf we go inter the chorus, which yer can play a *bit* louder – but not *too* loud, mind – 'coz I wants ter be able to 'ear meself!" (they both laughed) "an' then at the end, play them two chords a bit more slower, like, an' kind o' hold 'em a bit – sort o' – *tenderly*, like, when yer finish orf the song. Awright?"

Henry digested all this for a minute. Then he nodded enthusiastically.

This time the performance was very different, much improved. Henry felt like a real, *proper* accompanist. In fact the song sounded – well – *professional*. With those little touches, and the music being sometimes soft, and sometimes loud, and sometimes slower, and sometimes quicker, it was much more interesting to listen to, and *much* more fun to play.

Mrs McKittrick praised Henry highly, and said he was very intelligent and musical. Henry fairly blushed with pride. So keen was he to improve his technique, he asked Mrs McKittrick how he could get the pedal to make the music sound better.

"Well, guv, it's not so much the pedal itself wot does the job, as yer brains an' yer 'earoles." Henry looked bemused. "Yer see, each time yer play a new 'armony – a new chord, like, (Henry followed Mrs McKittrick's finger as it indicated the chord changes – he nodded) well, wot yer do is jus' before yer play a new 'un, yer lift yer foot off the pedal. An' then as soon as yer've played your new 'un, yer put yer foot back dahn again, quick, like, so it eckers. But yer 'ave ter do it quick an' clean, like, between each chord – that's where usin' yer brain an' yer ear'oles comes in, recognisin' when a new one's abaht to 'appen. If yer don't do it quick enough, the 'ole lot o' them chords'll run into each other, an' get all mushed up like different colours o' wet paint. See wot I mean?" Henry saw exactly what she meant. He tried to do as she instructed, but his feet and his fingers, and his brain and his ears wouldn't co-ordinate with one another, and he almost wore a hole in his grey matter in the attempt.

"Go slow, guv. Slow it dahn, like. Yer'll soon get the 'ang of it, honest. 'Coz yer dead quick on the uptake, you are. Jus' needs some practice ter get all yer bits ter stop fightin' wif each ovver, an' ter start workin' togevver, an' - look, see! Yer've done it! That's it, guv! 'Ere, that sahnds jus' the ticket! Wot did I tell yer? Yer've mastered the art of synchronised pedallin', an' it's only took yer a minute or two. Yer a genius, guv, yer a genius."

Henry was absolutely delighted at the results of his labours, and the fact that he was able to execute something with such a long and impressive name. *Sincronized pedlin!* It would take a fair bit of practice to get it really perfect, but ee, by gum, it were worth it! Just imagine how great he would sound when he'd got all these little devices in place! Fred might even give him a solo spot in time, if he really, really practised, and got really, really good. He was determined to do it. He would be a solo pianist. It would become his goal. He pictured himself, his hands flying over the keys, his feet a blur, the music clear, powerful, dramatic; the audience rapt with attention; the split second's silence at the end of his piece, followed by the tumultuous applause...

His tongue sticking out of the side of his mouth, Henry began to practice, slowly and carefully, listening for any clashes of harmonies, as his feet and fingers, and his brain and ears gradually began to work in tandem with one another.

"See yer, guv," called Mrs McKittrick, collecting her broom from the other side of the stage.

"See yer, Mrs Mac," called Henry, his fingers never leaving the keys, his eyes still glued to the music. "An' thanks very much for the tips...they were very 'elpful..."

Mrs McKittrick left him engrossed in his practice. As she departed, she noted with satisfaction that he seemed to have mastered the dynamics and pedalling in the first two bars. There was one heck of a way to go, but Mrs McKittrick was sure he would get there in the end. She smiled at the picture in her mind of young Henry, his eyes aglow, his hair tousled, his tongue sticking out with the concentration of it all.

"That's one good lad, there," she thought.

Shakespeare was right:

The man that hath no music in himself
Nor is not mov'd with concord of sweet sounds
Is fit for treasons, stratagems and spoils.

The music was there in Henry all along. It just needed a little miracle to bring it out.

* * *

Between this musical meeting with Mrs McKittrick and

the final night of the troupe's London run, Henry had put in a tremendous amount of hard work. The other members of Fred's band of players noticed he was improving daily, and congratulated him on his playing. He was modestly pleased, but knew in his heart he still had a long way to go before there was real magic in his music.

Whenever he met up with Mrs McKittrick, they would discuss things musical, and 'Mrs Mac' became his mentor. He was to be found daily putting all she'd said into practice. He worked like a slave.

None of the troupe liked to ask Mrs McKittrick what a woman with so much musical knowledge and ability was doing cleaning a theatre. It wouldn't have been polite. Perhaps she'd been from an educated family, but had fallen on hard times. If so, she wouldn't maybe like to talk about it, so they left the question unasked, and were just grateful she had taken such an interest in their troupe, and young Henry in particular.

Henry lived up to that interest in every way. He wanted desperately to do justice to all Mrs McKittrick's help and encouragement, to live up to her idea of him as being "very intelligent and musical". The final night of the troupe's appearance was his last chance to show her what he could really do.

On behalf of himself and his players, Fred had begged Mrs McKittrick to join them on a permanent basis, but Mrs Mac, though "most touched and flattered" said she had commitments elsewhere, and would be unable to take them up on their "most kind" offer. She told them she had given Mr Tomlinson her notice, as she would unfortunately be having to move away from London very soon. Mr Tomlinson had actually been extremely kind, and had given her a testimonial.

That night, everyone gave of their best, wanting to make the final performance something really special.

Winnie was on top form, singing so high in the last chorus, she sang, Fred swore, "notes only dogs could 'ear".

Marvel, Mrs Mac and the theatre cat continued to amaze

and delight the cheering crowd; Fred's powers of alliteration took positive flight in his introductions; Munro, Eddie and Albert raised the roof with the laughter they elicited that night; but most memorable (probably to all of the troupe) was *The Soldier at The Fair*.

From the second Henry first touched the keys, something magical happened. The notes of the piano seemed to become an orchestra. Sweet and gentle as flutes and strings, the introductory bars set the mood perfectly for the little love song which followed. Sophie's exquisite communication of the air's tender simplicity was admirably supported by Henry's interpreting the lyrics, just as Mrs McKittrick had advised him to. He enhanced the beauty of Sophie's performance, responding to her every nuance of tempo and dynamics, and the audience was mesmerised by the new and lovely interpretation of the well-known song. After Henry's quiet and gentle final chords, there was complete silence.

Then the theatre rang with appreciative applause. There were whistles too, and people cheering. As Henry and Sophie took their bows, there were more than a few tears in the eyes of their colleagues. That night, *Marston's Music Hall Magic* truly lived up to its name.

* * *

As long as they lived, none of the troupe ever forgot that night. Particularly young Henry, who almost burst with pride as he was kissed by Sophie, Winnie and Mrs Mac, slapped on the back by the men, and congratulated time and again by them all.

Fred's words were the icing on the cake.

"Well, Henry me lad, I think it's about time we put you in as a soloist."

Henry almost exploded with happiness. He thanked Fred ten times over, in ten different ways. Then he turned to Mrs Mac and said with great sincerity, "This is all due to you, Mrs

Mac. I can't thank you enough." He gave her an affectionate hug.

"No thanks necessary, guv," she said, "Yer did us prahd."

After the performance was over, the players were all exhilarated by the success. But it was tinged with a little sadness as they had at last to part company with Mrs McKittrick. They wished each other the best of good luck; but as they shook hands, more was said in the silence than in a thousand words.

She put on her old brown coat, stepped through the stage door onto the street, and turned and smiled at them all as they waved her farewell. Then she walked out into the rain, and no one at the Marlborough Theatre ever saw her again.

Funny thing, but no one ever saw the theatre cat again, either.

"You're just like your father," said Bess to young Kit, as she came upon the little girl one night in her sleeping quarters, impersonating the landlady of the local hostelry. Kit giggled. "He was a mimic, too – a good one," Bess continued, "he could speak any dialect he laid an ear to – and as for voices, he could convince you that he was a ten year old girl, or an ancient grandfather. He amused me for hours, he did – just like you do now. I think you have his ear, Kit. It's a gift – one which will come in very useful in future times, I'll be bound. But into bed with you now, my girl. Sleep is just as important as practising gifts. You have to have the strength to use them, you know!"

She kissed Kit goodnight, and closed the door softly.

Kit lay in bed, thinking. It would have been so nice to have known her father. She felt she almost knew him when Bess spoke about him, which she did, often. "It must be her way of keeping him alive," thought the little girl. "I hope someone loves me enough to keep me alive that way, when I'm no longer here." With such thoughts humming around her young mind, she soon fell asleep.

At breakfast the following morning, Kit asked Bess, "Was father learnèd, mother? I mean as well as being clever at acting?"

"Well yes, he was quite learnèd, I suppose," replied Bess, "though he always said he would like to have spent more time at scholarship, as education was an exceedingly good thing. And he was right, Kit. Learn all you can, my sweet. Travel; for you will gain much by travelling. You will learn of different places and people; their languages and cultures. You may then grow to be a tolerant and understanding person. Be knowledgeable, Kit. Be cultured. Know by doing. Acquit yourself well in Art and Music, Literature, Dance and Theatre. Study History, Mathematics, Geography, the Sciences, Religions and Philosophy. And read, read, read! You will find new worlds in books.

"Yes, knowledge is very important. But having the wisdom

*to apply it properly is of equal importance. Remember, Kit, knowledge is not ornamentation. It is to be used. And if it is to be used at all, it must be used for the good. Only the good, Kit; knowledge is a powerful tool which can be used to create or destroy; to aid progress, or to hinder it. Always remember that. Then you will be both knowledgeable **and** wise."*

Kit considered all Bess had said on the subject of her education. She determined to take her advice and stretch her knowledge and capabilities. She found knowledge to be useful, but also to be desirable for its own sake. She was particularly drawn to the Arts, and avidly studied Literature, Languages, Music and Poetry; sometimes to the point where she forgot to eat. Bess would affectionately scold her and made sure she learned to take good, nourishing food at regular intervals.

"It is good to see you feeding your intellect, Kit, and your spirit. But if you ignore the body which allows you to do so, all will come to an end. Understand this, Kit, and do so now. Later it will be too late, and you will regret not having paid the respect due to your body as well as your mind. And nothing in life is more bitter and insupportable than regret – it is an illness for which there is no cure. Think on these things, daughter, for every word I speak is true." By the time Bess had finished her speech, her face had taken on an expression Kit rarely saw, and the voice, usually so benign, had taken on a much more serious tone.

Kit duly took note, and committed her mother's words to memory, where on future occasions they served to save her from taking too much for granted her extraordinary gifts.

As Kit matured and her mind turned to thoughts of love, marriage and commitment, she questioned her mother about the implication of these gifts upon such a relationship. It was evident that from Bess's experience, marrying a mortal who did not possess such attributes presented problems. Kit felt that her ideal relationship would preclude such things as secrets; yet like her mother, in order to fulfil her destiny, she could not divulge her own gifts to any other human. And what *of her own children, should she so be blessed? Would they naturally be able to be recipients of these remarkable traits? Or would she be doomed to keeping her secret from them, too?*

"You will know if the Gifts can be passed on," Bess replied, "and to whom."

"You mean, if a Gifted has more than one descendant, only certain ones may receive the gifts, and others not?"

Bess nodded. Then she sighed. "That indeed must be a great burden. For secrets must then also be kept from siblings as well as offspring. I am glad that in my case, no such thing occurred. You are my only one, and to my everlasting joy, suitable for receiving the Gifts."

"If I had not been...suitable...?" Kit looked anxiously into Bess's eyes.

"Then the Gifts would have died out with me, when the time came for me to go on to The Great Adventure." Kit fell silent. She didn't like to think about that time.

"Is it possible to have all one's children enabled with the gifts?" she then asked.

"Yes, it is," said Bess, "but it's extremely unusual. It only ever occurs if both parents are Gifted."

"That must be a wonderful thing. To have all your loved ones share the gifts. No secrets, and so much to share with one another." Kit's eyes shone at the thought.

"It's what every Gifted would want for their own children. But it's rare, Kit, so very rare. You cannot choose whom to love, or who loves you. The Gifted are only born of love. It is impossible for us to be conceived in any other way. Hope, by all means, my dearest – don't let me stay you from hope – it's one of the sweetest things in the world. But be prepared to have to pay the price for having both your love and your gifts. There is usually a price to be paid for everything in this life."

1928–29

Faster than fairies, faster than witches,
Bridges and houses, hedges and ditches;
And charging along like troops in a battle,
All through the meadows the horses and cattle:
All the sights of the hill and the plain
Fly as thick as driving rain;
And ever again, in the wink of an eye,
Painted stations whistle by...

Like an unforgettable melody evoking a memory, the rhythm of the moving train danced Stevenson's poem in Kit's brain. With her eyes closed, she savoured the words which fitted so perfectly the sound and sensation of the huge iron beast; the pictures it conjured in her mind could be magically brought to reality, simply by opening her eyes. Yes! There it was – the painted station! And there the cattle! They were gone. In the wink of an eye. She smiled to herself and settled comfortably back in her seat. Kit *loved* to travel by train.

The sight of the massive, sweating engine clanking and hissing loudly to its majestic halt always made her heart leap. The masculine smells of the smoke and oil gave way to the more homely aroma of leather doorstraps as she climbed into the carriage and pulled the door shut. It always closed with such a satisfyingly solid, deep, baritone clunk. From her seat in the quiet of the First Class carriage, she turned her appreciative eyes upon the frosted glass lamps over the luggage rack; the mirror inlaid in the wooden panel between them; the crocheted antimacassars on the back of the seats. On the other side of the window was the noise and bustle of the platform; the sounds of hurried steps; travellers and luggage; porters and stationmasters; smiling folks meeting; tearful folks parting. Next, the shrill sound of the stationmaster's whistle, the cue for the journey to begin at last.

The engine cranked into life once more, and the train

started to creep forward. Slowly at first, as if the great iron monster was afraid of what lay ahead; then by degrees the speed began to increase, the big, black bulk moving forward with confidence and determination; finally, the familiar, joyous rhythm that sped the train along the shiny rails of Stevenson's poem, in perfect tempo with Kit's own heartbeat.

* * *

Lulled at last into drowsiness by the comforting lilt of the train's rhythm, Kit, alone in the carriage, finally surrendered to its mesmerising chant, and fell into a deep, relaxing sleep. It was as if she had fallen a long, long way, and had landed gently on huge, soft, black velvet cushions...

From the depths of her slumbers, she began to become aware of a change of rhythm; then footsteps tap-tap-tapping across her brain, a crescendo of sound; then, as if someone was speaking into a loudspeaker next to her ear, she heard the words "...only going to be going one stop..." They were accompanied by a gust of cold air, and Kit awoke abruptly as the door of the carriage slammed shut, and a large lady wearing a fox-fur stole sat down heavily opposite her.

Kit blinked herself awake, and shifted her position, sitting up straight, and crossing her legs, in order to avoid the various luggage bags which the woman had deposited on the floor, and on the empty space on the seat beside her. These were in addition to the luggage which she had placed on the rack above her. The woman panted and wiped her brow with a lace-edged handkerchief which was monogrammed 'M'.

Kit and her travelling companion exchanged glances, and smiled. Suddenly the lady peered through the window and waved frenetically to another, who stood on the platform, mouthing a message to her, which she obviously understood, for she smiled, and nodded, and waved madly as the train took off once more.

Kit tried hard not to look at the flattened body of the

beautiful creature which hung about the woman's shoulders. Its poor, thin, eviscerated legs and luxuriant brush hung limply down from her broad frame, the black bead eyes devoid of the fox's usual bright, intelligent expression.

The woman opened up her handbag and began to rummage around inside. Kit took the opportunity to powder her nose and touch up her lipstick, then snapped shut her bag and looked through the window to see how the journey was progressing. Still more fields, cows and painted stations...

She glanced over at the woman, who looked up at her from the depths of her bag.

"I can't find my ticket," said the lady, shaking her head in annoyance. "I know I put it in here, because I remember – Ah! Here it is!" She retrieved the ticket triumphantly, and Kit smiled back.

"They are so easy to mislay," she said to the woman, "I've often done the same thing myself."

The conversation started, it wasn't long before the lady had practically told Kit her life story. It was hardly a fascinating history, but Kit nodded politely, occasionally interjecting with "Oh really?" and "How lovely..." while the woman prattled on.

"...so I'm just going to stay with Ethel for the week – she only lives one stop along the line...very handy really..."

A peculiar sensation came over Kit. The woman's voice seemed to drift in and out of her hearing, and her senses told her she was being watched. How bizarre! There was no one to be seen in the carriage but her chattering companion, and she was most definitely not the perpetrator of the surveillance Kit was sure was taking place. She mentally shook herself out of this odd state of awareness and tried to concentrate on the woman's words. She glanced about the carriage during a brief lull in the conversation. Only luggage to be seen. The woman's suitcase and a hatbox on the luggage rack; shopping bags on the floor by her feet, and what appeared to be picnic basket on the seat beside her. Nothing else...no one else.

The train began to slow down.

"My stop," said the woman, gathering up her belongings. Kit stood up and lifted down the suitcase and hatbox from the luggage rack.

"Oh, thank you," said the woman. "I have such a lot of luggage, you'd think I was going to stay for a year!"

The train pulled into the station and came to a halt. The door was opened by a porter, who helped the woman onto the platform. Kit passed down her various bags and boxes, which the porter placed on a station trolley. Finally Kit handed out the picnic basket. As she did so, she felt the weight shift inside it. For the first time she saw the side of the basket. In it was a slot. Through the slot shone two blue eyes. They were surrounded by thick grey fur. A nose and a mouth appeared in the slot, and over the sound of farewells was the unmistakable sound of a cat's purr. Kit was surprised. She had been completely unaware of the animal's presence. And the woman never even mentioned it during the entire journey!

As the carriage door slammed to, and the train began to move, Kit was able to see the basket on top of the luggage trolley, through which the cat's face was now clearly visible in the daylight. The blue eyes met her own, and as the train pulled away, Kit's heart turned over. Was she mistaken? Was it a trick of the light? Or was it really true? As each held the other's gaze, and the distance between them grew, Kit could have sworn that the cat had smiled.

* * *

...and here is a mill, and there is a river,
Each a glimpse and gone forever!

The rural landscape now gave way to the urban sprawl of back-to-back housing in northern towns.

Kit pondered on the grey cat. *Had* something passed between them? Did the cat really smile at her? Or was this wishful thinking, auto-suggestion, a figment of the imagination, born of the desire to meet another of her kind? Kit had to admit to herself that this desire was becoming stronger within her. With her mother gone these many, many years, she had felt the need for the company of her own kind, of someone with the Gifts. She knew she may never in her lifetime know such joy again; but the hope would not be extinguished.

Perhaps the grey cat was simply a means to force her to fully acknowledge her innermost craving; after all, she did not often allow herself to dwell upon it. Maybe she should face up to the fact that she would always be alone in the world of the Gifted, as she had been now these two hundred years. She ought to be grateful for her extraordinary abilities, albeit the price of loneliness was a heavy one.

She sighed as she thought of the grey cat. If only it had been true. If only it really had smiled upon her...Ah, desire! How it makes fools of us all, the human and the Gifted alike!

She knew these words were wise ones, but even wisdom cannot lighten a heart heavy with desire.

* * *

Kit cast an affectionate glance at the black engine swathed in smoke and steam, looking for all the world like Monet's painting of *Gare Saint Lazare*.

Then she headed for the barrier, handed in her ticket and walked into the busy street outside the station.

She took in a deep breath that was almost snatched away from her by a strong wind which almost blew her sideways. So this was Lime Street. Liverpool at last. A city of ships and trading, merchant's mansions and the cobbled streets of the poor; well-heeled businessmen and shoeless urchins. Like many a port across the globe, a place of stark contrasts. It was her gateway to The New World.

But first a cup of tea and something to eat. A nearby café

took her eye; a welcome venue for cold, tired and hungry travellers.

A bell tinkled as she entered. A few customers sat at the tables, on which were blue checked tablecloths, clean and pressed, though slightly worn in places. Kit put down her suitcase and handbag next to an empty table, took off her coat and hung it on the back of the chair, then sat down to peruse the menu. Nothing fancy; mostly soup, sandwiches and various types of cake.

A waitress came to take her order. Kit decided upon tea and a scone. It would be sufficient, as she would be dining in style later that evening on the *Lauretania*. She caught sight of herself in the mirror which was hung on the wall opposite. She removed her cloche hat, which had been blown slightly askew in the wind, and shook her head. She smoothed down her silky brown hair which had been cut into the fashionable style of the bob. "An easily manageable coiffure for the girl about town," the London hairdresser had informed her. After wearing her hair long these past two hundred years, it had felt strange to begin with; but Kit had to move with the times – and she had to admit that despite the somewhat unflattering fashions of the day, at least the make-up was fun. On several occasions while out walking in Oxford Street in London, she had been mistaken for Pola Negri, which gave her an insight as to how awful it must be to be a film star, thwarted at every turn in trying to live your life in the normal way.

As she sipped her tea and enjoyed her scone, she could not help but hear the conversation of two women sitting at the table behind her. They spoke in the local accent, which Kit found one of the strangest and most fascinating she had ever heard.

"Mary makes the cakes fer this caff," said the first woman, in a deep, smoky voice.

"Oh, duz she? A nevver knew tha'," replied her companion in a high-pitched, girlish voice.

"Yeah. See tha' wot yer eat'n'? It's one uv 'er rock cakes.

Mind yer teeth. Thur not called rock cakes fer nott'n'."

Both women cackled.

The first woman spoke again. "She's gorran 'andy spot fer tha' bakery of 'ers, yer know. Very 'andy. 'Specially fer the fella oo 'as the shop nex' door. 'E's an undertaker."

The women cackled again, and continued their banter for some time, displaying remarkable ingenuity in the denigration of poor Mary and her cakes. Kit found their conversation amusing, and the delivery highly entertaining, but decided that having yet to find her way to the docks, she must take her leave of the café and its gastronomical and verbal delights, and head for the *Lauretania*.

She put on her outdoor things, paid the bill, gathered up her luggage and opened the door onto the cold street. The wind snatched up the cackles of the café women and hurled them out onto Lime Street. Kit closed the door behind her.

A cab journey later, she found herself on the quayside, gazing up at the most massive sailing vessel she had ever seen.

* * *

The rays of the setting sun slid across scurrying waves; petulant cries of seagulls were buffeted by a demented wind, uncertain of its direction, for on the way to the gangplank, Kit was thrown this way and that by its fierce intensity, and was grateful for the assistance of members of the ship's crew in helping her to board the liner without loss of life or luggage.

The kindly purser assured the embarking passengers that the wind would abate before departure and that a reasonably calm crossing could be expected, which put at ease those who came aboard pale-faced, and muttering dark references to the *Titanic*.

Kit's stateroom was very comfortable, and having unpacked her few, but well-chosen belongings, she set about exploring some of her surroundings before dinner.

The opulence! Rarely had she seen such splendour on land.

To find it at sea was nothing short of astounding. Sparkling mirrored bars, grill rooms and restaurants; designated smoking rooms; wood panelled walls and marbled bathrooms; elevators for moving between the decks; lounges with deep-piled carpets, tapestry-ed furniture, and plush velvet curtains and cushions. Domes of decorative frosted glass were to be seen above the lounge areas, making it even more difficult to believe you were aboard a ship. And the chandeliers! They were of extraordinary size and magnificence, reflecting on their surfaces light of every colour of the spectrum. The quality of the workmanship aboard this fabulous vessel was nothing short of breathtaking. Kit was enchanted. Cats are usually none too keen to cross water, she mused; but if they can do it in the comfort and luxury of the *Lauretania* then they might well be persuaded.

She decided to postpone her visit to the ballroom, tennis courts and swimming pool until the following day; it was nearing time for dinner. She returned to her stateroom to dress. Full evening dress was expected.

Kit selected a straight, sleeveless dress of black velvet, trimmed with black sequins from shoulder straps to waist, and laid it on the bed. Next, she chose a pair of black patent leather shoes, with buttoned straps. From her jewellery case came a stunning jet necklace with matching drop earrings. She laid these out on the bed in the scoop of the neckline of the dress, and surveyed the effect. She nodded. Just right for the occasion. Restrained, but glamorous. Classy. Bess would definitely have approved.

As she bathed, dressed and applied her make-up, Kit reflected on how useful Bess's advice had been to her; the education which she had advocated so strongly, and of which Kit had taken full advantage, had indeed always been of immense value. In this, the twentieth century, the financial rewards of an education were becoming increasingly evident. Now women too, were beginning to secure a stronger foothold in the professions which for so long had been the sole prerogative of men. The position Kit had recently acquired as a translator for a high-profile international law firm based in London, had been extremely well paid, and had facilitated her journey to the United States in comfort.

Kit had of course, throughout her life, taken work which allowed her to move in the world as a human. So many types of work she had undertaken! She couldn't recall even half of them now, she had lived so long. Some at least lodged in her memory; scullery maid, governess, waitress, secretary, musician, nanny, loom-weaver, fashion model, nurse, actress, potter, journalist, cleaner, seamstress, bus conductress, zoo-keeper, washerwoman, landlady, dairymaid...her entire history was a jumble in her brain. It's as well I'm not being asked to write an autobiography, thought Kit. I can barely recall the chronological order of the events of the last seven days, let alone those of the last two hundred years.

She finished her dressing, dabbed her wrists with her favourite French perfume and surveyed the results of her labours in the full-length mirror. The short, shiny, angular, bobbed hairstyle accentuated her high, rouged cheekbones. Her large, green eyes were enhanced with dark eyeshadow and kohl liner, the long lashes swept with black mascara. Her lips were a full, deep crimson. The black evening wear looked truly stunning. She stared in wonder at her reflection. She could barely believe that the young woman she saw before her was the same roughly-attired wench who had escaped the witch burning of 1723...

She closed the stateroom door behind her and made her way to the dining room.

* * *

Naturally the food was of an exceptionally high standard; course after course of beautifully presented delicacies, each plate a work of art. Colours, flavours and textures of exotic dishes vied with each other for the attention of the eyes and palates of the guests.

The courses were staggering. Fish and crustaceans; several types of fowl; roasted beef; grilled venison, and other game. The food was stunningly presented with colourful birds' feathers, fresh flowers...even cultured pearls and coloured glass 'jewellery'. All brought gasps of delight from even those who were accustomed to gourmet dining. Escoffier himself could not have faulted the gastronomic pleasures set before the glittering crowd of diners on the *Lauretania* that night.

Despite being a solitary traveller, it had been Kit's intention to avoid attaching herself to any of the families or other parties on board. She did not wish to be in the position of being a 'hanger-on', so upon entering the dining room, had taken her place at a table by a large potted palm, the better to enjoy observing, while remaining relatively unobserved.

She was in her seat for only two minutes before she attracted the attention of an American couple who were dining with their son at a nearby table. They simply would not hear of such a "gorgeous little lady" dining alone, and begged her to join them. They were on the way home to Texas. They had just 'done' Europe. What in the name of Heaven was such a "sweet young thing" like Kit doing, travelling without a man to escort her? Clancy here (the son) would be glad to act as her protector during her stay on "the boat", and she must tell them all about herself...if she was ever in Texas, she must look them up...

During the course of her time on the *Lauretania*, Kit was "rescued" from one party by another party, eager to claim her as their own. There were families with girls who looked of a similar age to Kit, with whom she enjoyed drinks, deck quoits or tennis matches. Elderly couples loved her company, for few young women of the day were able to talk about the past with such astonishing accuracy and affection. Socialites dropping names in unnaturally loud voices were a source of irritation to Kit, though none ever knew it; when she found herself pressed into their company, she treated them with courtesy, and spoke intelligently and appreciatively when asked what she thought of "dear Noel's" latest play, or "darling Gertie's" most recent stage performance. Kit was in great demand, for her wit, intelligence and culture ensured she was included as someone's guest in almost every event the liner had to offer.

However, the young men in particular were attracted to her. She could barely take a step, as she was surrounded by 'Bright Young Things' eagerly offering everything from a Screwdriver cocktail to a marriage proposal. A certain Algernon Barrington-Smythe, monocle-ed, chinless, and richer than Croesus, threatened to jump overboard if Kit refused to become engaged to him, but had to remain satisfied with a couple of Charlestons on the dance floor, and a promise that wherever she went in the world, she would never forget him. He was of course, Kit noted, somewhat 'squiffy' at the time.

The compliments paid to her were many and varied. She was "top-hole, old girl"; "the most divine creature ever to grace the universe"; "absolutely ripping"; "a real honey of a gal"; "a jolly good sport"; "a charming young lady" and "a cutie pie".

Thus Kit passed the days and nights on the *Lauretania* in the company of her fellow travellers; always pleasant and sociable towards them, but handling the young swains with a dignity and diplomacy which caused one elderly observer to inform her companion that "that young woman has an old head on young shoulders".

As at the end of all such journeys, there was much swapping of addresses and promises to write and call. Kit of course, at present, was of "no fixed abode", so managed to extricate herself from the somewhat difficult situation of having to provide knowledge of her whereabouts. She had naturally been given invitations to homes and offices the length and breadth of the Old World and the New, some of which she felt to be genuine. Her truthful reply to her new-found acquaintances was that she would always enjoy meeting them again.

The sound of the ship's siren, and the lapping waves were

forever to remain in Kit's memory, as standing on the breezy deck, she saw for the first time the land which was to become her new home.

She caught her breath, as with a frisson of excitement, she saw coming into view through the misty rain, the towering figure of the Statue of Liberty.

New York. *Noo Yawk.*

* * *

As soon as it had become necessary for Kit to be in possession of legal documentation, she had learned to furnish herself with the required papers. It was never difficult for a cat to gain access to an office building, and even on the odd occasion that a night-watchman might happen across her feline form and gently (or otherwise) eject her from the building, she was always able to find another means of entry.

Of course, these papers needed to be regularly updated, as Kit had the appearance of a woman of no more than say, twenty-five years of age; it simply would not do for her to be the holder of a hundred year old birth certificate. She had also, on occasions, to 'terminate' her existence for the purposes of recording a death certificate. She assumed many different names over the years. Physically and vocally a mistress of disguise, she provided herself with varied personae, and always had the relevant documents to hand. Sometimes she would assume an identity which had echoes of her original 'birth' name, Catherine Woods; but the pseudonyms bore little musical resemblance, and were occasionally foreign language versions. It would have proved impossible to detect her movements throughout the ages.

So, despite the fairly stringent entrance requirements to the United States, Kit passed through customs and the relevant agencies without difficulty. Then all that remained of the day's business was to find herself some suitable lodgings. Unsure of the length of time it would take to secure employment, and unwilling to risk the possibility of meeting fellow passengers from the *Lauretania* who may be staying in any of the grand New York hotels, she eschewed the luxury of the Waldorf Astoria or the Algonquin, and instead made her way downtown to find more modest accommodation.

First, she found a ladies' room in a restaurant on Fifth Avenue, and changed from the ultra-chic couture in which she had disembarked from the liner, into garments which would draw less attention when passing through the poorer districts. She left via the back entrance and began to wend her way through the New York Streets, taking in the sights, sounds and smells of the cosmopolitan city.

People of all colours, religions and accents thronged the streets. It seemed that whatever esoteric object your heart desired could be found in the shops which proliferated in every part of town. Bells jingled as customers entered and left these emporiums. Snatches of Spanish, Hebrew, German, French and Italian, the broad nasal accent of the Bronx, the soft brogue of the Irish, or the patois of the Latin or African American could be heard oiling the wheels of commerce. Kit marvelled. The whole world seemed to live in this vibrant city. She would learn much here.

In the cobbled streets of the suburbs, young boys strutted like miniature men, in long trousers, checked jackets and flat caps, or in Sunday-best suits and trilbies. From vents in the alleyways, steam belched forth, making the passers-by appear as if from fog; murky shapes looming in the distance, gradually coming into focus.

Passing through a street of nineteenth-century tenement buildings, she saw children playing on the sidewalks and swinging round the fire hydrants, watched occasionally by a man or woman sitting smoking or drinking on the stoop which gave access to the buildings. They gave her a cursory glance; the odd one smiled or nodded, and then being otherwise unemployed, went back to the business of doing nothing. Kit was content that she would blend in unnoticed in the heaving mass of humanity; the better to do the work for which she was fitted.

She turned a corner and her eye was caught by a shop, bright with the colours of fresh fruit laid out in rows on stands on the sidewalk outside. In the windows were an interesting and eclectic selection of packets, cans and jars. The sign above the business was written in black against a white background. It read:

B & B EDELMANN,
Purveyors of Fine Foods

It looked a very nice establishment, and one which caused Kit to stop dead in her tracks. For in the window hung a sign which said: HELP WANTED.

Kit never knew whether it was her feline instincts or her human pragmatism which drew her across the street to Edelmann's shop. Perhaps it was a little of both; but whatever the reason, she found herself entering the front door, placing her luggage on the floor by the polished wooden counter, and offering her gloved hand to the old grey-haired gentleman who stood behind it.

"Kitty Walden," she said in an American accent designed not to be particularly localised. She smiled as they shook hands. "I've come about the job you have advertised in the window. I believe you need help?"

The old gentleman smiled back, "Vell yes, I do," he said. "I take it you haf experience in retail?" His accent, as his name may have suggested, was German.

"Oh, sure," replied Kit. "But I'm afraid I have no references with me just at the moment..."

"No, no, no, that does not matter," interrupted Herr Edeleman, waving his hand as if to dismiss the idea. He smiled broadly. "I like the look of you. I think ve vill give it a try, ja? If you suit me and I suit you, ve vill vork OK together." His eyes conveyed a spontaneous warmth.

"Oh! Well, thank you so much... Herr Edelmann?" He nodded. "That's very kind of you. When would you like me to begin?"

"Vell, it is now nearly closing time," said Herr Edelmann, glancing at the clock on the wall behind him. "Perhaps tomorrow morning? About a qvarter to nine? Then I can show you vot is vhere and so on, before ve open up at nine, ja?"

"That'll be fine. I'll be here eight forty-five, sharp. And thanks again."

The old man nodded pleasantly. Kit picked up her luggage as some last minute customers walked into the shop and claimed the grocer's attention. She called goodbye to him on the way out.

"Goodbye Miss Valden. See you tomorrow." He busied himself wrapping goods, and attended to his customers.

Out on the street once more, Kit felt pleased. This was a good start. Now to find lodgings.

Two streets away, she found a small and somewhat dingy apartment in a tenement building. The rent was accordingly low. It was a roof over her head, and somewhere to put her belongings. She unpacked, and realised she was quite hungry. As she had passed a little Spanish restaurant on the way to the tenements, she had decided it would be a good place to eat. It didn't look expensive, and the aroma of the cooking which floated onto the street was so delicious, it would be a difficult place to pass without going in to sample its delights. So after a very tasty dinner in *La Cocina*, Kit returned to her rooms on the fourth floor of the building. She was very tired after her first eventful day.

But before retiring, she looked out of her window onto the New York skyline. It was beginning to darken by now, and the myriad lights of the city sparkled against the navy blue sky. A sight she would always remember. Millions of lights, millions of windows, millions of buildings, millions of people. Each with a story to tell. Kit climbed into bed, set her alarm clock, and fell asleep almost as soon as her head touched the striped pillowcase.

* * *

Kit and her employer worked very well together. They were soon on first name terms, of course, and "Kitty" and "Berni" became a formidable team. Kit's ability to speak to the customers in their own languages surprised and delighted Bernhardt. Takings increased. The customers enjoyed chatting to the pretty young assistant as she served with speed and efficiency, sometimes managing to keep several conversations going simultaneously.

"Vhere did you learn to speak all these languages?" asked Bernhardt, amazed.

"Oh, I just kinda pick 'em up, travelling around," said Kit. I just seem to have an interest in them, I guess."

After the first month, as they were packing away the stands on the Saturday evening, Bernhardt asked Kit about her lodgings, and whether she was happy there.

"Oh, they're fine," said Kit. "They'll do until I can find something a little bigger."

Not wishing to put Kit in a difficult position, Bernhardt tentatively, and with gentlemanly manner, asked if she would perhaps like to stay over the shop – there were rooms on the top floor above his own suite, which dear Gitta's mother used to occupy when she came over from Bavaria to stay with them. They were self-contained, as he and Gitta, God rest her soul, had made every effort to make things comfortable for their guest. He would not ask Kit for any rent. The rooms were not being used anyway...he would understand of course, if Kitty would find living over the shop uncongenial...

Kit was touched at his offer, and to his obvious delight, she said she would love to take him up on it; though she did wish to pay him rent. Bernhardt would not hear of it. He insisted that if she stay, she must stay rent free. Kit understood that he very much wanted her to be around, and replied that it would be lovely to have his company in the evenings, and improve her German.

At this, the old man was clearly overjoyed. Kit knew how lonely he was since the death of his beloved wife, Brigitte, four years earlier. Since Kit had come to work in the shop, a real change had come over Bernhardt. The worn look he had began to disappear; his watery old grey eyes had made him look far older than his seventy-six years; now they were brighter, and sparkled once more with life and humour. His weather-beaten skin seemed less lined, more tanned. Colour had returned to his cheekbones. His slim, frail frame stood straighter, and the thick, grey hair, which had lost its lustre, shone again, wavy and strong. Customers remarked how much better he looked since taking on his new assistant.

"Kitty is a great help to me in so many vays," he would say, putting his arm around Kit's shoulder and giving her a squeeze. Then he would look down at her with affection. "Ve are good friends, ja?"

"Ja*wohl!*" Kit would laugh, giving him a playful punch. She had become very fond of the old man.

So Kit moved into the top floor apartment above the shop, and in the evenings, when she was not exploring the city, she would sit and drink coffee with Bernhardt, and they would converse in German, Kit making only general comments about her own life; nothing which would invite further unanswerable questions. She didn't like to tell untruths to her old friend. Bernhardt would tell her about his boyhood in Bavaria, and how he met his dear Gitta, and of their son Wilhelm, who lived now in Berlin, of whom he saw little, but who wrote now and again. One day, Bernhardt said, Wilhelm would send for him, and he would have him live over in Germany with him and his family. One day, when Wilhelm was properly settled. One day.

He particularly loved to talk of Gitta. How beautifully she sang, how plump and fair and pretty she was. How the customers in the shop used to love her and her *kuchen*, the little cakes she made that sold so well. She was famous for her confectionery, Bernhardt said proudly. People would come from miles away for her tarts and biscuits and cakes. And she was funny too. They used to laugh a lot together, he and Gitta.

Occasionally the old man's eyes would well up with tears, and Kit could feel that the wound of his loss was very deep. Then she would squeeze his hand, or kiss him on the cheek, and before long she would have him laughing at some silly story or other she had concocted to bring him back into the world again.

Photographs of Bernhardt and Gitta, together, or by themselves, smiled out from the walls. Bernhardt had a framed one of himself and Gitta upon the wall of the shop. He couldn't bring himself to take it down, to put it with the other photos in his rooms. Even though she was no longer there to serve behind the counter, he wanted to feel she was still there in the shop with him. I know it's silly, he said to Kit, looking down at the floor as he spoke; but Kit took the old, veined, gnarled fingers in her own and told him no, of course it wasn't silly. It was a lovely thought, and not only that, it was a *true* one. She knew Gitta was with him all the time. She simply *knew* it. Kit spoke with such great conviction, that joy and comfort flooded through the old gentleman. He looked up and smiled. The belief and trust Kit saw in his eyes wrenched her heart. She truly loved Bernhardt. He was the grandfather she had never had.

* * *

For the first time in hundreds of years, Kit began to worry. Not for herself, because the centuries bore witness to the fact that she could always look after herself. No, the worry was not on her own account, but that of Bernhardt.

If he caught cold, she feared bronchitis. If he suffered from wind and she glimpsed him wincing with pain, she feared a heart attack. If he got up too quickly and became dizzy, she feared a stroke. She looked after him night and day. He thrived, the business thrived; but the old anxiety she had experienced when she was a young girl and had worried that some harm may occur to Bess, began to surface again.

The old man and Kit were devoted to one another. Bernhardt was always solicitous of her youth and encouraged her freedom. Kit reciprocated by watching over him like a mother hen. She would check that he was well supplied with whatever his wants before she left the shop, and would always look in upon him when she returned at night, to ensure he was safely asleep.

Once, unobserved, Bernhardt saw Kit stop on her way down the stairs. She looked at a photo of Gitta. "I'll take care of him," he heard her say. Then she ran lightly down the stairs to catch a bus uptown to buy new shoes. Bernhardt padded silently back to his rooms, his heart full.

"Gott sei dank für dieses Mädchen."

* * *

It was the beginning of December. Fir trees bedecked with baubles twinkled in the department stores. Snowy New York was laden with holly and mistletoe, Santa Clauses and reindeer; seasonal music drifted across the crisp, cold air.

One Sunday, Kit and Bernhardt dressed the shop with all the accoutrements of the festive season. The old man began to sing "Oh, Tannenbaum, oh, Tannenbaum..." Kit joined in and soon they were singing as loudly and lustily as if they were customers of a German Bierkeller. Suddenly they stopped. The doorbell was ringing insistently. They looked at one another.

"Who is that on a Sunday?" Bernhardt frowned.

"I'll get it," said Kit.

A stocky man in a large, fur-collared overcoat and black hat stood framed in the doorway. Without invitation, he pushed his way inside, elbowing Kit out of his path, slamming the door behind him. He strode over to the counter, behind which Bernhardt stood trembling.

"Twenty-five."

The old man looked back at him uncomprehendingly. Kit

rounded on the stranger.

"You're here to rob us? You swine!"

"On the contrary," replied the stranger, looking amused at Kit's spirited reaction. "I'm here to protect you. For only twenty-five bucks a week."

A protection racketeer! *Scum!!!* Kit's blood rose in anger. She went to Bernhardt who stood shocked behind the counter, and sat him down gently upon a chair in the corner.

"You're obviously just an errand boy," said Kit, looking the man up and down contemptuously. He bristled. "Whose errand are you running today, then?"

The hoodlum shot Kit a venomous glance and raised his index finger warningly.

"You mouthy broad," he snarled. "You have no idea who you're dealing with."

"You mean I'd tremble in my shoes if I knew the name of your big boss man?" Kit's delivery left him in no doubt that she was laughing in his face.

The man pointed his finger threateningly as he spoke. "Everybody trembles at Al Ferrino's name," he snarled. "He owns *everybody*." He curled his lip and smiled nastily as he saw Bernhardt draw in his breath quickly at Ferrino's name. He looked sideways at Kit and nodded towards Bernhardt.

"See? The old guy's got the message." He leaned over the counter and looked menacingly at the old man. "First payment is Friday. No excuses, just the dough. Or you'll find it'll start to get a little warm in here." He took a box of matches out of the right hand pocket of his coat, and struck one. He let it burn a second or two, laughing unpleasantly, then produced a half-smoked cigar from his other pocket. He lit it, all the while staring belligerently at Kit. She looked ready to strike the thug's pasty face, but Bernhardt laid his hand on her arm.

"No, Kitty, no. Please...no trouble." Kit knew he was speaking out for her own protection. And even in her fury, Kit was aware of the danger to Bernhardt of her continued provocation.

The man's eyes glittered in triumph and amusement at Kit's anger. He was used to witnessing impotent rage.

"Friday. Ten a.m." He sauntered out and didn't bother to close the door behind him.

Kit went to the doorway and watched as the lackey climbed into a Buick and drove away. She closed the door.

"Oh, Kitty, vot are ve to do? They vill take more and more. They vill ruin us." Bernhardt wrung his old hands in consternation.

"Oh no they won't," said Kit grimly. "Whoever else that scumbag Ferrino owns, he doesn't own us. And he never will."

* * *

On her forays into the city, Kit had met and befriended a number of New Yorkers of varied ethnic backgrounds, ages and occupations. She had learned much from them culturally and politically. One such acquaintance was a journalist who wrote for *The New York Clarion*. David Gerschowitz was an extremely good writer and investigative reporter. Kit admired his work greatly. They had met at the art exhibition of a mutual friend, and had immediately developed a rapport. Kit found him to be a man of integrity, in addition to being perceptive, knowledgeable and tenacious. Though Kit had by necessity to work alone, she felt that Gerschowitz could prove a powerful catalyst in her ensuing battle to bring Ferrino and his poisonous cronies to justice. History had proved time and again that empires fell. Empires built upon fear, corruption and betrayal fell even faster.

Unsure of which officers in the NYPD were on Ferrino's payroll, Kit decided that the damning evidence which she intended to obtain and use against him would be safer in the hands of *The New York Clarion*.

Kit wasted no time in beginning the task of collating the necessary material proof of Ferrino's illegal and immoral activities. At night, when Bernhardt was safely asleep in bed,

Kit would quietly leave the shop, and in various disguises, human or feline, she began to shadow those closest to Ferrino, and amass information useful to her cause.

She told Bernhardt to place the twenty-five dollars to be collected each Friday in a brown envelope. "Put it on the counter," she said quietly to the old man. "Make him pick it up himself. Don't give him the satisfaction of handing it to him personally. It's not a gift. He's stealing from us. He should be made to feel that. This money is buying us time, Berni. We won't have to do this for long. My sources tell me that Ferrino's days as the big cheese hood are numbered. Trust me." Bernhardt did.

There were times that Kit needed to be out of the shop during the daytime, to ensure she was in the right place at the right time for collection of her information and evidence. She found plausible excuses to leave the shop in Bernhardt's capable hands while she went off on these excursions. She would go out on the pretext of picking up some interesting new foodstuffs which she was sure would sell well, or slip out to the bank for some small change – they were running low in the till, or a trip to the post office was necessary to send some money to a friend in need. She disliked having to make up these stories, but could not tell the old man the real reasons for her journeys; he would have been worried sick for her safety. She didn't wish to be the cause of any more distress.

Little by little, Kit collected her evidence. She knew the address of every hidden gaming joint, illegal still and narcotics factory in and around New York, and how corrupt officials received their cuts; in many cases, she knew their names and addresses. The information would be useful in the raiding and shutting down of operations, putting a dent in Ferrino's takings; but what she needed to remove him completely was hard evidence, of the kind that had put Pisano away. Of course, Ferrino and other 'bosses' had learned their lessons from the Pisano saga, and although it was common knowledge that they were obtaining money illegally and evading tax, proof was difficult, if not impossible to come by. They were just too damned good at covering their tracks.

However, one Thursday evening, Kit got a lucky break. She had left Bernhardt sitting comfortably by the fire listening to the radio. She'd called in to tell him she was off to meet some folks in the city. What she really intended was to keep her ear to the ground at a night spot where some of Ferrino's mob hung out.

"Haf a good time, Liebchen," said Bernhardt. "Be careful. Don't be back too late."

Kit assured him she would do as he bid, and took a bus into the city centre. Looking out of the window, she spotted one of Ferrino's men going into a small eating house. Not a fashionable or expensive restaurant, like Ferrino's crew would normally frequent, but a diner, which sold cheap food to the down-at-heel. She got off the bus immediately, two stops earlier than she had originally intended, to follow up this lead. Going down the empty alleyway behind the diner, she slipped into a doorway. Taking a handkerchief from her bag, she rubbed her eyes to smudge her make-up and make her look unwashed. Then she wiped off her lipstick, and donned an unattractive old felt cloche, and some scruffy flat shoes she kept in her bag for moments of quick disguise. Stooping her shoulders, she tottered slowly towards the diner. She had aged herself twenty years.

Inside, she ordered a mug of coffee, and sat down on the opposite side of the room to Ferrino's man. No one in the diner took any notice of her whatsoever. She slowly sipped her coffee and looked out of the front window onto the street, a blank, tired expression on her face. The perfect kind of client for this gloomy emporium. But her hearing was feline; as sharp as the edge of a cut-throat razor.

What she heard made her pulse race with delight, though she sat as if in a trance and held her mug in her two hands, as if grateful for the warmth.

They spoke in low voices, Ferrino's crony and the

chubby man opposite him; no one in the place could have heard them. Except Kit.

It became apparent that Ferrino's man had been appropriated by a rival boss. At present, he was in the fortunate position of being paid by two masters. When he finally betrayed Ferrino, it seemed, he was on the promise of a trusted position in Joey di Parma's organisation, and would have more dough at his disposal than Ferrino would ever have put his way. It appeared, at the behest of di Parma, this Ferrino man, Valdano, had been keeping accounts of the Ferrino business. Accounts of the type that could render him as useless as Pisano. With Ferrino rotting away in the State Pen on a tax evasion charge, di Parma would be in possession of a huge empire, with the added bonus of no one on the scene being big enough to challenge him. It was the only way to get Ferrino out of the game. His protection was legendary. He seemed to have a small army at his disposal, and artillery that would be the envy of a Latin American republic. Some had tried, and had failed, to kill him. Stories of the dreadful repercussions for the attempted assassins and their families ensured the attempts were few and far between. Making Ferrino a guest of the State Penitentiary was by far the safer option for di Parma.

Valdano was to have his appearance changed, a huge amount of funds, a new name, and run a slice of the action himself in Chicago, away from the clutches of the NYPD. A nice reward for the act of betrayal. Such were the mores of the underworld.

"Di Parma wants those books tomorrow night."

"Sure thing, Frankie. He'll have 'em."

"You got 'em at home?"

"You kiddin' Frankie? With Ferrino in and outa my house? He uses it for meetin's, sometimes. Couldn't run the risk of 'em at my place. I don't want my brains decoratin' the walls for my kids to see. Get wise!"

"Where, then?"

It would have been difficult to decide who was listening

more intently, Frankie, or Kit.

"Gotta key for a lock-up in Grand Central."

Frankie nodded. "Yeah. That's good. Delivery at eight tomorrow night, then. If you want your walls to stay the same colour."

"Right," Valdano said, trying to disguise his nervousness, "don't worry – I'll deliver. There won't be any problem."

Oh, but there will, thought Kit. If you think for one moment, Valdano, that a man like di Parma can be trusted, you are a fool. A greedy, naive, unprincipled fool.

Frankie got up and left first. Valdano sat a few minutes more, threw some coins on the table, then made his own exit.

He was unaware of an unkempt woman coming out of the diner and hobbling a few yards behind him. Perhaps he had a lot on his mind.

* * *

By the Saturday morning, things had moved on apace. Valdano's body had been found in front of the lock-ups at Grand Central, a bullet through his back. One of di Parma's men, Kit was pretty sure, had lain in wait, and as Valdano was opening the locker door, had used a gun fitted with a silencer, to do away with him.

Not that it would have done the murdering thug much good, thought Kit. Because I've got the account books.

* * *

It had been a piece of cake to get into Valdano's house, while he and his family slept. To change from human, to feline, to human form once more, and to place the locker key securely in her own possession, took no more than a few minutes. Then followed a trip to Grand Central Station to collect the account books. Kit dropped them off back at the shop, slipping them under her bed, before quietly returning to

Valdano's to replace the key.

Good work, she thought with satisfaction, as she lay in bed, taking stock of the night's achievements; then fell into a sounder sleep than she had had for some considerable time.

* * *

Since Ferrino's heavy had paid them the first visit, Kit noticed that Bernhardt had lost his sparkle; he became nervous and forgetful, and nearly jumped out of his skin if the doorbell rang. It may only have been a window-cleaner ringing for payment, but the old man trembled as if the caller could have been the Grim Reaper himself.

It pained Kit to see Bernhardt like this. She did her best to ease his anxiety, but knew the only way to relieve it completely was to put Ferrino and his ilk entirely out of commission.

She felt that though much of the evidence she had amassed should have been sufficient to send him to hell and back a thousand times, the cunning of Ferrino's team of lawyers may yet result in his evading justice by denying any association with the politicians, law enforcers and businessmen whose names appeared in the secret account ledgers. *They* most certainly would deny association with *him*. Proof was needed that these ledgers were not fabrication.

Kit looked at Bernhardt and saw the fear in his eyes. Thousands – perhaps millions of people in New York must live with such fear because of that scum Ferrino and his bullies. Kit was almost sick with anger. She shook with fury as she thought of the horrific acts he had committed against good, decent, hard-working people.

But she must not give in to blind, hot hatred. That was the enemy of thought. What was needed now was cool, intelligent planning. Like the cat she was, she would watch, wait, stalk, bide her time. Then she would move in on her quarry and bring him down.

* * *

To the already long list of professions, Kit was about to add 'Photographer'. She obtained a good quality camera and a roll of film. Tonight was to be her first assignment.

The previous Saturday night, in the ladies' powder room of a cabaret club frequented by Ferrino's henchmen, Kit had overheard a conversation between the wives of two of his heavies. She remained hidden in a toilet stall, as the women discussed 'The Big Party', which Ferrino was throwing at a 'safe house' just outside New York. The party of course, didn't include the wives and girlfriends of the Ferrino mob; it was to be a 'men only' gathering. This in fact was the nub of the conversation. The women were griping about their exclusion. They feared that 'women of ill repute' would be at this shindig, while they were forced to remain at home. Kit smiled wryly to herself. Women of ill repute! The irony! These dames were gold-diggers living off the misery of the innocent.

Apparently, those of the mob's women who knew about it had been sworn to secrecy about this gathering of Ferrino's. Of course it didn't stop those two from discussing it. After all, they both knew about the party, and anyway, there was nobody else about, was there?

Kit was sitting on the toilet seat, her feet pulled up off the floor.

The women looked about them. The stalls were all shut. No sound. No feet.

They snapped shut their clutch bags and Kit heard their heels click on the marble floor as they left.

The sleuthing had at last paid off big time. She couldn't believe her luck! She now knew the house in which Ferrino was to be schmoozing his important guests. They must be very important if he's using a 'safe house' outside of the city, and keeping these VIPs away from the eyes of the world, and the chattering tongues of the mob women. Kit knew the time and the place. It seemed like this gathering could end up a turkey shoot. At least of the photographic kind.

* * *

The night before Ferrino's Big Party, Kit took a trip to the mansion where it was to take place. She needed to 'case the joint', find out how the land lay. It was important that she knew her way around. She had to plan her escape routes – with so many of Ferrino's heavies about, she could take no chances. There would be only one shot at this. The opportunity would not come a second time, and the safety of thousands of others, as well as her own, was dependent on the mission going without a hitch. It would be a dangerous one; like Daniel going into the lions' den. Give me the lions any day, thought Kit, rather than this pack of evil swine. In feline form, Kit made a thorough inspection of the venue.

It was a large and beautiful mansion, built in the Mock-Tudor style, and set in grounds of fair acreage. The walled gardens were immaculate, and landscaped with mature trees and shrubberies, rockeries, statues and fountains. There was the odd arbour and gazebo too; plenty of places where a cat could hide, unnoticed, on the approach to the house.

Opposite the house, on the other side of the road, was a wooded area in which Kit had parked the Austin Seven she had hired. There was a fairly wide, but winding track through the woods, probably made over the years by the cars of drivers with secret assignations, amorous or otherwise. The track finished at the far edge of the wood, and accessed a narrow lane, which led, via unlit back roads, to the state highway into New York city.

There were likely to be guards on duty in the grounds, the night of Ferrino's bash; perhaps on the road outside the house. And they would be armed. There may even be dogs. A lot of forward planning would be required.

Back in the woods, Kit resumed her human shape and

climbed into her hired car. She started up the engine and set off through the woods back to the city. A strange way this, for a young woman to spend a Friday night.

* * *

Some years ago, Kit had come across an old khaki bag, used by a soldier in the Great War. She had sewed into it thick, waterproof lining, and further camouflaged it by gluing on artificial leaves of various hues. Thrown upon the ground near any kind of bush or shrub, it was impossible to recognise as anything other than natural vegetation. It had proved exceptionally useful on many occasions. She drolly called it her 'Kit Bag'.

The next day, while Bernhardt was taking a nap after lunch, she put into it the necessary items for her evening's work. Six lead crystal drinking glasses; half a dozen well-wrapped thick slices of raw beefsteak; a bottle of champagne; her make-up bag and hairbrush; several packets of fast acting barbiturate powder, and a blonde shingle wig. Ensuring the camera was loaded correctly, and closed up in its leather casing, she put it into the bag with the other items. The 'Kit Bag' was then inserted into a large, plain, brown paper shopping bag, of the type she and Bernhardt used in the store. She placed the package under her bed.

"I think that's all I'll need," thought Kit. "Apart from one heck of a lot of luck."

* * *

After an early dinner with Bernhardt, Kit went back to her apartment to dress for the evening ahead.

She put on a fashionable above-the-knee dress of brown velvet; it was fringed in layers all the way down to the hem, and had a slit on one side which reached to the thigh. Over her shoulders was a matching brown velvet cape, which reached to the floor. On her feet were brown leather shoes. A long string of pearls and matching earrings completed the outfit. She was well-coiffed and made-up. Surveying the effect in the mirror, she was satisfied with her choice. Pretty, but practical. Very practical.

She retrieved the brown paper parcel from beneath her bed, picked up her car keys, and went in to say goodnight to Bernhardt. She knocked softly on his door.

"*Komm, Liebchen*," he called. Kit opened the door and stepped inside his living room.

"*Sehr hübsch*," he said, smiling. All dressed up! You are off to a party?"

"Sure am," said Kit. "I'm just going to drop off these groceries to a friend of mine on the way."

"You never stop vorking," said Bernhardt, shaking his head. "Even vhen you are going to a party. You take care, now."

Kit smiled. How right you are on all counts, she thought.

She kissed Bernhardt goodnight, closed his apartment door, took a deep breath and exhaled slowly.

OK Kit, it's party time.

* * *

Kit brought the car slowly to a halt in the woods, and turned off the engine.

From her 'Kit Bag' she took the blonde shingled wig, and using the rear-view mirror, adjusted it over her own brown bob. She brushed it through and patted it into position, then applied a darker shade of red, glossy lipstick over her existing colour. Next, she kohl-ed her eyes with darker, thicker lines, and rouged her cheeks with a deeper shade of rose. An earthy brown eye shadow and several coats of black mascara later, turned her into the blonde vamp she may have to play before the night was over.

The meat, though a little high due to lack of proper

refrigeration, she was satisfied would be appetising enough to any dogs she may encounter. She rubbed the meat with a few packets of sleeping powder, wrapped them up again and replaced them in her bag. Then she cleaned her hands with a cologne-moistened handkerchief. A few squirts of cheap perfume, and Kit was ready for action.

Taking the bag with her, Kit climbed out of the car, closed the door gently, and made her way to the edge of the wood which faced the gates of the Mock-Tudor mansion.

It was dark, but well in advance of the time for the party to commence. Kit had a few things to do before the arrival of the honoured guests.

Making sure no one was watching, she crossed the road to the house, and from outside the perimeter wall, peeped through the iron gates. No one was in sight.

She slipped quickly in through the gates and slid behind a huge evergreen bush, which stood inside the perimeter wall, next to the gate. There was not much room, but no matter; all she needed to do at present was to take the camera from the bag, and hide the bag itself behind the bush. She peered through the branches. Still nobody about. Good.

The next part of the plan was to cross the lawn and deposit the camera in a hydrangea bush, one of many different shrubs which bordered the path which ran across the front of the house. The hydrangea was directly opposite the dining room, which contained a long banqueting table. Kit had assumed that this would be the single place in which she would be able to photograph the entire bunch of Ferrino's low-life cronies together. Disparate photos of small groups in various parts of the house would not be nearly so useful to her cause, as well as being more dangerous to obtain. She needed proof that they were all part of the same, sordid set-up.

Kit could not afford for anyone to look out of a window of the house and see a woman crossing the lawn, carrying a camera. The nature of its structure precluded it being safely absorbed into her body matter. As a cat, she could not carry it.

It must be on site, ready for use when the time came. As much as she possibly could, she intended to stay in feline form, assuming human shape only when absolutely necessary.

She slipped the brown velvet cape over her head, covering the blonde wig and most of her face, and ran across the lawn as quickly as she was able, keeping her head low. Reaching the hydrangea bush, she brought out the camera from under her cape. She pushed it into the centre of the bush, hard into a thick tangle of stems, from where it could not fall. In a trice, she became a tabby, at the precise second that a light was switched on in the dining room. Kit lay down under the bush and turned her green eyes upon the lighted window. Uniformed catering staff were laying out the table. Kit's eyes narrowed in satisfaction. She had been right. They would all be there.

She glanced upwards. There was a slice of quarter moon in the sky, which was almost entirely eaten up by clouds which relentlessly passed over it on the way to a new destination. Kit inwardly rejoiced. It seemed house and grounds were to remain in shadow. So far, so good. She padded slowly and silently back to the bush next to the gate, and settled down quietly behind it, hidden between the bush and the garden wall. A perfect place from which to watch the arrival of the VIPs.

About fifteen minutes later, a lackey came out of the house and walked down the driveway to the gates. He opened them wide, in preparation for the entrance of the vehicles, then returned to the house once more.

Kit's acute hearing picked up the sound of the first car engine well before the vehicle swirled in through the gates. Her eyes shone bright with concentration.

In the back of the chauffeur-driven car sat the Mayor of New York.

Kit's heart beat fast in anger. The Mayor! Such sickening betrayal of the people of New York. She felt more strongly than ever how important her task was to be. Her eyes were narrowed in contempt as they followed the mayoral car up the driveway. It stopped at the front door of the mansion. The chauffeur got out and opened a door of the car. The Mayor emerged. The huge wooden door of the mansion was opened and the Mayor entered. The door closed. The chauffeur turned the car around and drove back through the iron gates past Kit's watching eyes.

No cars were to remain on the premises, then. No attention was to be drawn to this gathering in any way, shape or form. Ferrino was taking no chances, 'safe house' or not.

A second car arrived to deposit its contents at the front door of the mansion. It contained the Chief Commissioner of Police.

Kit could have cried out loud. What chance do any of us have if the Chief of Police is in league with these villains? If he props up the criminal underworld, not only does he fail in the task for which he is paid – to protect the innocent – he actively and knowingly harms them! Kit was aghast.

But no more so than when she saw the last of the dozen cars make its entrance to the den of vice. For it contained Judge Roy Wilkinson.

Kit almost burst with the enormity of this final injustice. Undoubtedly Ferrino's most expensive insurance policy, Wilkinson had not only betrayed the people, he had entirely violated the American Constitution, and the very foundation on which civilisation itself was built – The Law. The Law, the strongest bastion against the oppression of the innocent.

Kit felt her fury fuel the energy that she needed to carry her through the rest of her mission. It was now more than a mission. It was a crusade.

But before she began the night's work in earnest, she had to regain her cool, feline objectivity. She must subsume the natural human desire to confront the unjust and go in with guns blazing. She sat for some time, until her rage abated, and she felt more in control of herself.

It was only then that the sensation broke through. She had experienced it before, momentarily, in the past. In moments of extremis, she had had the feeling that somehow, she was not alone. It was so brief as to cause Kit to think it was only her imagination, and she would put it down to a surge of self-induced courage, and would plough on with renewed vigour. But tonight she felt it more strongly than ever before. This time she allowed herself to surrender entirely to its power, to reach out through the sensation and beyond, to its source. The calm, the strength, surged into her mind, her body, the very fabric of her being; and with it, the spirit of another entity outside of herself seemed to surround her, to envelop her with its presence. She listened to it with her very soul, stretching her senses beyond their limits.

She knew it to be Bess.

It was deep, wordless, joyful. The moment reached towards eternity, then gently let go its hold, and Kit was left with the knowledge that now found, this means of communication would not be lost to her. Never in her life had she felt so strong, so whole inside.

She was ready at last.

* * *

Kit walked softly between the iron bars of the entrance gates and out into the road. No guards. Obviously Ferrino was determined that no attention would be drawn to the house that night. But once inside the grounds, and outside the house itself, it would be a different kettle of fish. She must be prepared.

In her vigil behind the bush at the gate, Kit had noticed that most of the cars contained women of the type that men called 'broads'; over-painted, dressed to the nines in party clothes. The loose-tongued pair in the ladies' room had been right. Women other than themselves were the order of the night. They were doubtless chosen for the traits that were the bricks and mortar of Ferrino's empire, and without which such empires could not exist; an unholy trinity of flaws: they were greedy, compliant and easily intimidated. If it became necessary, Kit would have to pretend to be one of them.

Still in feline form, Kit crept towards the house, keeping hidden behind bushes and shrubs, and made her way to a holly bush which stood in the border near the front door to the mansion. She sat down underneath it and waited a moment or two. She could hear voices to her right. Guards. One came into view. He was carrying a pistol, doubtless fitted with a silencer. Another guard walked round from the back of the house to join him. He also had a pistol, tucked into a holster round his waist; from where she sat, Kit could see it under his open jacket. And he had something that the first guy didn't. A dog.

Damn! Kit tensed. The dog would surely pick up her scent. But the dog didn't seem to be aware of her presence at all. In a flash, Kit realised why. The cheap perfume she had applied must have disguised the feline scent, rendering her neutral to the dog's sense of smell. It would appear that luck was on her side once more.

The guards wandered off to the left, smoking cigarettes. Two so far. Kit needed to see if there were more. She crept round the right hand side of the building, then around the back, keeping in the cover of the vegetation. Nothing. Only one more side to go. Voices. Kit slipped under a bush and lay low. She saw the glow of two cigarettes, and the eyes of the Alsation dog she had seen earlier. The same guards! Just two, and the dog. It figures. Any more men moving around outside the house all night would draw attention. Ferrino obviously thought these two heavies were sufficient. They must be two of his most vicious henchmen. Kit let them pass. They strolled round the back of the house. They must be literally doing the rounds; a regular clockwise route. Good! So far things were going well. But the next step was to be more challenging. Time to move.

Kit made her way quickly back to her headquarters at the bush by the gate. She slipped behind it and resumed her human form. From her 'Kit Bag', she took out two glasses, and set them down on the soil, for stability. Then she retrieved the champagne bottle, opening it as quietly as she could. It made a soft popping sound, almost inaudible. She poured out champagne into each glass, and leant the bottle against the wall, pushing it down firmly into the earth to stop it falling. It was then but the work of a moment to take out two packets of the swift acting barbiturate, and add them to the glasses. She stirred the foaming liquid with the index finger of her right hand, wiping it dry on her cloak. She patted the blonde wig into position, smoothing down any stray curls, and picked up the champagne glasses carefully. Stepping through the shrubbery onto the lawn, she bent down to wipe the bases of the glasses carefully on the grass, to remove any trace of soil. Then she did the same with the soles of her shoes. Very slowly, in order not to spill any of the champagne, she made her way through her carefully planned route to the right hand side of the house. She stood just at the corner near the front of the building, but out of sight of anyone who should come through the front door, and see her standing on the pathway.

The right hand side of the house was in darkness. The action was going on in the rooms at the front, which were brightly lit with chandeliers. The dining room, at the front, ran from the left of the front door, about halfway along the house. The rooms which continued alongside it were lit, but unoccupied. From the right hand side of the main entrance door, the rooms that ran the length of the front were unlit. Ferrino and the rest were in the dining room at the banqueting table.

It was a good time to effect the next stage of her plan. Even so, her heart beat a little faster. This was where the going could get tough. She was going into the lions' den. And two of the lions were now coming into view. She took a breath and made her move as they walked towards her.

"Hey guys!" she called softly in a babyish, nasal Bronx, "here! Al told me to give ya dese. He must t'ink ya desoyve it!!" She giggled girlishly and tottered on her high heels as if slightly squiffy herself. The guards looked at one another and

Kit's heart stood still. Perhaps they knew she wasn't one of the dames on the guest list. One of them spoke.

"Well, whadya know? Al must love us after all."

The men both laughed and took the glasses from Kit.

"Yeah, well who wouldn't? A couple o' gorgeous guys like you..." She fluttered her eyelashes and simpered, noting with satisfaction their greedy draughts from the glasses.

"Noyce dawgie," she said, patting the Alsation's head. The reply was two thumps and a tinkle of glass as the heavies hit the path. Kit, fearing that the dog may raise the alarm, patted her thigh and ran onto the lawn, as if beginning a game with him.

"Here boy, good boy," she said softly and encouragingly. The dog cocked its head on one side as if deciding on its course of action.

"Come on, boy, see what I've got for you!"

These were words the dog loved to hear. He bounded after her towards the shrubbery, which they both reached simultaneously. They ran behind the bushes next to the perimeter wall, the dog panting eagerly. At last they reached the bush by the gate. Kit wrestled the meat from her bag, and the dog, scenting beef in prime condition, almost dived into it headfirst. He gulped it down without persuasion, enjoying every mouthful. He never quite made it to the third slice, because he began to feel rather drowsy...he laid his head on the soil. Kit lifted him behind a bush nearby. He was sleeping soundly. Kit left the remainder of the meat under the bush near him, in case he should waken, though she doubted that would be likely. She ran her hand up the length of his nose and patted him softly on the head. "Perfect qualification for Ferrino's mob," she noted to herself as she rose and adjusted her cloak. "Greedy little tyke."

Now for the guards and the glasses.

Under cover of the dark night and her brown cloak, Kit made for the right hand side of the house. The two heavies lived up to the description. Overfed, gluttonous fools, thought

Kit, as she lugged the first over the lawn to the shrubbery by the perimeter wall. She was panting by the time she got him hidden behind a large budleia, and propped him up against the wall. Needing to check that there was no-one coming out of the house to interrupt her task, she made her way along the wall behind the shrubs until she reached the part which faced the house. Suddenly, she heard a noise from the area of the front door. Oh, no! It was opening! If the second guard was discovered on the pathway, it would all be up. And she had yet to take the photograph. *Damn!*

She stood behind a high, thorny bush, watching, her heart pounding fiercely. Two people stood on the doorstep. Kit craned her neck to get a better view. It was a maid and a waiter. They were talking; the waiter was smoking. They made no move; must be taking a breather during a break between courses, thought Kit. Still, she had no time to lose. She needed to move that other guard.

In a flash, she became feline, and streaked across the grass, back to the right hand side of the house. Regaining her human shape as she reached the slumbering giant, she bent down to drag him across the lawn. He wouldn't budge. Oh Boy, was he heavy. For once, the sheer panic she felt at that moment lent Kit the strength she needed to move him the first stage of the journey. She almost cried out in pain, her muscles ached so, but with her heart thumping like it would burst through her ribs, she set to again, yanking, dragging and pulling, until hot and shaking, she finally got him behind a massive holly bush, and propped him up against the perimeter wall. She slumped down next to him, unable to move, nauseous with the effort.

Hearing the sound of the front door closing, she crawled along the wall until she had sight of the door. No one there. The caterers must have gone back inside. She had to get the photograph before much more time elapsed. And there was still the broken glass on the path to clear away. It would raise suspicions if anyone was to come out of the house and find it. Kit pulled a few branches down from a nearby bush, and with difficulty, snapped them off. She would use them as a brush to remove the worst of the broken glass. Feeling tired still, but driven by fear of discovery or failure, Kit made her way as quickly as she was able, back to the path on the right side of the house. Her excellent feline night vision allowed her to see the broken shards. She swept them with her home-made broom from the pathway onto the soil, then threw some soil on top of the glistening fragments, until they were invisible. The broom she threw under a nearby bush.

Now for the photograph!

She wished she wasn't feeling so shaky from her physical exertion. Trembling would be fatal at this time, of all times. She needed her feline calm. Changing now back to her tabby self, she padded to the hydrangea bush, where she had concealed the camera. Lying down underneath the bush and closing her eyes, she tried to breathe slowly, and to relax her muscles. She thought back to the moment when she had felt the presence of Bess. It was a calming thought. She remembered that wonderful feeling when Bess communicated to her that she would never be alone. It gave her the inner strength she needed. Resuming her human form, she stood, cloaked in the darkness, ready for the final and most important task of all.

Calmly, and with determination, she reached into the hydrangea and withdrew the camera. Lowering her covered head, she stepped across the pathway to the cover of the wall next to the dining room and quietly prepared the camera for its work.

One important factor remained; the dining room windows. She didn't want the camera flash to catch the window glass. It would ruin her photograph. To enter the dining room herself, in order to ensure windows were open, would of course be impossible. Should they be closed now, she planned to access a maid in the kitchen and ask for directions to the bathroom. She would then tell her that Ferrino had asked for some windows to be opened – the dining room was getting stuffy.

Ferrino's request was hardly likely to be ignored. The windows would be opened for sure.

Thankfully, none of this became necessary. The window nearest to her was ajar; the temperature inside the dining room had indeed risen during the course of the meal, and a waiter had been despatched to open some windows. Kit thanked her lucky stars.

Keeping low, she peeped through the opening nearest to her. Not a good angle. She could not include all the diners within that shot. She guessed the same would apply to the window furthest to her right. The middle window seemed to her the best option. Creeping low under the window ledge, she stopped at an open window roughly between the other two.

Slowly, she raised the camera to the top of the ledge. My God! A superb shot! As ever, Shakespeare provided the apt words for the occasion.

All my pretty chickens in one fell swoop!

She held her breath, and pressed the shutter three times in rapid succession. Each time, the flash seemed to light up the universe.

Kit hugged the camera under her cloak and ran like the wind.

* * *

For five long minutes her tabby form lay behind the bush by the gate, watching, listening for any sign that the occupants of the house were aware of her presence. Nothing. No sound but a victrola, which began to filter through, as the diners moved to another room to begin the next stage of the evening's entertainment. Kit recognised the song as *Wild*.

He's wild,
And she's wild,

And you're sure wild,
And I'm real wild,
And folks out there they think we're losing our grip –
Ha Ha!
Pip Pip!

If all goes to plan tonight, Ferrino, thought Kit, your grip will be considerably loosened. Ha Ha. Pip Pip.

Still, she was immensely relieved. If the flash had been noticed by the diners, they must have put it down to being the flashlight of the guards outside on their rounds. The drunken company carried on with their revelries well into the wee small hours, by which time Kit had shapeshifted once more, gathered up her bag and hit the highway.

Never had she been more relieved to see the inside of her little bedroom on the top floor of Berhardt's shop.

Kit lay in bed, shaking with the exertions of the crusade. She had been in danger throughout; that she had returned unharmed was little short of a miracle. She gave inward thanks for the cosmic aid she felt she had undoubtedly received.

Next was to see her friend Manny Goldblum, and ask him to develop the film. She'd waste no time, but do it tomorrow, Sunday.

"Anything for you, Kitty," Manny had always said, "any time."

She hoped and prayed the photographs would be successful. To have gone through the strain of this night for nothing would be soul-destroying.

She needn't have worried.

They were purr-fect.

* * *

Now she had her hit-list, Kit worked tirelessly at this, the most mammoth task she had yet undertaken. She watched. She waited. She sleuthed and she shadowed. When it came to

Ferrino and his associates, no stone was left unturned. No legal documents or real estate purchase papers were left unread, no bank statement ignored. Even trash cans were subject to her scrutiny. She was going to make damned sure she would bring the whole stinking edifice of Ferrino's empire tumbling down.

Bit by bit, she assembled the hard evidence. The paperwork. The proof of transfer of monies from Ferrino's accounts to the members of corrupt officialdom. No matter how hard both sides of the unholy alliance tried to cover the tracks of their underhanded dealings, Kit found the means to uncover them again. The aliases and false bank accounts had to be signed by somebody. Signatures existed. Handwriting could be compared. The dates of the acquisition of cars, jewellery, furs and travel documents of these arrogant villains would be difficult to dismiss as coincidences. There were far too many of them. And Kit, of course, had the receipts.

In her various disguises, posing as an undercover cop, she made enquiries germane to her case against Ferrino. As a result of the photographs in her possession, she was able to ascertain from bank clerks that one or other of these criminals had opened or drawn upon an account, using a name it was now clear was patently not his own. The clerks could recognise and point out the villains using these aliases in a court of law. More than one of the clerks, Kit discovered, had cause to want to see Ferrino go down. Members of their families had been victims of his reign of terror.

It was an exhausting time. Working in the shop by day, sleuthing in the evenings, and sometimes far into the night, was beginning to take its toll on Kit. One day, Bernhardt noticed that she looked very tired, and persuaded her to take a rest when the shop was not too busy.

"Go get some sleep, Liebchen," he said. "You vill get ill if you don't get proper rest."

Kit was grateful and did as she was bid. She had told Bernhardt that presently she was helping some friends of hers with various projects, but soon she would be finished, and she and Bernhardt could resume their evenings together. Kit knew he missed their conversations, and felt bad about having to leave him; but she also knew she had to complete her task, for only then could she and Bernhardt, and thousands of others reclaim their lives and enjoy peace of mind at last.

* * *

David Gerschowitz too, was not idle when it came to Ferrino and his mob. As a result of his own subtle investigative efforts, he had also begun to gather information. He knew the task was immense. It could take years; but sooner or later, there was always a weak link in a chain, and Gerschowitz kept his ear to the ground, hoping for a means to find it.

The breakthrough came sooner than he had dared to hope.

Kit, having stalked, was now ready to pounce.

* * *

One Monday morning, a cheery young errand boy stepped out of the elevator and whistled his way along the corridor which led to Dave Gerschowitz's office on the first floor of *The New York Clarion*. With his left hand, he adjusted his flat cap, which, being too big for him, was slipping backwards off his head. He pulled it down over his face at a jaunty angle, then grabbed his brown paper parcel with both hands and headed towards the sound of clacking typewriters.

The door was ajar, and he shouldered his way in, still whistling his tune.

"Delivery for Mr Gerschowitz," he said to the guy nearest the door, who was taking swigs of coffee, his eyes glued to a script.

The journalist looked up, and inclined his head towards a desk in the centre of the room.

"The guy with checked jacket on his chair."

"Thanks." The boy walked purposefully over to the chair

which was indicated.

"You Mr Gerschowitz?"

"Yeah. Sure am."

"Special delivery for you, sir." The boy handed the parcel to Gerschowitz.

"Thanks." He reached into his pocket and handed the boy a tip.

The lad nodded his thanks. "You're welcome." He pulled his cap tightly over his forehead and sauntered off down the office, his hands in his pockets, and resumed his whistling again. It grew fainter as he retraced his steps down the corridor and jumped aboard the empty elevator.

"How the hell did you get in there?" said a woman's surprised voice as the elevator doors opened onto the ground floor.

By way of reply, the tabby streaked between her feet and out onto the street.

* * *

David Gerschowitz cut the string and opened his package. On top of the enormous dossier was a scribbled note:

from a well-wisher

Puzzled, he opened the file at the first page. On it was a photograph of Ferrino in the company of the Mayor, the Police Commissioner, Judge Wilkinson et al, in obvious high spirits and congenial surroundings...

Gerschowitz's eyes widened. As he continued to turn the pages, he whistled through his teeth; then the office was brought to a standstill as he jumped up from his chair and smashed his fist triumphantly on his desk.

"*Hot damn!*" he yelled. "We got 'em!! WE GOT EM!!!"

* * *

As with every tumbling edifice, the rats began to run. And the pest control officers were there to catch them.

The message went out loud and clear: after "might is right" inevitably comes "right is might". Justice at last. A job well done.

Kit and Bernhardt were strolling down at the waterfront, one Sunday afternoon in the Spring. The sun was shining and the air felt clean. Kit stopped. Bernhardt turned to see what Kit was looking at. It was the Statue of Liberty. They looked at each other and smiled.

And Kit could feel it. Bess smiled too.

* * *

"Goodnight, Berni, darling. Sleep well."

"Goodnight, Liebchen."

Kit kissed him goodnight. They gave each other a warm hug.

Those were Bernhardt's last words. During the night, he joined Gitta on The Great Adventure.

And in the morning, when Kit found him, he looked peaceful and happy.

Yet, try as she might, Kit was unable to stem the tears.

Kit's education would not have been complete without touching on the subject of The Great Adventure.

"Mother," said Kit one day, shortly after her seventeenth birthday, "do only the Gifted go on to The Great Adventure?"

"I'm sure all creatures do, my love, gifted or otherwise. But the Gifted live much longer, and know without doubt when their time has come."

"Is it a sad time for them?" Kit asked anxiously, tears threatening as she spoke.

"No my dearest, I'm told it is not, by those who then went on before me. Why should it be? It is simply the start of a new form of life, not an end of a life altogether. Think of it as a well-earned rest from the rigours of the earthly life you have experienced before; a different way of being."

"What kind of being?" asked Kit.

Bess laughed. "Now how can I tell you that when I haven't experienced it myself? But I can tell you Kit, I have no fear of it; no more than I would fear travelling to the next county. And neither will you when the time comes, of that I can assure you. I've seen many a Gifted go before me, and never a one was afeared."

Kit pondered on this. She pondered on it for years to come, and as time went on, she began to accept The Great Adventure as if it were simply a journey she would make one day when she felt like it.

1947

THE NEW YORK CLARION, September 14, 1947

THIS WEEK'S SHORT STORY for the CLARION is written by the celebrated detective story writer ROYSTON CHALMER. It is based upon an actual case.

THE LADY FROM LARAMIE

In most detective fiction, it seems that all you have to do is *cherchez la femme*. The *femme* who kick-started the whole affair that Monday morning didn't need much in the way of cherchez-ing. In fact, she cherchez-ed me.

Black leather shoes with gold and diamond and buttons on the ankle straps, were attached to feet which were attached to legs that went all the way up. They were *long* legs. The dress was a little black number you could describe as figure-hugging. And let me tell you, that dress sure had plenty to hug. In all the right places. A black sable wrap and hat nicely set off the gold and diamond necklace and matching earrings, which seemed to be quite happy sitting there in a haze of French perfume, which had to have cost a million bucks an ounce.

As she slinked through the door of my office, she turned a smile on me which could have melted all my shirt buttons if two of them hadn't come off already that morning. There was no doubt about it. She was the classiest looking piece of trouble I'd clapped eyes on in a long while.

"Mr Philip Murdoch?"

I nodded.

"Paulette de Vere." She stretched out a hand wearing a long black leather glove that went up her arm a few feet. On the third finger of the left hand was – you've guessed it – a gold and diamond ring. This dame was dripping with dough from head to toe. And something in those beautiful baby blues told me she wanted to stay that way.

I offered her a seat, indicating the chair on the opposite side of my desk, but she didn't sit down. She couldn't. It was already occupied by the tabby cat who'd appropriated me and my office last Wednesday.

"Your cat?" she asked, looking from it to me with a smile of amusement playing across the glossy red lips.

"Oh, sorry," I said, and went round the desk to scoop up the bundle of fur. Somehow knowing it was eviction time, the tabby stood up, stretched, and jumped from the chair to the desk, and then into a pool of sunlight on the top of my filing cabinet, where she lay languidly surveying the scene through half closed eyes.

"Thanks." My client-to-be sat down, crossing her shapely legs at the ankle.

"What can I do for you Mrs de Vere?"

"I'd like you to find my husband, Hector. I haven't seen him since yesterday morning. He didn't come home last night, and he never called me to say he wasn't coming home. He never does that. He always calls me if he has to stay out overnight. I'm worried that something might have happened to him."

"Have you been to the police?" I asked, "filed a Missing Person report?"

"Oh, of course. I've just come straight from the station house."

"Then..."

"You're wondering why I need you, too."

I smiled. She smiled back.

"Well, as you probably know, my husband is a wealthy man." That was the understatement of the century. Hector de Vere was one of the fattest cats in the country, a businessman of renown, a mover in all the right circles, all of them gilt-edged. Suddenly she looked anxious.

"I'm afraid – I'm afraid he may have been kidnapped, or something awful like that. The sooner he's found, the better.

I'd feel a whole lot happier if you were on the case, as well as the police."

I nodded, and asked her all the usual questions about work schedules, the places he frequented etc. There wasn't a lot to go on – the guy could be anywhere. After all, this is the twentieth century. You can get a long way in twenty-four hours. I asked for her address and phone number and sat with my pencil poised; but she opened her purse and passed me a card all printed out fancy, with name, address and her number. The fluted edges were tinged with gold. At the top was an embossed picture of a cowboy astride a horse, hat held high in hand. The name of the house, printed below, was 'Laramie'.

"Why 'Laramie'?" I asked, having heard that de Vere had had the house purpose built by an expensive firm of New York architects.

"Hector's a big fan of the Wild West," she replied, looking amused again. She looked real pretty when she did that thing with her lips. "The house is built ranch-style. When he retires, he wants to go out West and build a real *big* ranch, and breed horses – you know, racehorses. It's always been his dream." Suddenly she looked desperately and earnestly into my eyes. "Please, please find him, Mr Murdoch. Please."

I assured her I would do my best, and we came to the usual financial agreement – fifty bucks down for expenses, the remainder on completion.

As she got up to go, her eyes fell upon my bookshelf. Amongst the phone directories and street maps, she spotted my leather-bound volume *Twentieth-Century Poets: ee cummings*.

"Is this yours?" she asked, with obvious surprise.

"Sure."

"You read poetry?"

"They tell me that's what you're supposed to do with it."

"Well, you do surprise me!"

"So I see."

"Oh – I didn't mean..." She looked rather embarrassed.

"Well, I guess you wouldn't expect a gumshoe to have ee

cummings on his bookshelf," I said, and smiled at her to make her feel more at ease. She smiled back. It had kinda been a smiley sort of morning so far.

She made her way to the door, and I opened it for her in what I hoped was a gallant but business-like manner, and after further reassurances of my best attention to her husband's disappearance, we said so long, and she left. She made her way down the staircase, and I have to say she looked every bit as alluring from the back as she did from the front.

The black sable was followed by a different pile of fur, as the tabby jumped down from the cabinet and shadowed Paulette de Vere step for step, out of the building and into the street, looking for all the world like a feline sleuth.

But maybe that's just my poetic imagination.

* * *

Shortly after, I went out to lunch. Well, strictly speaking, 'out to lunch' just meant I grabbed a pastrami on rye from the deli on the corner and munched it as I walked along, thinking about the de Vere case.

Paulette de Vere had certainly wasted no time in reporting her husband missing. Short, balding, pug-faced de Vere sure was lucky to have a dame like her so avid for his company. Now I'm not so worldly-wise and hard-bitten as to believe a young and beautiful wife can't be head-over-heels in love with a plug-ugly spouse like Hector; oh no, I wouldn't read poetry if I didn't believe in the finer aspects of the human soul. All I'm saying is, my finer instincts told me that I smelt a rat. In my game, I've smelt 'em more often than Pest Control, and this one stank big time.

Sure, she was quick off the mark to get things moving as soon as she thought he'd disappeared. Maybe just a little *too* quick. And she sure didn't give me a hell of a lot to go on. Needle in a haystack info. Yeah, she was real earnest in her plea for me to find him. Her face was the picture of pleading earnestness. But those big blue orbs told me a different story. I began to feel genuinely concerned for the welfare of poor, rich Mr de Vere.

I picked up a newspaper and a few items I'd run out of; milk and coffee and suchlike. I'd been through a lot of milk since Puss arrived. On the way to the checkout, I lifted a can of cat food. The picture on the front made the stuff inside look so good, I wished I was a cat. I thought about that for a minute or two. Yeah, life was real simple if you were a cat. No work, no taxes, and always some sucker like me to provide the necessary when times got rough. If there was such a thing as reincarnation, there was no doubt in my mind what I'd like to be next time round the block.

I went back up to my office, planning on making a phone call to Hector de Vere's gentleman's club, to see if he'd been there on Sunday; it would be a start. When I unlocked the door, the tabby was there to welcome me. Must have come through the window, which was left ajar. I made a mental note not to provide access to my office again – after all, anyone could get in and rifle through my filing cabinet. Well, I guess that's all they could do. There sure wasn't anything else worth looking at.

The tabby was purring insistently, so I opened the can, spooned out some food onto a saucer, and poured some fresh milk from the new bottle into another. I set them both down on the floor, and the cat continued to purr with obvious satisfaction as she hungrily, but delicately ate the food. I watched her for a moment as she picked up the chunks of meat with ease and grace; I found myself smiling. "You varmint," I said aloud. "You've got me for a real sap."

Suddenly, under my desk to the right of the animal, I caught sight of what looked like a small square of paper. I bent down and dragged it out. It wasn't one of mine. Too small. It was from a notepad. A de Vere notepad; on the top was embossed the cowboy on his horse. It must have fallen from Paulette de Vere's purse as she handed me the address card.

Funny neither of us noticed it fall. As I lifted it up, I saw there were actually two pieces of paper, one tucked snugly underneath the other. They were blank, but that didn't matter. There were impressions from the pen of a writer with a heavy-ish hand.

I took the sheets over to the window, where the light was better. The top sheet simply read: 'Jumbo 10.30'. The one underneath had a slightly lighter impression; but it was still possible to see what was written: W: 5489. W: could be someone's works telephone number. The top sheet presented what seemed to be a more obvious piece of information. Somebody was meeting somebody at the Jumbo Club at ten-thirty. This joint was a night-spot for those with an elephantine bank balance. The rich and their hangers-on frequented it; the champagne and cabaret set. It was a block or so further on from my office. There was no guarantee that the '10.30' on the note-sheet referred to tonight, Monday night; but since it was at least something to go on, I thought I'd play a hunch and turn up there anyway.

* * *

I'd probably hand the fifty bucks Paulette de Vere gave me straight over to the bartender, the price of the booze in the joint was so steep; I should have asked for two hundred up front for expenses. Oh well, no use whining about that now.

I arrived about ten-fifteen and decided to nurse a long, cool beer and keep in the shadows. Didn't want to be seen by Mme de Vere if she was here for a tryst. As it happened, I struck lucky. She was.

Around ten-forty, she made a low-key entrance dressed in black satin and lace. The diamonds weren't all that low-key, but they weren't too ostentatious in a place that look like the clientèle had just raided Tiffany's.

Paulette de Vere made her way over to a plush, high-backed booth, upholstered in red velvet, and managed to install herself without drawing any attention. I watched from the shadows at the far side of the room. There was a fair crowd on the dance floor, so when Mrs de Vere was quietly joined by a young, mustachio-ed guy with black, wavy hair, it wasn't difficult to make my way unnoticed through the throng and take a seat in the unoccupied booth behind them.

I hadn't missed much. They were still at the 'hell to get a cab' stage. Then the conversation took a different turn.

In a lower voice, though not inaudible to me (I was listening real close) Mrs de Vere suddenly said:

"Well, Lennie?"

"Couldn't be better."

"Good. It shouldn't be too long before the will is sorted out, then we're home and dry. In the meantime, I'll see the readies are in place for a job well done." Then her voice took on a real sense of urgency. "Uh-oh. Make like you've just sat down at the wrong table, and get the hell outa here. I've just seen the Van de Burghs arriving, and if they see me they'll come over."

Lennie did a fine performance; a quick and unobtrusive apology for mistaking his booth, and he was gone. The Van de Burghs did indeed spot Paulette, and Mrs Van launched loudly into enquiry as to Paulette's and Hector's well-being. Fortunately for Paulette, she didn't wait for an answer, but went on to tell her (and everyone within a ten foot radius) of her simply mah-vellous vacation in Europe.

At this point, under cover of Mrs Van's diatribe, I extricated myself from my seat, and disappeared through the crowd on the dance floor, out into the street. I jumped a cab and went straight home to get some shut-eye. After all, now I had a lead or two, I had some real sleuthing to do the next day.

* * *

Tuesday morning, I picked up a newspaper on the way to the office. The headlines 'TYCOON FOUND MURDERED' and Hector de Vere's picture underneath, somehow came as no surprise. A guy walking his dog did my job for me, and found de Vere, shot in the head and buried under a heap of garbage bags in a back alley. The poor sap would never get his horse ranch after all.

I rang the de Vere residence and asked to speak to Mrs de Vere. The maid who answered said Madame was too distressed to come to the phone. She assured me that she would pass on my condolences to Mrs de Vere, and hung up.

In the light of Hector's demise, and in view of what I'd heard the night before, I now had even more work to do than I had previously envisaged. There were puzzles to be solved, ones which for the satisfaction of my own curiosity, and for the sake of plain justice, I had to address. And let's face it, business was hardly booming, so I had damn all else to do with my time.

A further puzzle awaited me when I reached my office. Another piece of paper was on the floor when I opened the door. The cat trod on it as she wound herself through my legs, the usual expectant purr greeting me as I went in. I bent down and tousled her head as I picked up the sheet, which appeared to have been shoved under the door.

> with all
> the cummings
> and goings
> you maybe miss
> the hitman
> maybe miss

A poem in the style of ee cummings. Who had written that? I read it again. 'The hitman.' Something to do with the de Vere case? Who could have penned a poem like this? They would have to be pretty well read to have come up with this; phrasing, typography – definitely in the cummings style. It had all the earmarks...and the ambiguity.

you maybe miss
the hitman maybe miss...

The murderer may have missed de Vere. Hector could still be alive...the story fed to the papers by de Vere and the police, to pretend that the hitman had been successful, giving them time to track down the assassin, Paulette de Vere playing along, acting the distressed, bereaved widow. But then, what was all that about in the Jumbo Club? It didn't add up. I looked at the lines again. In ambiguous cummings style 'the hitman maybe miss' could mean 'the hitman may be Miss'!

"The hitman may be a woman," I said aloud. Puss mewed. I poured her some milk.

* * *

A phone call to the morgue convinced me that de Vere was dead. I knew one of the guys that worked, there, Billy Feldman. He'd dealt with the corpse, and he said the widow had identified the body.

The mystery poem continued to puzzle me. I was sure in my bones that Paulette de Vere had had something to do with her husband's death, though, given the gist of the conversation with Lennie, she hadn't been present when the gun was fired. She wasn't then, the 'Miss' in question. Was Lennie the guy with the finger on the trigger? If so, why the 'Miss'? I couldn't figure it out, so I did something I could do.

I lifted the phone and dialled the number I guessed may be Lennie's place of work, the one left imprinted on the 'Laramie' note-paper. A secretary answered the phone.

"Hello, Millhouse and Bernstein, how can I help you?" She sounded pleasant and efficient, not one of those broads who talk to you through gum with the phone on her shoulder while she files her nails. Firms hire far too many of those dames these days.

"Hello," I said briskly, "is it possible to speak to Lennie, please?"

"Which Lennie would that be, sir? Old Lennie, or young Lennie?"

"Er...young Lennie, I guess."

"Oh, Lennie Kravitz. Will you hold a moment please sir, while I try to connect you?"

"Sure. Thanks."

After a brief silence, there was the sound of a phone ringing. The call was answered by a voice which I recognised as that of the mustachio-ed guy in the Jumbo Club.

"Hello, Lennie Kravitz speaking. What can I do for you?"

As I had no idea what kind of business Kravitz was in, I decided to go for the old faulty telephone line routine. I didn't want to raise any suspicions in him by asking fool questions.

"Hello, my name is...hello?" I tapped the cradle rest of the telephone several times and repeated "Hello...hello?" as if I couldn't hear him for the fault on the line. Then I replaced the receiver, imagining Kravitz shrugging and putting down the phone.

Now I knew the name of Mrs de Vere's suspected accomplice, and where he worked. It was fair to assume Kravitz wasn't entirely unknown at the Jumbo Club. He was evidently the type to hang around the wealthy. If he's working for a living, he sure wasn't one of them. I thought I'd go nurse another beer and make some discreet enquiries.

As I left the office, I put some catfood and milk down outside the door, before locking it. Puss began making inroads into the first course of beef and gravy.

"This Jumbo Club is costing me next year's income," I muttered to the cat, who I'd gotten into the habit of talking to. "You couldn't lend me twenty bucks, could you?"

By way of reply, she purred deeply through the thick gravy.

* * *

It was hardly likely that Paulette de Vere would be seen at the Jumbo Club so soon into her widowhood, so the risk of seeing her there was negligible; which was just as well, as I was there to get the low-down on her boyfriend. As it happened, he wasn't in the joint either, which made snooping into his private life a little easier than it otherwise might have been.

Every now and again, the enigmatic poem kept rattling my cage. The only person I could think of who knew my penchant for the poetry of ee, was Paulette de Vere. And she sure wasn't the type to pastiche poetry, or come to that, to kindly drop clues about her husband's murderer. So it still remained a mystery. I'm none too keen on unsolved mysteries. However, once again I had to put the thought of it out of my mind; I had some poking around to do on the Kravitz front.

I swivelled my eyeballs around the club, standing at the bar with my beer. If it got much more expensive in here, you'd need a mortgage on a packet of peanuts. I hoped I'd get the SP on Kravitz before my booze ran out.

My investigative exploits began by starting up a conversation with a girl who was sitting on the bar stool next to me. Her back was to the clientèle on the dance floor. She faced the barman.

"Hey, Barney," she said to him. "Hit me with another of those Manhattans, will you?"

Barney finished polishing the glass he was working on, fixed the cocktail and put it down in front of her. I found myself saying: "This one's on me." I'd probably be sharing catfood with Puss for the next two months, but what the hell. She turned to me and smiled.

"Thanks," she said.

"Brent Rickman," I introduced myself; I didn't want Kravitz to hear Philip Murdoch had been asking questions about him.

"Kate Bentham."

She was something else. She'd have put Paulette de Vere in the shade had she been stood next to her. Yeah, and her diamonds, too. It was hard not to stare. She was tanned, a real Riviera tan; smooth skin, great curves, which you could see real easy from the way the gold satin snuggled up to them; dark brown hair you wanted to jump into, and what eyes. Green as emeralds. Shaped like almonds. The long, black lashes swept up and down in a slow, languid way as she spoke. She put me in mind of the cat that had adopted me. This Kate could adopt me any day.

After some initial pleasantries during which she told me she didn't come here a lot, just when she was flush and wanted to spoil herself, and I made some not so funny remark about the prices being higher than the top of the Empire State, I managed to get started and do my PI thing.

"Do you know Lennie Kravitz, by any chance?" I asked. "I'm told he comes here from time to time. A mutual friend asked me to look him up if I was in the Jumbo. I've never met him – just thought if he was here, I'd say hello from Charlie." I thought Charlie would be a safe enough name. Everyone in New York knows a Charlie.

"Oh, sure. I know Lennie. But he ain't here now." The speech and accent had a tinge of the Bronx about it, but not so strong as to flatten your beer. "He was in earlier. He's probably gone to The Cavalier. Spends a lot of time there. And a lot of dough. Big gambler, is Lennie."

The Cavalier was a casino where you could make or break your fortune in the blink of an eye. Only big time gamblers usually played there. It was no back-room gaming house, but one where the serious money could be found. Where Kravitz got the money to play at The Cavalier, one could only surmise. He would have to have either a big salary and a lot of luck, or some very rich friends indeed.

"Personally, I think it's a mug's game," I said, taking a slightly deeper draught of my beer. I felt I could drink up and go fairly soon, to follow up this casino thing; see where

Kravitz hangs out when he's not schmoozing Paulette de Vere – just throwing her money around the roulette tables. It would be a shame to take leave of the lucious Kate to shadow a creep like Kravitz, but if I've learned one thing as a PI, it's never to let the trail cool down.

I was sorry I'd taken such a big swig of the Jumbo Juice, because what the lady had to say next started up a trail even hotter – and in a different direction.

"It sure is a mug's game, replied Kate. "That's maybe what Laverne was telling him, when she was talking to him before."

"Laverne?"

"Laverne Delmar." As she spoke, she turned and looked towards the cabaret singer on the stage, and then returned to her drink. She took a sip.

"She's not bad," I said. "Nice voice."

Laverne Delmar was crooning an old Andrews Sisters song, and not handling it at all badly.

"She and Lennie know each other?" I asked, nonchalantly.

"Well, I don't really know how well they know each other. I just know she sings here every now and again. They looked like they were having a serious conversation, though. Maybe she's an old girlfriend of his or something, and he was trying to give her the brush-off. Anyway, he seemed a bit uncomfortable, and left right after. Talking of leaving," she said, "I really don't wanna be rude, but I have to go. I have to be in the office by eight-thirty tomorrow. Some of us have to work for a living, you know." She grinned. "Thanks for the drink, Brent. It sure has put me on the right road. I hope I can do the same for you sometime."

"Sure thing. Nice talking to you, Kate. I'd offer you a lift, but I came by cab." I indicated the drink.

"Subway's only a step away, I'll be on my way home before you finish your drink."

"Safe journey," I said.

"See you around," and she patted me lightly on the

shoulder as she left, the scent of her perfume drifting past as she swept by.

"Be seeing you," I said. I hoped I would. I don't like to ask for a phone number when I meet up with a woman the first time. It looks pushy. I hate pushy. I figure if she wants me to have her number she'll offer it. But I hoped I'd run into Kate again. Maybe I'd start taking the subway more often.

* * *

The trail that I followed as a result of what Kate had said about the conversation between Lennie Kravitz and Laverne Delmar proved much more useful than hanging around The Cavalier and staking out Kravitz. It was a damned sight cheaper too.

I took a cab back to my apartment, and since I'd only had the one beer at the night-spot, I took my car, parked it outside Jumbo's, and waited for Laverne Delmar to emerge.

It was around two-thirty a.m. when she finally appeared, alone, and clicked her way on high-heeled shoes towards her parked car. Other revellers from Jumbo's spilled into the parking lot and ambled, tottered or staggered towards their own autos, making the usual coming-out-of-a-night-club sounds. Engines started up, and the noisy clientèle hollered their goodbyes into the night air.

So, starting up my engine and crawling out amongst the line of cars did nothing to draw attention to me as I left Jumbo's and headed out onto the freeway with the rest of them, keeping a safe but observable distance between my car and Laverne Delmar's.

She turned off the freeway. One or two other cars as well as mine turned off too. It was only on the road she finally swung into that she left the traffic completely behind. Not wanting to follow her into what appeared to be a cul-de-sac, I drove on past, continuing a few yards before stopping the car, getting out, and closing the door as softly as I could. The cul-de-sac wasn't brightly lit, but I could see her car go into a driveway. I stayed out of sight, behind a hedge which bordered the road I'd parked on, and only when I was sure she'd had time to gain access to the house did I make my way to her driveway. The house was big and expensive, with a landscaped garden containing mature trees and shrubs. I stood quietly in the shadow of a huge oak and watched the house.

Laverne Delmar could be seen moving between lighted rooms upstairs. She appeared to be alone – there was no evidence of anyone else present. One by one, the lights went out, and after a safe time elapsed, I crept towards the house. There was a double garage attached, the door open, no cars inside. There was only Laverne Delmar's car on the premises, and that was left parked on the gravel driveway. She was too tired, maybe, to be bothered to drive into the garage and close the door.

I made my way across the lawn and looked around the ground floor. One window was slightly ajar. It was the work of a moment to climb inside the house; I found myself in what appeared to be a study, or office of some sort. I could make out a desk, chairs, and occasional tables set with lamps. I chose to use my trusty flashlight, rather than turn on a lamp. The drawer of the desk wasn't locked. It contained an address book. I looked, but there was nothing under 'K' for Kravitz. I tried 'L' and came up trumps. Lennie's name was there all right, and his works telephone number. I replaced the book and closed the drawer. On a shelf near the desk were a few books. On the spine of one of them was printed 'Hillingdon High Yearbook, 1938'. I lifted it down carefully.

Inside, were pictures of the class of '38, Laverne's face amongst them, smiling up from the page. Except that the name underneath was not Laverne Delmar. It was Dora Kravitz. Was Laverne Delmar Lennie Kravitz's wife? Did they marry when she was still at high school? If so, how did he manage the upkeep of his wife, a house the size of this mansion, and his gambling habit, all on an office salary? Paulette de Vere sure wasn't going to hand dosh over to Lennie to keep his wife in the lap of luxury. But then, she may not know he had a wife.

My flashlight fell upon the answer to Dora's identity. Dora was not Lennie's wife. But she may be his sister. A wedding photo on a table revealed the happy couple who inhabited this palace. Laverne, or should I say Dora, and her husband Robert Bellamy. My heart went down to the basement and up to the penthouse before returning to its rightful floor. He was a big time thug and a crook. Into narcotics, illegal immigrants, protection, and probably a whole lot more he hadn't been caught at yet. And I was in his house. But not for long.

I made for the window, switching off the flashlight before I climbed out into the garden. There was no sign of Bellamy here, though – or his car. I knew he drove a Rolls; he was pictured with it in the paper a couple of weeks ago, when he was photographed handing a large cheque to some charity or other. All the hoods did that; made sure they appeared squeaky clean.

Dora's car was parked unlocked in the driveway. There appeared to be nothing of note in the interior; nothing in the glove compartment, on the floor, or seats. As I walked softly around to the trunk, keeping my steps as light as I could on the gravel, I turned on the flashlight. It illuminated the ground beneath the car. There was a dark patch glistening on the gravel. Oil. A few more patches revealed themselves along the driveway. For all the money Mrs Bellamy had access to, she had a leaky car.

I opened the trunk and looked inside. Nothing there. From habit, years of experience in the gumshoe trade, I ran my hands down the sides of the trunk's floor. Nothing. No! Wait! What was this? I retrieved a small, hard object about the size of my thumbnail. It glistened gold. With the trunk lid up, shielding the flashlight from the house, I examined the object, close to the centre of the beam. It was a cufflink. This one had a cameo setting. And the picture on the cameo was that of a cowboy astride his horse, hat held high. No bozo could convince me now that there was no link between Dora Kravitz/Bellamy and Hector de Vere. Here it was in my hand. The evidence had to remain where I found it, if it was to be worth a damn, so I slid the cufflink back to where it had come from, completely out of sight, but not completely out of reach.

I closed the trunk softly, and made my way quickly back to my car. On the way home, I turned things over in my mind. How did de Vere's cufflink get into the trunk of Dora Bellamy's car? She evidently wasn't aware that it was there. If de Vere had lost a cufflink and an innocent Dora had intended to return it to him, she surely would have put it in her purse, or the glove compartment, not in the trunk, to roll around or get lost. No, it was more likely that the death of Hector de Vere had more than a little to do with Mrs Dora Bellamy. I had a feeling that not only his cufflink, but Mr de Vere himself had occupied that trunk. The cummings-style poem jumped back into my head. The hitman maybe Miss. Miss Laverne Delmar. Miss Dora Kravitz. Or even Mrs Dora Bellamy.

* * *

On Wednesday morning, I arrived at my office a little later, to find the tabby sitting patiently by two empty saucers, and two hefty cops outside my door. One of them was Pat O'Malley, an Irish guy whom I'd known a long time in the course of my professional work. He was an OK guy, O'Malley; an old-fashioned cop, straight, wasn't on the make like some of them, and hated those who were. We'd done each other a few favours over the years. He had a new guy with him I hadn't seen before. O'Malley introduced the rookie as Mike Benson. We shook hands, and I unlocked the door.

Puss ran ahead of us into the room.

"This yours?" O'Malley asked, nodding towards the tabby.

"Kinda. I guess so. Sort of invited herself a week or two ago."

"That's cats for you," said O'Malley, and drew up a couple

of chairs for himself and Benson.

"What can I do for you, Pat?" I asked. As we spoke, I washed up the saucers, fed the cat and made us some coffee.

It appeared that O'Malley had dropped by to ask me to confirm that Paulette de Vere had had an appointment with me on Monday morning. In the light of Hector's untimely departure from this mortal coil, everyone who knew him was under suspicion, including his grieving widow. O'Malley informed me that not only had de Vere been shot, but drugged beforehand. I asked if the cops had found anything of value to assist them in their quest for the murderer. O'Malley said they didn't have much to go on. Just some oil and gravel on de Vere's shoes, and a cufflink missing. Otherwise, he was as well-dressed in death as he had been in life.

I told O'Malley what I knew. Benson listened closely and wrote fast. I didn't, of course, say I'd snooped around the Bellamy house in the early hours of the morning, or dug around in Dora's car trunk. I wouldn't want to put O'Malley in the position of having to do me for unlawful entry or any of that stuff. I simply said I'd become interested in the case and my enquiries led me to believe there was a connection between Laverne Delmar, Lennie Kravitz and Paulette de Vere. And that I'd followed Laverne home, and noticed her car was leaking oil in the gravel driveway. I suggested a search of her house and car might turn something up – no problem in getting a warrant now, with the gravel and oil evidence, surely? Reasonable cause for a search, wouldn't you say?

O'Malley was grateful. He promised to let me know of any new developments. He and Benson left, and I sat down and poured myself some more coffee. The mystery of the cummings-style poem (of which I'd said nothing to O'Malley, as it was hardly hard evidence) continued to plague my brain. Even the tiniest inkling of who the writer had been continued to elude me. No one, other than myself, Paulette de Vere and the cat were present when my penchant for cummings had been discussed. I was pretty sure Mrs de Vere didn't write it. I sure didn't.

"That just leaves you, Puss," I said sternly to the tabby. *You* must have penned that poem. After all, as Conan Doyle wrote; 'When you have eliminated the impossible, whatever remains, however improbable, must be the truth.'" The cat stood up on the chair she occupied and arched her back. She turned her green-eyed, unfathomable gaze on me for a moment, then curled up in a circle, with her tail around her, and closed her eyes. I laughed. She purred.

* * *

New developments on the de Vere front came thick and fast. Between O'Malley's low-down from the Police Department, and the daily papers over the following weeks, the facts of the case became clear.

There was no one at home when the cops arrived with a search warrant, at the Bellamy house. Dora's car was still in the driveway. Fortunately, the search of the car provided the necessary evidence; the cufflink was retrieved. The cops figured that if she was involved in the death of de Vere, Mrs Bellamy must be headed for an airport to make a getaway. She sure wasn't likely to stick around the States with a murder rap even a remote possibility.

Wednesday afternoon, a warrant for her detention was issued. Phone calls to the airports brought to light the fact that she had booked an early evening flight to Rio de Janeiro. She never got there, of course. The cops, to her surprise (and no doubt, horror) were there to pick her up, along with her leather suitcase containing fifty thousand dollars in cash, and the gun which shot Hector de Vere – she'd foolishly kept it, presumably for protection in Rio. The fingerprints of Paulette de Vere and Lennie Kravitz on the suitcase made it impossible for any of them to deny involvement with one another.

It transpired that Dora Bellamy had agreed to do the dirty work for Paulette de Vere, and Dora's brother, Lennie Kravitz.

Paulette was to pay her fifty thousand dollars to do away with Hector de Vere; the dough was meant to give her a new start in South America, away from her increasingly brutal gangster husband. She was to take a new name (which seemed to be a hobby of hers) and disappear amongst the colourful hordes in Rio. Paulette of course, was then to inherit Hector's vast millions, and she and Lennie (and likely Dora too) were to enjoy themselves on the spoils.

Dora had timed things nicely. On the Sunday night, Hector de Vere left his gentleman's club alone. As he usually enjoyed a drink or two there, he hadn't taken his car, and was intending to take a cab home, it being his chauffeur's night off. Before he could hail a cab, a young (and rather attractive) girl fainted in front of him. Simply collapsed on the street. He picked her up and she began to regain consciousness. When she had come around fully, she said she'd been feeling unwell, but that it wasn't the first time this had happened; she'd be OK, her car was just around the corner. Hector wouldn't hear of her driving herself home in that condition. He'd take her home. So Hector, poor sap, did his good deed like a gentleman should, and off they went back to Dora's. Her husband, Robert Bellamy (with whom Hector was naturally unacquainted) was away 'on business' in New Orleans, so Dora, now 'recovered', had the house to herself, and the time to effect her plan to escape from her financially stable, but emotionally miserable life.

She offered de Vere a drink, but he said no, he'd had enough that evening, but a cup of coffee would be nice. It was the last cup of coffee the poor guy was ever to drink. Drugged and unconscious, Dora dragged him to her car under cover of darkness, and lugged him into the trunk. It must have been hard work, but the fruits of her labours would be substantial, so a little breathlessness was hardly to be complained of. At this point she (sensibly) didn't shoot him. Blood in the trunk would have been a dead give-away.

She drove back to the city, down an alleyway, and pulled the still unconscious Hector out of the car. Making sure there was no one around to see her, she took the gun, fitted with a silencer, and gave him one shot to the head. She buried him under a huge pile of garbage bags, and hi-tailed it back to her house.

The next day, Monday, Paulette de Vere (who made certain she and Lennie had alibis at the time of Hector's death) went to the police, and to Mr Philip Murdoch, to report Hector missing; playing the worried wife to throw the cops off the scent.

On the Tuesday, Paulette went to the bank and withdrew fifty thousand dollars in cash, to enable Dora to get out of the States and ensconced in Rio. Unknown to Mrs de Vere, however, the cashier, thinking that such a large amount of cash may be a blackmail or kidnap payment, took note of the serial numbers, as was policy with that particular bank for large cash withdrawals. So dear Mrs de Vere could hardly deny association with Dora's payout. Not to mention her and Lennie's dabs all over the suitcase. Sure that no one would suspect Dora (she'd never even met de Vere, only knew him from newspaper photos), they were careless, and wore no gloves as they handled the money and put it in Dora's suitcase. They had also compounded the situation by driving up to the Bellamy house to deliver the cash on Tuesday, managing to get oil and gravel from Dora's driveway on the wheels of Paulette's car.

The evidence against these three dopes was so irrefutable, there was simply nowhere for them to go but the State Pen. Dora had attempted to get her sentence lightened by turning State's Evidence against her husband, giving the cops all she knew about his illegal operations. I'll bet it was like everybody's Christmases and birthdays all rolled into one, down at the fifteenth precinct that day.

The thing that must have been particularly galling to Lennie and Paulette was that in the end, it was to have been all for nothing. They could have saved themselves a lot of trouble if they'd known about Hector's insurance policy, and his will.

Suspecting that Paulette was cheating on him, and unhappy about the low company he'd heard she'd been keeping of late, Hector had put a clause in his insurance policy, that if he was to die by any means other than natural causes, no insurance was to be paid out. He also changed his will, unbeknownst to Paulette, leaving his millions to be divided up between his favourite charities; he had no other living relatives. All he'd had was Paulette. A dumb broad who paid an even dumber broad to introduce his intellect to some lead. You kinda had to feel sorry for the guy.

Well, the case was solved all right, but I hadn't really had one hell of a lot to do with it. It was a really a Case-That-Never-Was as far as I was concerned. I suppose I was sort of instrumental in justice being served, and all that kinda stuff, but I sure as shootin' didn't get my 'case completion' fee from Mrs de Vere, and under the circumstances I wasn't about to ask for it. I put it all down to experience and resigned myself to being a poor guy again. I guess things could be worse. Look what can happen to a rich one.

The mystery still remained, however, as to the author of the 'cummings' poem. It still remains a mystery to this day. Well, you can't solve 'em all. Well, perhaps *you* can. Answers on a postcard please, to *The New York Clarion*.

What probably surprises you as much as me about this whole shebang, is the fact that throughout the entire thing, not once was I slugged over the head, or beaten up by sadistic cops and left to rot a few days in a police cell.

However, a month or so later, when the papers had gotten fed up with the de Vere story, things had returned pretty much to normal in every way. That is, I was sitting alone in my empty office, waiting for something to turn up, without even the cat for company (it disappeared after the de Vere case was wrapped up – obviously went looking for its kicks elsewhere now all the excitement was over), when there came a knock on my office door. A guy came in asking me to find his wife. She was last seen in Chicago.

I duly booked my ticket to the Windy City. Two days after I started the case, I woke up in my hotel room with a lump the size of a baseball on my bruised and bloodied face, and before I could wash off the haemoglobin, two heavies from the Chicago Police Department were staring me in the kisser, asking me why I was keeping company with the Mob, and would I grace them with my salubrious presence down at the station to "help them with their enquiries".

But hell, that's another story.

As they returned from market one day, Bess and Kit stopped at the top of the hill overlooking the wooded valley below, and sat down to rest before continuing with their load. They were carrying cloth as well as the usual foodstuffs, for Bess had decided upon making a new dress for Kit – one which better fitted her burgeoning shape, and which she could wear on special occasions.

"'Clothes maketh the man,'" quoted Bess, "but they can do a lot of good for a woman too – if you have the eye for what best suits you. Don't underestimate the power of dress on the human being, Kit. I could write a book about it. Always look your best, if at all possible."

Bess herself was a fine figure of a woman, and still turned heads as she wove through the market each Thursday afternoon. Kit was very proud of her mother, and though she enjoyed being with her friends, time spent in Bess's company was fun and pleasurable – and always informative. And Kit loved to learn. So it wasn't long after they sat down to get their breath that Kit returned to the subject with which she was so naturally preoccupied: the Gifted.

"Must the Gifted not use their abilities once they have passed on the gifts to others?" asked Kit.

"Once they are passed on, they are no longer able to be used by the Bestower. So the Bestower must be extremely careful that they are passed on to the right recipient, and at the right time," Bess replied.

"But they don't...they don't have to...to go on to The Great Adventure as soon as they have bestowed the gifts...do they?"

*"Oh, no, they don't **have** to. Like The Great Adventure, they can choose the time when they give their gifts away to others. But many may choose to make the two events very close together."*

"Why?"

"It's because it feels right for them. The Gifted can choose whenever to effect any of these Changes. They know when the time is right. It's an enviable advantage that we have over the

human race, the business of knowing when the time is right. What makes humans so fragile and vulnerable to the whims of Fate is that in their lives, timing is everything, and they rarely have control over it.

"We are lucky, Kit, very lucky; when it comes to the great Changes in our lives – we have the power to choose the time."

1959

"Susie! Sit still and settle down, now. This is a *test*."

"Miss Lanyon, Ralph Adams keeps pulling my hair and I can't think properly." Susie turned and glared at the smirking Ralph, then looked beseechingly at the teacher, who cast her eyes heavenwards and threaded her way impatiently through the rows of desks until she reached the culprit.

The boy turned his blank-faced stare of wide-eyed innocence upon her once too often that morning. Miss Lanyon leaned down and in a threatening undertone spoke few, but telling words to the class bully, which were inaudible even to those around him. He was in a desk by himself behind the unfortunate Susie. Ralph cast down his eyes and jutted his jaw, wriggling a little uncomfortably in his seat. Everyone present wondered what Miss Lanyon had said to so discomfort him, but nobody dared make a sound, for it was obvious that the usually calm and even-tempered teacher was in no mood for disruption.

Miss Lanyon returned to her desk and sat down. Unbidden, the class resumed work at their Math test. The only sound to be heard was the breeze rustling the branches of the cherry blossom tree which stood next to the open window of the classroom. Miss Lanyon allowed her attention to briefly wander from the children as she watched some of the pink petals fall from the tree to the ground below. Soon there would be a pink carpet upon the grass; then the blossom would disappear from the tree until next spring. She measured her years in the school by the number of times she had seen the tree bloom. This was the fifth time she had seen its glories...summer would be here soon...would she still be here to see the tree flower another year? Or would she by this time next year be Mrs Clayton Hadfield, living in style on Long Island?

A faint commotion interrupted her thoughts, and brought her attention back to her charges.

"Miss Lanyon, Angélique Fluck's wet herself."

The class was soon in an uproar. Desks and chairs scraped the floor as children in the vicinity of Angélique's desk leapt out of the way to avoid the urine which leaked into the aisle and formed a puddle under the chairs of those nearby.

Miss Lanyon sprang up and immediately took control.

"Come and stand here," she ordered the children nearest to the wet area. They needed no second bidding, and made their way hastily to the front of the classroom by the window. She hurried over to Angélique and took her by the hand, calling to Susie Bell as she did so, "Go and ask the janitor to bring a mop and bucket, and some disinfectant, Susie, please."

Secretly rather pleased at being chosen to perform this important task, Susie glanced around at the envious faces of her classmates and said, "Yes, Miss Lanyon," rather more loudly than was necessary, and skipped off down the corridor, glad that Angélique's misfortune had resulted in some kudos for herself, and had put paid (for the moment at least) to the dreaded Math test, which Susie knew she would have flunked anyway.

Miss Lanyon sat Angélique on the floor in front of her desk, whilst quieting the excited class. She had to go and see if there was still a spare pair of girl's panties available in the cupboard in the staffroom.

"Now, I have to go to the staffroom," said Miss Lanyon. "I'll be back shortly. There must be no noise. Miss Blaine's class is also doing the Math test this morning, so I repeat: no noise." She looked sternly around the classroom. The children sat still and quiet.

From where she sat on the floor, Angélique looked up at the teacher, her small grey eyes staring out of her plump, round, face, mucus running from the nostrils of her short, flat nose. Poor kid, thought Miss Lanyon. I don't think she even knows what's going on.

Looking round the classroom once more, the teacher left, closing the door softly behind her. Her footsteps gradually faded as she headed down the corridor to the staffroom.

When they could be heard no more, the classroom erupted. Like a lynch mob, the children exploded into a roar of jeers and laughter, of angry shouts and nasty jibes.

"Don't you know what a toilet's for?"

"You've made a mess of my new shoes! You filthy pig!"

"No wonder you're smelly, Angélique Fluck."

"She's *always* smelly! She's probably never ever had a bath."

"If she did go in a bath, she'd think it was a toilet!" Ralph Adams basked in the howls of laughter from the class. Except for the two children who weren't laughing.

Angélique sat staring uncomprehendingly at the jeering faces in front of her. And another small girl at the front of the room watched the scene in pain and horror, tears streaming down her face, unseen by the remainder of the mob. Poor, poor Angélique. With each new cut, and the accompanying laughter, a shard of pain went through Evie's heart. Why were her classmates behaving like this? What made them say such dreadful things? It was awful. *Awful*.

Judy Merrell suddenly caught sight of Evie crying.

"What's the matter with you?" she asked Evie.

"Everybody's being horrid to Angélique," replied Evie, tears choking her as she spoke.

"So, what? She's too stupid to know what's going on, anyway. Anyone would think it was you that was being laughed at."

Evie was dumbfounded. She could barely formulate a reply.

"But it's not right," was all she could manage through her sobs, "how do you know how Angélique feels?"

"What's up with Evie?" A few of the other girls had come over to see this new drama.

"Oh, she's just a cry baby," scoffed Judy, then returned her attention to Angélique, who had been playing with her shoe. The buckle had broken, and the shoe came off her foot, revealing a greyish coloured sock, so worn that her big toe stuck out through the hole. Gales of laughter greeted the sight. Fingers pointed anew, the voices grew raucous. Evie's anguished sobs were drowned by the din. Angélique's face began to crumple, her little fat body began to shudder, but the taunts were relentless.

The latch clicked. A grim-faced Miss Lanyon stood framed in the doorway.

Tears started to flow from Angélique's eyes, making two clean tracks through the grime on her face. She turned her tousled head and gazed up at Miss Lanyon with a look that suddenly spoke a thousand words.

Little Evie thought her heart would break. Only her own sobs could now be heard in the terrible silence that followed. Miss Lanyon's eyes spoke a thousand words, too. She stood and looked at the children with such contempt as to make them shrivel to their very souls.

Quietly they began to return to their places, and remained in silence, held by the expression in Miss Lanyon's eyes. For what seemed a lifetime, she looked directly at them, one by one, holding their gaze until they lowered their eyes in shame.

She bent down, lifted Angélique up, and set her on her feet. She took her by the hand. Only then did she speak.

"Come with me, Evie," she said in a low voice to the sobbing child. "I want you to come and look after Angélique for a while."

Evie rubbed her eyes with her soggy handkerchief, swallowed hard, and made her way over to where Angélique stood. She took hold of Angélique's hand, which was stained and wet from the tears she had wiped across her face.

Miss Lanyon led the two little girls out of the classroom, leaving the door open as she did so. The only sound to be heard were their footsteps as they walked along the corridor.

* * *

"Children can be so *cruel*," said Mrs Prenton, shaking her head despairingly, as the events of the morning were discussed in the staffroom that lunchtime. "People think that they are all so sweet and innocent. They can be simply dreadful."

"Like a pack of ravaging hyenas," agreed Miss Wade.

"And Miss Lanyon's class are only nine years old, for heaven's sake," said Mrs Mayhew. "What on earth will they be like when they're sixteen?"

"They're not all bad," sighed Miss Lanyon. I think they do have a conscience. And then look at little Evie Thurston. A more sweet-natured child would be hard to find. She's always looked out for Angélique, since she first came to us. Evie tries to include her at playtimes, even though Angélique's incapable of any meaningful input to the games. It's quite touching, really. Evie was awfully upset when the class got at Angie."

"Yes, Evie's a nice little thing," said Mrs Prenton. "I taught her brother Arnold. He's a good little fellow, too."

"Some kids are so unlucky," said Miss Shearley. "I mean, when most of them get the measles they just get over it, and that's that. But apparently about one in a thousand get complications like Angélique did, and end up with encephalomyelitis."

"What exactly *is* that?" asked Miss Blaine.

"Well, it's a condition that affects the nervous system. Even if you recover from it, it can leave you with a mental handicap, and incontinence, as in Angélique's case."

"How awful," said Mrs Prenton. "You'd never think that measles could end up doing so much damage. It makes you realise just how fortunate you are when your own children survive unscathed." Everyone nodded in agreement, and they sat in silence for a while.

"Well now, to more cheerful things," said Miss Moorcroft, the Principal, putting down her coffee cup and smoothing her skirt. "I've found our celebrity to open the new gymnasium." This was greeted by a murmur of interest from the others.

"I've asked Rocky Wilde to do the honours."

The surprise in the staffroom was palpable.

"You mean *the* Rocky Wilde?"

Miss Moorcroft smiled and nodded.

"Well, I'll be darned!" said Mrs Mayhew, adjusting her spectacles and patting her chignon, which she was sure had fallen into disarray at the news.

"Who is this...Rocky...er..." asked Miss Wade, she of the horn-rimmed spectacles and flat, sensible shoes.

"He's the lead singer in the rock n' roll group 'Rocky Wilde and The Stormraisers'," replied the young Miss Shearley. "He's a very handsome guy." Realising that her last sentence was delivered in a rather too appreciative tone, she added in a matter-of-fact-manner, "His record is number one in the hit parade at the moment."

"Good heavens!" gasped Miss Wade. "Could we not have asked a famous sportsman or something? I mean, after all, we are opening a gymnasium, not a concert hall, Margaret."

Miss Moorcroft grinned at her deputy. "Rocky Wilde – or should I say Norman Perrin –"

"Norman Perrin! No wonder he changed his name," exclaimed Miss Shearley, and the women laughed.

"– Norman Perrin is actually a member of this community – or at least his family is – I taught his father years ago in Chicago. The family now live here in Kingsville. It seemed sensible to have a local celebrity – it keeps down the expenses," said Miss Moorcroft, nodding knowingly at Miss Wade, and the others laughed. Miss Wade was always looking for ways to save the school money. "We'll earmark someone to play host to our celebrity –"

"I'll do it Miss," squeaked Miss Shearley, to the amusement of her colleagues. "Well, I am the youngest," she said hopefully, and got a playful smack on her wrist from Miss Wade.

"Now girls," admonished Miss Moorcroft in a mock-headmistressy voice, and they all chuckled.

"I thought the best way to do it would be to get the

children to each write their names on a piece of paper, which they place in an envelope. Then we'll put all the envelopes in a box and I'll draw out the one who'll do the job."

"That's a good idea," said Mrs Prenton. "When will the draw be?"

"Thursday afternoon I'll draw the envelope," said Miss Moorcroft, "but I'll open it in front of the children on Friday afternoon. It'll be all the more suspenseful and exciting for them. Not to mention being an excellent way of getting them to be good! They'll get to know on Friday afternoon *if* they've been nicely behaved." This suggestion naturally met with great approval. "The opening ceremony will be next Tuesday," continued Miss Moorcroft, "so it'll give us time to brief our host or hostess as to their duties before the big day."

She suddenly stopped and cocked an ear towards the playground outside. "Do I hear the bell? I think I do. All right, ladies, back to the grindstone."

* * *

The boys and girls ran towards the school bus, or awaiting cars, or strolled in twos and threes homewards at the end of the afternoon. Due to the events of the morning, those in Miss Lanyon's class left in a more subdued manner than usual, as their teacher had made it clear by her demeanour that she was still very displeased with them for their appalling behaviour towards the unfortunate Angélique.

Evie couldn't stop thinking about the situation, and after the others had gone home, and she waited for her mother to pick her up from school, she sat on the bench near the cherry blossom tree, which stood on the grassy verge between the classroom and the roadway.

The picture of Angélique surrounded by taunting classmates would not leave her mind, and, as she imagined what it must have felt like to be in the poor girl's place, tears welled up once more, and before long, she was sobbing softly, wiping her tears on the sleeves of her coat and feeling very unhappy.

Evie could not forget Miss Lanyon's words through the staffroom door as she sat outside it, waiting for Angélique.

"Just climb out of your wet panties, Angélique, there's a good girl. That's it...oh dear, you've dirtied them too. We'll have to give them a good wash before we give them back to your mother. Here now, let's clean you up – hold up your dress like a good girl. That's it. Oh *dear*..."

Evie felt so humiliated for Angélique. How awful to have to have someone clean up your mess... The modest and fastidious little Evie couldn't imagine anything worse. Her sympathy for Angélique reached new heights. She wanted to move out of earshot, not wishing to add to Angélique's troubles by being party to this embarrassing scene. But she couldn't move away from her seat in the corridor. Miss Lanyon had told her to stay there and wait until Angélique came out. She had asked Evie to sit with Angélique in an empty classroom while she telephoned Mrs Fluck to ask her to come and collect her daughter. Angélique was to be excused school for the rest of the day, as she was obviously unwell.

"There Angélique. Nice dry panties. You'll feel better now."

The door opened and Miss Lanyon came out holding Angélique by the hand. Evie jumped up, and dried her face with the back of her hand. She smiled as brightly as she could at Angélique. Angélique smiled back.

"Right, you two, just go and sit quietly in the room opposite. I'll only be a minute or so telephoning Angélique's mother."

Evie and Angélique went into the empty classroom and sat down at a desk near the door.

"Are you going home now, Angélique?" asked Evie. Angélique looked at her, but said nothing. Her attention wandered and she looked out of the window into the playground.

"You can come and play handball in the playground with me tomorrow, if you like," said Evie. Angélique turned to look at her, a blank expression on her face. Still she said nothing. Evie knew there was something wrong with Angélique's brain, so she didn't mind when there was no answer. She liked it when Angélique smiled, though, as she sometimes did. It showed she wasn't unhappy all of the time. They sat together in strange, but companionable silence.

Miss Lanyon came into the room.

"You can go back to class now, Evie," she said. "Angélique's mother will be here in a few minutes. I'll be along soon."

Evie got up to go. Angélique made a sound and reached up to get hold of Evie's hand.

"I'll see you tomorrow, Angélique," said Evie, giving Angélique's hand a squeeze. Angélique let go and stared out of the window again. Miss Lanyon nodded her thanks to Evie, and the little girl left the room and made her way back to the classroom. Before she could reach it, the bell sounded, signalling lunchtime. But Evie wasn't very hungry.

As she sat now, on the bench by the cherry blossom tree, Evie's mind turned from Angélique's present to her future. Poor Angélique. What would happen to her when she was grown up, and maybe had no one to look after her? How would she live then? Evie sighed a shaky, sob-ridden sigh. She wondered where her mother was. It was much later than the time Evie was normally collected.

Suddenly she felt the bench on which she was sitting shake, as if somebody had sat down next to her. She looked up. Somebody *had* sat down next to her. It was a lady in a flowered print dress. She looked at Evie with concern.

"You OK, honey? You look a little sad," she said. "You been crying?"

Evie nodded.

"Has someone been mean to you?"

Evie shook her head. "No, not to me. To Angélique."

"Oh, I see. Is she your friend?"

"Yes," said Evie instinctively, though she knew that she and Angélique were not really friends in the way you normally understand friends to be. It wasn't really like that at all.

"Angélique's...not...not very well," said Evie. "And the others were making fun of her and it just isn't fair."

"No it sure is *not*," replied the lady. "In fact it's really *awful*. People can be so nasty sometimes. But it's good Angélique has a friend like you, huh? That more than makes up for the others, I'd say."

Evie looked at the lady, whose eyes, she noticed, were very green. Evies's eyes were green too. But not as green as the lady's.

"I don't think Angélique has a very good time," she confided to her new acquaintance. "Being...ill and all." Evie's eyes clouded once more.

"Well now," said the lady, leaning towards Evie in a conspiratorial fashion, "I happen to know that Angélique is gonna have a real good time – and very soon, too."

Evie looked at her in astonishment. "How do you know that?" she asked.

"Because...well, I'm gonna fix it that she is."

Evie's eyes were as big as dinner plates. The lady answered her unasked question.

"Let's say I sometimes do special favours for special people." She slowly winked one of her green eyes.

Evie believed her. "Sort of like a fairy godmother?"

"Yeah, sort of."

Evie began to smile. "Wow," she said softly. She looked into the green eyes again. "Where do you come from?" she asked.

"Cherry Blossom Heights," said the lady.

"Where's that?" asked Evie.

"Oh, not far from here," replied the lady airily. "Say! You've got green eyes, like me," she said suddenly, looking into Evie's with a warm, open smile. Evie nodded. "Only real special people have green eyes," said the lady. "Do you know, I think you're gonna be lucky as well as special. Honest! Hey, is that your mom?"

A car drew up at the kerb, and a blonde woman waved from the driver's seat.

Evie jumped up. "Oh yes!" She waved to her mother, then turned to the lady.

"Thank you," she said. "Thank you very much for..."

"Yeah, sure," said the lady. "You take care, now. And watch out for Angélique." She smiled and winked again.

Evie ran to the car and climbed in beside her mother, who greeted her apologetically.

"Hi, honey, sorry I'm late. Traffic lights were out coming into Kingsville." She gave her daughter a kiss. "Who was that lady you were talking to?"

"She's..." Evie knew her mother wouldn't believe she was a fairy godmother.

"She's a friend of Angélique's."

Evie and her mother turned to wave through the car window, but the lady with the green eyes had vanished.

* * *

On Thursday afternoon, the children sat riveted in the school hall as Miss Moorcroft felt inside the box of envelopes and carefully drew one out. Every child in the room hoped fervently that the slip with their name was the one inside it.

"Bet that's got my name on it," whispered Ralph Adams to Judy Merrell, as Miss Moorcroft held the envelope aloft.

If they had all had X-ray eyes, they would have known that Ralph had won his bet.

* * *

On Friday afternoon, it took a little while to quiet the pupils down as Miss Moorcroft entered with The Envelope, which had been sitting in the drawer of her desk overnight. When order was restored, she slit the seal with her brass letter opener and slid her hand inside. The atmosphere was electric. The children held their breath; all eyes were on the white slip of paper. The silence could have been cut with a knife.

"And the lucky pupil who will be hosting our guest Mr Rocky Wilde...is..." She glanced down at the paper and tried to make out the scrawled misshapen letters upon it. "Ah yes – it's Angélique Fluck."

* * *

The teachers agreed, as they began to assemble the pupils in the new gymnasium for the opening ceremony, that there was more than a touch of poetic justice about the way things had turned out. Since it would have been difficult for Angélique to manage the task alone, little Evie Thurston was the obvious choice to aid Angélique in her important role. The girls had practised their greeting (Angélique said 'Hello' when prompted by Evie) and after Evie's vote of thanks to the guest upon arrival, Angélique was to say 'Thank you' when Evie gave her the sign.

On the day of the ceremony, Evie was more nervous for Angélique than she was for herself. She wanted Angélique to show everyone that she could do a good job, and get lots of praise, instead of being jeered at, like she usually was. As the other pupils were settling in the gym, the two girls sat in the lobby, awaiting their famous guest.

* * *

It wasn't a sunny day; it was rather grey overhead – looked like there may be rain, in fact – but a little thing like that didn't stop Rocky from donning his 'shades' before driving off in his shiny black automobile. As he drove, he checked his appearance in the rear-view mirror, and smoothed his slicked-back hair with his right hand, expertly bringing his quiff into the position he felt made him look Maximum Hip. He narrowly missed hitting a pink Chevrolet which had drawn up alongside him, and he grabbed the steering wheel just in time to avoid collision, braking hard as he did so.

"Punk!" called the driver, and put his foot to the floor. The Chevy took off like a rocket, and left Rocky, somewhat shaken, tootling along in the inside lane, thanking his lucky stars that his guitar on the back seat hadn't hurtled through the front window and ended up on the highway, reaching Kingsville before he did.

Rocky turned up the collar of his leather jacket, pushed up the sleeves to just below the elbow and resumed feeling hip again. He felt he would look more cool if he leaned his left arm on the car door with the window open, and flicked the wheel with his fingers like Dean and Brando did in the movies; so he opened the window, rested his elbow in the required place and immediately regretted it, as the wind through the open window ruffled his just-combed hair and sent his quiff down to the end of his nose, where the strands parted company and covered his eyes, obscuring his vision.

"*Tarnation!*" he hissed, pulling the car over to the sidewalk, and drawing to a halt. He switched off the engine and rolled up the window again. Feeling impatiently inside his pocket for his comb, his heart nearly stood still. No comb! NO COMB! Panic threatened to overcome him, until he realised that there were alternative pockets in his jacket, and that he had probably chosen the wrong one. Maybe it was in the left inside pocket. He threw up his left arm to reach inside the jacket with his right hand, and cracked his elbow on the window glass.

"OW! *Oh, Man!!*" He hit the steering wheel in annoyance and the horn sounded. And sounded. And kept on sounding. The thing just wouldn't stop. Rocky didn't know what to do to stop it. He didn't know anything about cars. He just drove 'em. But he couldn't drive this one making such a darned awful racket – the cops would be on him like ducks on a June bug. It had to be stopped before he could get going again.

He looked at the dashboard. It was full of switches and buttons. He switched and he buttoned, and lights went on, and lights went off, and the windscreen wipers went like crazy. So much so, that one of the rubber blades shot off and disappeared over the hedge at the side of the road.

"*Jumpin' Jehosophat!!*" he yelled, smashing his fists down angrily on the steering wheel. "OW!!!" he howled as his finger bones met the hard surface. But the horn stopped. Praise the Lord for that, at least. Alleluia. He rubbed his hands to ease the pain.

Then he switched and buttoned some more, until the status quo was established, and he heaved a sigh of relief. He was going to have to get somebody to explain all this stuff to him before he went out in this heap again.

Rocky rubbed his elbow, which he was sure would have a bruise the size of Boston, and having retrieved his comb, resumed the important task of repairing his coiffure. He looked at himself in the mirror. *Geez Louise*, he looked like something from a sci-fi film. He set about making himself gorgeous again, and when satisfied with the result, he practised his hip smile in the mirror – the Elvis one, where he raised one side of his top lip. Instead of producing a wry, sensuous smile, the face in the mirror sneered back rather nastily at him, so he decided he'd need a bit more practice before he'd perfected that one, and did a Paul Anka smile instead. Yeah, that was cool. He'd use that one today. Probably better anyway if he was going to be around little kids.

He started up the engine and slid out onto the road again. His watch showed he was running a little late, but no matter. He'd make up the time by going like a bat out of hell when he was sure there were no speed cops around. This car could sure fly when it wanted to. The car, however, didn't want to fly. In fact, it didn't want to go at all. It slowed to a halt another two hundred yards further down the road. Rocky couldn't believe it. Until he looked at the petrol gauge.

"Aaaaaargh!" he screamed, and hammered his fists on the dashboard, forgetting they were already sore from their previous encounter with the steering wheel. "*Aaaaaargh!!!*"

He caught sight of himself in the mirror. His face was contorted in pain and rage, ruining his pin-up image. But worse. His hair was a mess again.

* * *

"I do hope he won't be...gyrating," said Miss Wade in an undertone to her colleague, pursing her lips as she did so.

"That's what rock singers do, Ethel. They gyrate," replied Miss Moorcroft quietly, with a twinkle in her eye.

"Well it's to be hoped he'll keep it to a minimum. It all seems rather unseemly, if you ask me. Anyway he's seven minutes late already. Not a very impressive start, is it?" Miss Wade surveyed the assembled children as she muttered her reply. They sat expectantly in their seats in the gymnasium, watching the teachers, but unable to hear their *sotto voce* conversations.

At the rear of the gym, Miss Lanyon and Miss Shearley supervised those at the back.

"I wonder what kind of car he'll drive," mused Miss Shearley, "I'll bet it's a big, shiny, expensive one, whatever it is."

Miss Lanyon nodded. She saw Miss Moorcroft and Miss Wade heading towards the lobby, so she went up to take their place in front of the children. She glanced at her watch. If Rocky Wilde didn't turn up soon, the pupils would begin to get restless.

Out in the lobby, the Principal and her deputy checked on Evie and Angelina, still sitting patiently inside the entrance door, then went outside to await the arrival of The Main Event. As they emerged from the lobby, they heard the sound of a vehicle's engine, and smiled at one another in relief. Then:

"Oh my, what on earth..." said Miss Moorcroft.

A truck containing a small flock of sheep swept into the school grounds. It stopped outside the main entrance. There was the sound of a door slamming, then the truck took off again, leaving in its place a young man in jeans and black leather jacket, hopping unsteadily from one leg to the other as he flicked straw from his shoes. He came to a standstill and adjusted his hold on his guitar case, which threatened to escape his grip.

Miss Moorcroft and Miss Wade looked at one another in disbelief. The young man realised he had an audience, and went into Hip Mode. He loped his way in cool and groovy fashion towards the middle-aged ladies who stood at the school door, slicking back his hair as he did so, his facial expression a cross between his Paul Anka smile and a Bill Sykes leer.

"Oh dear Heaven, what *have* we let ourselves in for?" muttered Miss Wade between clenched teeth.

"Well, at least he's here," said Miss Moorcroft, through a forced smile.

As he reached the ladies, Rocky could see they were doing their best not to show the displeasure they felt at his time-keeping – not to mention his unorthodox entrance – and immediately his manner changed into that of a kid caught with his hand in the cookie jar.

"Ma'am. Ma'am." He politely acknowledged each of the women and shook hands with them both. "I'm real sorry I'm late...car trouble. I hitched a lift with a farmer..."

So *that's* why you're looking a little sheepish, thought Miss Moorcroft wryly, but she smiled and said all's well that ends well and glad to meet you, etc., etc., and asked him if he'd like to start the ceremony straight away, or freshen up first. To her immense relief, Rocky agreed to perform the ceremony straightaway, sing a song to the children, and then leave immediately afterwards so that he wouldn't keep them late at the end of afternoon school.

"Before we go in, Norman," said Miss Moorcroft (Rocky felt several degrees less cool at the mention of his real name),

"I need to give you some information about the pupils who will act as your welcoming committee this afternoon."

* * *

Evie and Angélique jumped to their feet as Rocky entered the lobby. Evie's heart beat quite fast, but she managed to remember her lines.

"Hello Mr Wilde," she said. "Thank you so much for coming to open our gymnasium. It's very kind of you to make the time to come to see us."

"Hello," said Angelina. "Hello. Hello. Hello."

"It's real nice to meet you," replied Rocky, and shook each of the girls' hands. He smiled at them. A big, friendly Norman smile.

"Thanks for asking me," he said.

"We've put a stool up on the rostrum for you in front of the microphone," said Miss Moorcroft, "is there anything else you need?"

"Just two more chairs – on either side of the stool, if that's OK," said Rocky, "for these little ladies."

* * *

Having duly declared the gymnasium officially open, Rocky did what the children had all been waiting for, and launched into his song. He launched the whole school right in there with him. They joined in the song with the words he asked them to sing.

"*Doo-Be-Wop-Bom,*" they sang lustily, before Rocky completed the line "*Doo-Be-Dom-Bom*".

Underneath the ear-splitting singing, Miss Blaine was just about audible as she remarked loudly to Mrs Prenton that she'd never heard the pupils sing '*Rock of Ages*' with anywhere near the enthusiasm they were currently displaying in their rendition of '*Doo-Be-Dom-Bom*'.

"Doo-Be-Dom-Bom
'm a-rockin' with my baby
Doo-Be-Wop-Bom
I'm a-jivin' with my gal
Doh-Be-Kam-Bam
She's a groovy little lady
DOO-BE-WOP-BOM!
Doo-Be-Dom-Bom!"

"We're gonna sing this just once more," said Rocky, after he had quieted the excited children in what seemed like a micro-second, "but this time we're gonna have some help from our friends. Angélique here, – did you know that 'Angélique' means 'little angel'? – well it does." He reached into the pockets of his jacket as he spoke. "This little angel here on my right will be blowing me some notes on this harmonica here," he handed Angélique the instrument, "and this little princess here on my left will blow me some notes on this harmonica here." He passed the other instrument to Evie.

"Blow us a couple of chords, Princess," said Rocky to Evie.

"Zee!! Zee!!" blew Evie.

"Yeah, groovy!" said Rocky appreciatively.

"ZEE!! ZEE!!" blew Angélique loudly, copying Evie.

"Ter-ri-fic!" said Rocky, giving Angélique a high-five. "OK. One more time, kids."

He strummed the guitar loudly and rhythmically. Miss Shearley began to clap on the beat, and soon the children and the other teachers were providing the backbeat. By the final chorus, the roof of the new gymnasium was in danger of coming off, the singing was so loud.

"DOO-BE-WOP-BOM!
DOO-BE-DOM-BOM!!!!!"

Rocky's fingers twanged the last chord with a punchy fortissimo. There was a split second's silence, then:

"BOM BOM," said Angélique. "BOM."

Tumultuous applause and laughter followed, and Rocky raised Evie's right arm and Angélique's left, like they were two World Heavyweight champions at Madison Square Gardens. There was a flash from a camera. This was the picture that would appear in the *Kingsville Chronicle*.

Evie thought she would explode with happiness. She looked over at Angélique. Good! She was smiling!

They took a bow, like Rocky asked them to.

As Miss Moorcroft made her way over to the rostrum to make her vote of thanks, and to dismiss the pupils, Evie and Angélique held out the harmonicas to return them to Rocky. He tousled their hair, smiled his Norman smile and said, "Keep 'em. You've earned 'em. Thanks for your help, kids. You were *great*."

* * *

The last of the pupils had left the building. The teachers congratulated Rocky on his performance.

"You were really great with those kids," said Miss Shearley, her admiration for Rocky now sky-high. "If you ever get tired of being America's Number One Rock Singer, you could come and work here. You'd make a great teacher." There were murmurs of agreement.

Rocky grinned. "You know, I might just do that!"

"Well, Norman, we're going to have to get you home, if your car isn't running," said Miss Moorcroft. As she spoke, each of the women was thinking the same thought, but only one of them got the words out, almost before the Principal had finished her sentence.

"I'd be happy to drive you home," said Miss Wade.

"I'd be honoured to have you drive me, ma'am," said Rocky. "I'll get my guitar and I'll be right with you." He hurried over to the front of the gym and jumped lightly onto the rostrum.

"So no gyrations then," said Miss Moorcroft quietly to Miss Wade, a grin threatening to break out as she spoke. "He turned out quite a nice young man after all, wouldn't you say, Ethel?"

"He's groovy," said Miss Wade.

* * *

As always happens, the pupils of Kingsville Junior High grew up and went their separate ways. Evie's parents had left the district a few months after Rocky's visit, and so Evie went to a new school in another state.

It was years later, when she was grown up and expecting a child of her own, that she ran into Susie Bell. Naturally, Evie asked about Angélique. Susie told her that Angélique had died the year after Evie had left.

After taking her leave of Susie, and saddened by the news of the death of her friend, Evie reflected on the events of her childhood at the Kingsville school. How glad she was now though, to know that she had been part of the happiness in that short life. Good things *did* happen for Angélique, just as the green-eyed lady had predicted. Strange that Evie had not seen the woman before or since that day; stranger still to think that as a child she had believed her to be a fairy godmother. Evie smiled at the thought. The green-eyed lady was just a grown-up, cheering a sad child. The fact that what she had said came to pass, was just another of life's odd coincidences.

When Evie's child was born, her husband Ben, looking into the eyes of his baby daughter for the first time, remarked fondly that she looked...well...so *angelic.*

Then there's only one name she could possibly have, thought Evie.

Bess had always been sensitive to the fact that when it was time for her to part company with her daughter, and go at last upon The Great Adventure, it could be a difficult time for Kit.

So, as with all other aspects of Kit's life, Bess endeavoured to prepare her well, and began to introduce the idea of the journey to the unknown when she felt the time was right.

She spoke with shining eyes and bright voice of how she looked forward to The Great Adventure to come; how wonderful and exciting it must be; how the future held possibilities of which she'd never dreamed; how she would have capabilities beyond her wildest imaginings, unfettered by even a thing so marvellously constructed as her own miraculous body.

She often took Kit to the woods, where in the dappled sunlight, they laughed and picnicked and sang and talked and played silly games until the darkness fell. Then they would sit under Bess's favourite tree and watch the stars come out, picking out the constellations, and marvelling at the shape and colour of the moon; listening to the night creatures and feeling part of the natural world around them.

Then they would walk home in the sweet, cool air, and go to bed with the sounds and sights of the day and night to swirl them into the world of sleep.

That old oak tree, Bess often said, would make a wonderful starting point for the journey to The Great Adventure.

1974

Sherilynne pushed the last strand of hair through the elastic band at the nape of her neck, and sat back in the chair in front of the dressing table, trembling with the effort. Under the glare of the unshaded light bulb hanging off-centre in the smoke-stained ceiling, she rested against the arms on the cheap wooden chair and looked at herself in the mirror.

She'd lost count of the times she'd been told how much she resembled Diana Ross. Well, she didn't this morning. Not unless Diana Ross had one eye the size of a golf ball and dried blood on the cut above her eyebrow, and purple, puffy flesh distorting the left side of her face. Far from adorning the stage at the Apollo, Sherilynne felt she looked as if she'd done fifteen rounds at Madison Square Garden. It was difficult to see out of her left eye, since it was almost closed. All she could make out was a mound of flesh, once her right eye was shut.

She couldn't even cry. She was all cried out last night. All she felt was a sick, trembling feeling in her body, a numbness in her spirit. She sat for a while, grateful for the chance to be alone, quiet and safe at last in the empty apartment.

The sudden sound of the doorbell made her jump; her heart began to race. Would it be Duke? Had he forgotten his key? Would he be standing abject in the doorway with a "Sorry, baby" ready upon his lips? If he was still crazed, he'd have kicked the door in by now. It could be someone else.

Sherilynne felt the little blobs of swansdown feathers soft on the soles of her feet as she manoeuvred them into her grubby, pink satin mules. She slowly rose, pushing back the chair, wincing from the pain of her bruised body. Tying her pink towelling bathrobe close around her, she shuffled out of the bedroom and towards the apartment door in the living room. She reached for the handle, and with an effort, opened the door a half-inch, peering anxiously out onto the landing with her right eye.

The Lord be praised. It's only Roxy.

Roxanne's smooth black skin and cheery smile could be seen over the top of the big brown paper grocery bag she held in front of her. Sherilynne opened the door for her friend to enter, turning away as she did so, saying "Hi, Roxy, come in" as she made her way slowly across the living room to open the curtains to the daylight.

"Hey, girlfriend, it's past twelve o'clock – you only just got up?" Roxanne's voice registered amused surprise. Sheri was usually an early riser.

As the curtains opened and light flooded into the room, Roxanne's tone changed.

"Oh gee, Sheri! What's happened here?"

Table and chairs lay fallen, ashtrays and stubs, empty beer cans and pizza boxes, cups, cutlery and plates lay strewn around the floor. Roxanne looked up and saw her answer written in blood and bruises on her friend's face.

"Oh, for Heaven's sake," Roxanne said, her voice low, her face registering horror and pity. She put down the grocery bag and went over to where Sherilynne stood. As she hugged her close, she felt Sherilynne wince with pain.

"Honey, we need to get you to a doctor." Roxanne released her hold and looked into the puffy face.

But Sherilynne shook her head. "Nothing's broken. A doctor can't make the bruising go away any quicker. It'll go in time."

Roxanne set the furniture to rights, and sat Sherilynne down in an armchair. Their eyes met, and Roxanne suddenly burst out angrily:

"He's gone too far this time! He coulda blinded you! You gotta leave him, Sheri. You *gotta*. He'll kill you one of these days." Then, seeing the tears start down her friend's face, she asked more gently, "Jimmie wasn't here, was he?"

Sherilynne shook her head again as she dabbed at her face with a Kleenex.

"No. He stayed over at Eloise's last night. It's the twins' birthday today and Eloise is gonna take them all to the zoo today."

"Well, thank the Lord for that at least," said Roxanne. "Look, you had anything to eat this morning?"

Sherilynne didn't reply; her lips were trembling. She was fighting back tears.

"I didn't think so," said Roxanne. "You need ham and eggs. And hash browns. And coffee. Something to start building you up."

"I don't have ham, Roxy. Or hash browns, or eggs. I don't think there's even any coffee, either. There's not much of anything."

"Well, I've got all of 'em," said Roxanne, picking up her bag of groceries. "I'll go fix us some. Stay right there and chill, girlfriend."

Sherilynne smiled gratefully through the tears, and Roxanne disappeared into the tiny kitchen, where Sherilynne could hear her clattering about, retrieving the necessary cookware.

Sherilynne sighed a deep, sob-ridden sigh, then dried her face once more with a fresh Kleenex. Slowly, she reached forward to the floor, where a crushed pack of cigarettes lay. There were two good ones left. She kept one for Roxy, placing it on the coffee table nearby, and found a box of matches next to the armchair. She lit the cigarette and drew on it, the smoke she exhaled creating a fug about her. She closed her eyes.

She knew in her heart that Roxy was right. It wasn't fair on little Jimmie to grow up in a home where he saw this kinda stuff. He was only five now, but it wouldn't be long before he understood what was going on. She'd seen the effect on kids from homes like that. Hell, Duke himself had grown up in one. Jimmie was such a cute, loving kid. She didn't want him ruined, ending up like his father: brutish, feckless, cunning. Of course Duke wasn't always like that. He could be romantic and charming, sweetness itself.

A picture of Duke enfolding her in his arms, whispering, caressing her, sprang into her mind. Sweetness itself. Her heart contracted and the tears began anew at the memory.

Sweetness itself. When he wanted something. Money, usually, to pay his gambling debts. Or maybe to take some girl out on the town. She didn't know. She didn't want to know. While she thought that she was his only woman, while he was sweet to only her, she kept on paying the price of her marriage to Duke. She paid over and over: in fear, in poverty, in the frequently increasing bouts of violence when he came in drunk. She paid the price in anxiety when he came through the door; was he drunk, sober, sweet or sour? Would he take the last of her hard-earned cash and leave her to worry about where the next meal was to come from, how she would buy Jimmie his next set of clothes?

But he was her husband. She had promised to love him until death. Her throbbing head became worse as the tears turned into sobs. Till death do us part.

Next time, it might do just that. And Jimmie would be left without a mom. Marriage shouldn't cost this high a price. Loyalty shouldn't be rewarded with cruelty.

An overwhelming feeling of grief for lost love, a hopelessness and utter despair crashed like the angry sea into her brain, her heart, her soul. But as always, it lay silent and unexpressed inside her, like a lead weight, the fear of the consequences of its communication to Jimmie, or even Duke himself, forcing it back inside her, where it stayed, poisoning her very being.

She controlled the subsidence of the wretchedness with a skill born of long practice. Roxy was in the kitchen, only yards away. Sherilynne had enough to occupy her without contending with the appalling maelstrom of emotion which threatened to destroy this present little oasis of normality. Once more, with the by now familiar effort, she pressed the torturing feelings back down inside her, and waited for the welcome numbness to take over, for the dregs of sanity to return.

Roxy came in from the kitchen with two plates of eggs,

ham and hash browns. She placed them on the table with two knives and forks. Then she went back into the kitchen and brought out two cups of black coffee.

"Come on now, girlfriend, eat," she said, putting the cups down next to the plates. She helped Sherilynne to the table and sat down opposite her.

"No talking, just eating," said Roxy. "We can talk later. Eat, drink, calm yourself down."

Sherilynne nodded and made an effort to smile. The two ate and drank in silence. Roxanne noticed that Sherilynne moved her jaw slowly; it must be painful for her to eat, Roxy thought; but she said nothing, and let her friend continue with her breakfast. She probably can't even taste this, Roxy surmised, but she needs food inside her. She'd be in a worse state without it.

Having finished the breakfast, they took their coffee back to the armchairs, and Roxy lit up the cigarette Sherilynne had kept for her. Sherilynne didn't want to smoke, she said, she'd just have her coffee. Roxy waited for her friend to speak.

"He was *real* drunk this time," Sherilynne began, by way of explanation. "I don't think I've ever seen him so bad." She sighed. "I guess it doesn't really matter what started it all off," she said in a low voice, and then fell silent.

"Heaven forgive me, Roxy," she suddenly sobbed, "but after he'd left, I just wanted him dead." Roxy nodded. "It's the first time the thought has ever come into my mind," Sherilynne continued more agitatedly. "I thought...I thought it's the only way. I've left him twice before, but he always finds us, and he swears he'll be different this time, but it only last a coupla weeks and then it starts over...I just don't know what to do. He won't get help. I can't help him. I've tried everything. But he just doesn't want to change. Why should he? He has his own way no matter what I do or say. He'll never be any different, I know that now. I feel so bad, wishing he was dead. I don't really want him to die, but I just can't go on like this. I'll never be free, Roxy, never. Not 'till I'm dead myself."

Roxanne took a deep draw on her cigarette and exhaled slowly.

"Look, honey," she said quietly, "there are women out there demanding liberation. And they'll get it, believe me. And you're in here crying your soul out, and wasting your life on a no-good jerk like Duke. Don't get sad, get mad. And don't just get mad, get even. Get a life for yourself and little Jimmie – while you've still got legs to walk with. If you stay here, Sheri, you'll be blinded, maimed – or worse. Get outa here – I mean *out*. Outa New York. We'll get the money together somehow. Take a plane to Oregon or somewheres. Get a proper job. Go to college – Geez, you were the brightest in the whole class at school, though you wouldn't think so to look at you right now. It's an awful waste of a life. You got brains. You got beauty. You just ain't got spirit. That punk's knocked it outa you."

"Roxy, you know how it is," replied Sherilynne, "every time I make a buck he gets it outa me somehow. He can't get it by sweet-talking me any more, so now he's started to take it by force. How am I supposed to get money together for plane tickets? I can't even go to work today – I can barely move. I haven't got a dime for Jimmie's dinner tonight, let alone the price of plane tickets. And geez, Roxy, *anything* could happen in the meantime. I don't know where to start."

Roxy pursed her lips and stubbed out the butt of her cigarette. Persuading her outa here's gonna take some time, she thought.

Suddenly there was an almighty crash and the apartment door was burst open, falling askew into the living room as it parted from the highest of its hinges.

* * *

The tabby trotted along the sidewalk close to the walls of the tenement buildings. In the afternoon sunshine she stopped on a stoop on the sunny side of the street, and since she could see no one in the hallway through the open front door, she sat down on the lowest step to clean her fur. Then she stood up, shook herself, and padded up the remainder of the steps to the cool interior of the hall, out of the sunshine. This looked to be a place where she could do somebody a good turn.

She looked about her. A typical run-down tenement building, with old wallpaper, scuffed and torn; dark brown wood on the doors and dado rail, and on the uncarpeted staircase which led to the narrow landings. A bicycle was leaning against the wall at the foot of the stairs in the hall, just outside a door on which there was painted the number one. A galvanised bucket and a mop had been left halfway up the stairs, as if whoever was cleaning the staircase had gotten fed up and gone for a coffee break. Although no one could be seen or heard on the ground floor, there were voices which seemed to be raised in argument from an apartment on the floor above. The tabby could just make out two womens' voices and a man's; then the sound of falling furniture and a scream. She began to ascend the staircase.

As she did so, there was a crash up above; what sounded like a door falling to the floor. A tall black guy sharply dressed, hurtled across the landing and began to sway down the stairway, shouting obscenities, his eyes red-rimmed and wild. He turned on a stair and yelled up again at the two women who stood holding on to one another at the top of the flight of stairs. They were trembling and ashen-faced. Despite their obvious fear, one of the women shouted back at him.

"Don't you ever *dare* lay another finger on her!"

As she uttered the words, the man shouted further insults and turned on his heel, staggering on down the staircase. He tried in his drunken state to grab the handrail as he did so, but missed his hold and stumbled unsteadily onwards down the flight of stairs. Halfway down, he was aware of the long handle of the mop, and the bucket on the next stair to his left. At the precise moment he swayed to the right to avoid them, a movement at his feet caught his eye, and there was a yowl of pain from the tabby as he trod heavily upon her tail. The cat struggled to free herself and became entangled between his ankles, and the man, now having no option but to lurch forward to the next stair-tread, suddenly lost his balance and fell headlong down the remainder of the flight of steps. His arms flailed; the fingers of his left hand caught fast in the wire basket attached to the back of the bicycle. The cycle fell to the floor, followed a split second later by his body which crashed down heavily upon it. His spinal cord snapped with a sharp crack. His neck broken, he moved no more, but lay lifeless in an awkward heap at the foot of the stairs. The only sound now was the back wheel of the bicycle spinning slowly to a standstill. Blood dripped silently onto the wooden floorboards from his right eye socket into which the left brake handle was forced upon impact.

Mrs de Souza came out of apartment number one and drew in her breath sharply, putting her hand over her mouth.

From the landing above, Roxy and Sherilynne looked down in stunned disbelief.

The tabby, sick with fear and shock, trembled uncontrollably, unseen in the shadows of the corner of the landing, where she had fled from the man's huge bulk. Her sweaty fur stood out from her body.

I've killed a human. I've killed a human.

* * *

Kit had finally left the tenement building far behind her, barely aware of the world outside her mind. Her body moved through the streets of New York, but her brain was largely unaware of its whereabouts. The muscles moved and propelled her body forwards, but in total shock, her mind went out of control. It frantically trod the same fleeting, unwelcome pathways, over and over again.

I've killed a human. I've killed a human. I didn't mean to. I didn't mean to do it. I've killed a human. I'm here to help them, not to kill them! Not to kill them!!! I've killed a human. What can I do? What can I do? What's to be done? What can I do? What's to be done?...

Kit had become completely unaware of her surroundings. She was mentally exhausted and physically ill through lack of nutrition, for she had no knowledge of the needs of her own body. She moved without purpose, her soul sick to the point of dying.

Her fur was dull and patchy; her ribs began to show; the whites of her eyes became a sickly yellow, the rims red, the green eyes pale. The once curved claws were worn down to short, flat stumps. She didn't feel the presence of the ticks and lice which began to drain what little life was left in her. The pads of her feet were almost worn away with the constant, slow, inexorable motion forwards, forwards, onwards, onwards...

I've killed a human...I've killed a human...What's to be...

With a soft thud, Kit's body fell to the ground. In the grey light of dawn it lay thin and still, a heap of bones and fur upon the cold, hard sidewalk.

* * *

Rosy Dawn Lopez was part Cheyenne on her mother's side; her father was Mexican. Her parents told her that she was born on a morning with a bright red sky, the like of which had never been seen before. If she had been born a boy, her father said, they would have given him the name of Red Sky; but since she was a girl, they called her the more feminine 'Rosy Dawn'.

Rosy Dawn politely insisted on her full Cheyenne name at

all times, and refused to acknowledge the shortened name of 'Rosie'. She strongly felt the blood of her Native American ancestors flowing in her veins, and despite being a modern girl, working in a big city, in Manhattan she experienced a closeness to nature every bit as powerful as that her great-great-grandparents felt for the magnificent landscape of their youth.

It was Monday morning, and her room-mate Rachel Steiner was just leaving for work. Rachel called goodbye, and the door clicked shut. Rosy Dawn had no sooner stood up from the breakfast bar than the door was heard to open, and Rachel's voice was heard again.

"Rosy Dawn! Rosy Dawn! Come here quickly!"

Thinking that her friend had suddenly been taken ill, Rosy Dawn hurried into the hallway where Rachel took her arm and led her down the steps of the stoop. She pointed to where the wall of the building joined the steps of the stoop.

"Oh!" said Rosy Dawn. She ran down the steps and crouched by the wall. Then she looked up at Rachel.

"Leave it to me," she said. "You get off now, or you'll be late. I'll take it into work with me. I'll call you later."

Rachel nodded, said goodbye once more, and hurried off towards the subway, checking her watch as she did so.

Rosy Dawn lifted up the animal, carried it into the apartment, and closed the door.

* * *

"Lord, it's in a bad state," remarked Gus Petersen, as Rosy Dawn placed the tabby on the operating table in her boss's surgery. "Where d'you find it?"

"My room-mate Rachel found it by the stoop this morning, on her way to work."

"Lucky she did. Another hour and this puss would've been a gonner. Burn those damned ticks off while she's still out. And zap the fleas. Looks like she's nearly used up the ninth one this time around. There's aways to go before she'll catch any more mice. I'll leave her in your hands, Rosy Dawn. Work some of your magic, OK?"

Rosy Dawn smiled and nodded. It was the first time Mr Petersen had called her 'Rosy Dawn'. He usually addressed her as 'Miss Lopez'.

She liked to work for him. He had the reputation of being one of the best vets in New York. Rosy Dawn was studying in the evenings, to work her way to college. There was going to be a long and demanding time ahead of her; a veterinary degree didn't happen overnight, and it was costly. But the experience at Petersen's surgery was invaluable. She was very lucky to have a position here as his receptionist/assistant. Even when it meant she had to deal with unpleasant things like ticks.

She started on the first of them, a fat, white brute, right by the tabby's collar. For the first time, she noticed the disc which had somehow become tucked inside the brown velvet band around the cat's neck. She turned it to the light to read the inscription.

"Well, Kit," she said to the unconscious animal, "you couldn't have found a better place to conk out in the whole of New York. Somebody up there is sure looking out for you."

* * *

"I can understand her tucking into the beef and chicken the way she does, and the fish of course, but have you ever known a cat to eat French fries? Or chocolate cake? You know, Mr Petersen, she'll eat practically anything – she's the most extraordinary feline I've ever come across."

"I figure she thinks that anything that's good enough for Rosy Dawn Lopez is good enough for her. You two are real pals, huh?"

Gus Petersen and Rosy Dawn were watching Kit relishing the last remnants of the chocolate cup cakes they were eating at lunchtime.

"You know Rosy Dawn, you wouldn't believe that's the same animal you carried in here six weeks ago. You've done a real good job. I have to say, that cat was sure on the edge when you brought her in. It was fifty-fifty whether or not she'd survive. You've got a real gift with animals. This one in particular seems to appreciate your efforts."

Kit jumped onto Rosy Dawn's knee and brushed her face against Rosy Dawn's cheek. Then she settled down into a plump circle of sleek fur and purred contentedly, her eyes closed, her chin resting comfortably on her tail.

"Yeah, she's real special," said Rosy Dawn, stroking the velvety nose. "It really didn't seem fair to leave her alone at home, and anyway, she seems to like my company. You don't mind me having her here while I'm at work?"

"Oh, no. She's no trouble. She doesn't even twitch a whisker when we get the rodents in to treat. She's a funny little critter." As he spoke, he scratched behind Kit's ears, then rose to put away his coffee cup.

Rosy Dawn carefully lifted Kit off her knee and put her on the cushion of a chair in the corner of the surgery.

"Time for work, Kitty," she said.

* * *

Rosy Dawn didn't know it, but she'd done much more than simply to heal the body of a dying cat.

When Kit had first regained consciousness, it was her physical condition of which she first became aware. The weakness and hunger began to assault her senses, her mind now solely aware of the fact that the body's well-being was its first consideration.

Into her consciousness came thirst; Rosy Dawn provided water to slake the all-consuming dryness which had come upon her. Kit lapped some water. She slept. She awoke and took the nutrient-enriched milk which Rosy Dawn proffered. With the strength the liquids began to awaken, came the tiny nag of hunger. Rosy Dawn gave her mashed meat and gravy, into which she crushed antibiotics and vitamins. Rosy Dawn stroked Kit's fur. Then she allowed her to sleep, undisturbed.

Kit slept the sleep of the dead; deep and dreamless. Her tortured mind and exhausted body gradually began to repair themselves. Strength of body begat a healing of spirit. Little by little, Kit grew stronger. Memories of childhood and her former existence began to surface, coming together like a jigsaw puzzle, allowing her access to the story of her life.

As if by some unnamed instinct, the memory of the day of the fatal accident presented itself only when it felt Kit's mind was ready to deal with it. It slipped in slowly, a drop at a time, a kind of slow-motion replay, allowing her to see it for exactly what it was – an unavoidable accident; a collision of factors, of which it would have been impossible to alter the timescale of each individual event, a series of unplanned occurrences, devoid of intent, and culminating in a disaster which would have been unforeseen by any of the protagonists. An accident in the true sense of the word.

At first, the memory caused an increased rate in Kit's heartbeat. She knew she would always regret having been the cause of a human's death, albeit it was unintentional. The scene would remain vivid in her mind as long as she lived. But she knew Fate had decreed it, and she must learn to accept it. And this she gradually did as the weeks went by.

She stayed in Rosy Dawn's apartment by night, and at the surgery during the day. In truth, Kit admitted to herself, at this particular time of her life, it was exactly what she needed, physically and spiritually. Rosy Dawn was a gifted healer of bodies and minds, who had a unique ability to empathise with creatures of a different species to herself. She seemed to know how they felt physically; how they psychologically perceived the events which were taking place around them. She would communicate through her eyes, her hands, her voice, the pace of her movements. Frightened creatures became becalmed in her presence, allowing her to work her magic. Rosy Dawn had been born to this vocation. She felt it was a privileged calling.

One day, Kit vowed, she would repay Rosy Dawn. When she was fully healed and could effect the change to her own human form, she intended to repay Rosy Dawn in the best possible way. When she could effect the change to her own human form...

One evening, Rosy Dawn had bathed and had washed her hair, and was sitting in front of her dressing table mirror fetchingly attired in rust-coloured check blouse, a beige suede calf-length skirt, and long, rust-coloured leather boots. Kit was sitting on a chair in the bedroom, cleaning her fur, occasionally stopping to look up at Rosy Dawn, who was putting the finishing touches to her make-up, applying a rust-shaded lip gloss, very becoming against her bronze skin.

Kit ceased her own grooming, her right paw momentarily stopped in mid-air. Her little feline heart lurched. She could almost feel the sensation of applying the smooth, moist colour to her own lips. It seemed so long ago that she had performed such a simple, feminine act. She sat down, tucking her front paws beneath her, and watched through her intelligent green eyes the motions of the hairbrush through Rosy Dawn's long, blue-black mane; the deft movement of her slim fingers as she created one long, shining braid down her left shoulder. The muscles in Kit's body experienced the same sensation of plaiting the silky tresses, as the memories in her brain began to stir. A tiny bolt of frustration and desire shot through her heart; but immediately it did so, she realised the positive nature of this desperate need. She was ready to attempt the transformation to her human, female state.

The idea began to excite her. This was good; but she also knew that she was very much out of practice, that any sudden attempt could do more harm than good. She remembered the half-baked attempts of her early youth, when she was in perfect health; to rush headlong into such an important venture so soon after her illness could result in the kind of fiasco that would only ensure a lonely lifetime as a side-show freak. No, she must bide her time, tune into her body, prepare her mind thoroughly for the event. She must recall and mentally practice every aspect of the transformation, leaving nothing overlooked. Every minute detail of order and execution must first be planned in her agile brain, as a professional musician would resurrect a long-unplayed piece.

She would spend the quiet nights as her benefactor slept, to prepare carefully, to discipline herself completely for the important task ahead, when she could at last return to her human form and repay the goodness of Rosy Dawn Lopez.

* * *

Fate had already shown Kit the consequences of inauspicious timing; now its caprice was to do quite the opposite.

It was a Monday evening. On the previous Saturday night, Rachel had been invited to a party at a colleague's parents' home in Queens. Being tired, and feeling a little out of sorts, she had been loath to go, preferring to stay at home with a pizza and a book.

"Oh, Rachel, you should go," Rosy Dawn had said. "I'm sure it would do you good. Put on the Ritz and go enjoy yourself. You can sleep all day tomorrow if you want. Books and pizzas you can have anytime. Invitations like this don't come that often. What do *you* say, Kit?" Kit made a tiny squeak by way of reply and the girls laughed.

"Well, OK, you've both persuaded me," said Rachel. "I guess you're right, I'm beginning to be an old stick-in-the-mud. I'll go! I'll wear that new cream trouser-suit I bought in Bloomingdales' sale. I haven't had a chance to wear it yet."

"There you go!" said Rosy Dawn. "You'll look a million dollars. You can borrow my long cream chiffon scarf if you want."

"Great! Thanks."

So off Rachel went, and that night she met Abe Solomon

at the party. Their mutual attraction and rapport was immediate. The rest, she would say on their golden wedding anniversary, was history.

At the party, Abe had asked Rachel to go to the theatre with him on Monday evening. Naturally, she had accepted, and Rosy Dawn was delighted for her friend.

"While you're in the theatre holding hands with Abe, think of me slaving over a hot notepad," she grinned, as Monday was one of her night school classes.

So the girls dropped kisses on Kit's head and left for their respective venues.

It was in fact that very evening that Kit felt at last she was ready to effect her transformation.

* * *

The moon was full that night; Rosy Dawn and a few of her classmates decided to take a walk down at the waterfront, and having worked themselves up an appetite, to stop by at Mae's Diner before going home.

Rachel and Abe on leaving the theatre, and not wishing to take leave of one another until the last possible moment, found a Portuguese restaurant nearby, and shared a seafood paella while they discussed the play. They lingered over coffee afterwards while they decided where to go the following evening.

Alone in the moonlit apartment, Kit closed her eyes and breathed deeply. She relaxed her muscles, and prepared herself psychologically for the task. She must feel alert and positive, ready to seize the precise second when she was physically and mentally at her optimum; any slight hesitation during the process would result in failure. Only a negative psychological state could hinder her change to human form. She knew that the Gifts would have been taken from her forever had she killed a human through malevolent intent; as this had no way been the case, Kit knew instinctively that the Gifts remained intact within her.

However, she had no idea how the outcome of the change would be after so many months of non-transformation. Would she be as she had been before her illness? What of the clothing which she had last assimilated? Would she have suffered any lasting damage to her human body? She didn't know. It was outside of her experience. But she would soon know. The answers to these questions were but a moment away.

She opened her eyes and summoned every ounce of positive energy she could muster. Body and mind were as one. The process began, and though more slowly than before, the familiar feelings of stretch and growth and strength seeped through her being, following their instructions via the neural pathways she had mentally trod so often in her mental preparations.

It was completed.

Kit looked down at her newly emerged form. From her shoulders hung limp strips of clothing, rags which barely covered her body. Only a third of what she had worn before her last transformation now existed. She recognised the remnants of a white silk chemise; coloured flags of floral print from the dress she had been wearing; threads of lace from an underskirt; now battered shoes, ripped at the toes, the heels threatening to part company with the soles. It was evident that much of the mass of the clothing had disintegrated while she had starved; the rest may well have been expelled from her body in other ways of which she had been unaware during her mental and physical withdrawal from the world. It was now time to see how her human form had fared.

Crossing the living room floor to the bedroom, Kit closed the curtains and switched on the light. Slowly and carefully, she stepped out of the shoes, and then began to remove every shred of the materials which clung to her body. Then she stood in front of the full length mirror and surveyed her reflection.

With immense relief, she saw that she was as she had been before. A little thinner, perhaps, but otherwise the same lithe body; the same shape, the same skin colour. Her dark hair had its usual thick texture; it rested on her shoulders, framing the familiar features.

She smiled and nodded. Rosy Dawn had healed her completely. She had given her back her extraordinary life.

Kit gathered up the remnants of clothing and threw them into a refuse sack. She slipped into Rosy Dawn's bathrobe and slippers, and under cover of darkness, threw the sack into a trash can at the front of the building, where they would be disposed of the following morning. She went back to the apartment and closed the door.

Having returned the robe and shoes to their rightful places, Kit proceeded to turn herself back into a tabby. With the perfect result achieved, her confidence flowed, and to her great delight, the following minutes of practice resulted in several changes from human to feline form as quick, as effortless and as accurate as any she had ever before accomplished.

When Rachel and Rosy Dawn came home that night, their little companion was curled up asleep in a furry circle upon the couch.

* * *

The time had come for Kit to take her leave of Rosy Dawn and Rachel. There was of course, a great sadness to the parting, but Kit had planned the event to be as painless as possible – she wished to spare the girls anxiety, and to bring her relationship with them to a satisfying conclusion as quickly as she was able.

Rosy Dawn and Rachel remarked upon Kit's display of affection to them, when late on Monday night they returned from their respective venues. She was, they noticed, particularly sweet, placing her paws on their shoulders and brushing her face against their cheeks, and purring so loudly, Rosy Dawn said, she could have been heard in Long Island. The girls hugged her to them, and played with her awhile, then

Rachel said "'Night, Kitty" and went off to bed, leaving Rosy Dawn touching Kit's soft nose with the tip of her own. Then Rosy Dawn laughed, lifting Kit's front paws from her shoulders. She kissed her on the head.

"Bedtime, now," she said. "'Night, little Kitty."

Rosy Dawn put Kit down gently on the couch, and stroked the purring cat once more; then she turned off the light, and Kit heard her soft tread as she entered her bedroom and closed the door with a quiet click.

* * *

Kit had a calling deep within her. She knew what she had to do, where she must go; she knew not why this inner prompting had suddenly manifested itself, but it could not be ignored.

But before she could obey the voice within her, she had a debt to repay. And no matter how strongly the voice inside her called her, her obligation to Rosy Dawn had to take priority.

So, just before daybreak on Tuesday morning, Kit changed her form to her human self, and opened the window of the apartment's living room a crack; just enough for the body of a cat to slip through. Then in a flash, she became once more the sleek-furred tabby of the night before.

Her green eyes looked around the apartment for the last time, and she sent a silent, heartfelt "Thank you" to the sleeping girls within.

Then she turned and lightly sprang to the windowsill, and was through the opening and down on the ground within a heartbeat.

* * *

An overpriced 'couturier', 'Les Femmes', stood on the corner of Third Avenue. It was really just a glorified frock shop, but the owner had pretentions the size of her bank balance, and made a fast buck from women with more money than sense.

Kit decided that this was the ideal place to 'kit' herself out for free, since she needed female clothing in which she could take a cab back to her own apartment. To travel there from the city centre as a cat would be far too exhausting. She had, of course, no money for public transport; at least she could pay the cab driver when she arrived home.

So at nine o'clock, as the doors were opened and the first customers arrived, Kit slipped in amongst them, unnoticed. She hid under a rack of ankle-length dresses which were conveniently located next to the fitting rooms.

When she was sure there were no assistants or customers in her immediate vicinity, she emerged, and in a trice completed her transformation. She quickly grabbed two dresses, complete with hangers, and placing one in front of her and one over her back, moved quickly into the empty fitting room and disappeared inside a cubicle.

She bit the price tag off one of the dresses (she noted the cost was ten times the worth of the garment) and put it in the pocket. She pulled on the dress. Hm, a bit on the big side, but no matter, at least it covered her – and her feet, for she had no shoes. It was a plain jersey wool dress in a rather boring beige colour, with a round neck and long sleeves. Nothing at all eye-catching, which exactly fitted the bill. She didn't want to attract attention as she was making off with the goods.

As she pushed back the curtain of the cubicle, the fitting room assistant appeared from the shop floor. Unfazed, Kit swept past her, assuming a haughty look and a Boston accent, pushing the second dress at the girl as she did so.

"Completely unsuitable," she said, and not waiting for a reply, swanned out of the shop and straight into a yellow cab, which as luck would have it, pulled up for her as she emerged from 'Les Femmes'. She gave the driver her address, and sat back in her seat, breathing a controlled sigh of relief.

The cabby swung expertly through the New York streets,

and Kit looked through the window at the familiar skyscrapers with a now nostalgic affection. She was going to miss New York. Who knows if she'd ever see it again?

"Right here'll do fine," said Kit, and the cab pulled to a halt. Kit explained her purse was in her apartment, that she'd come out without it by mistake.

"Do you want to come up to the apartment for the fare, or would you rather wait in the cab?"

"I'm a good judge of character. I'll trust you. I'll wait here," grinned the cabby.

Kit smiled and ran lightly to the lift in the lobby. It took her right to her apartment door on the first floor. Thank Heaven, no keys to be bothered with, she thought, as she tapped in her code on the electronic keypad. She grabbed her purse from the bedroom, and within a couple of minutes, the driver was paid and Kit was back in her own familiar surroundings.

She sipped a cup of coffee as she went through the mail which had accumulated. Apart from bank statements, there was nothing of any consequence to deal with; junk mail mostly. The rent on her apartment was paid by Direct Debit, so there would be no problem with irate agents looking for the payments due over the last few months. It was easy to disappear for a while in New York.

Kit loosened the velvet band around her neck, and took it off. Next to the engraved disc with her name, Rosy Dawn had added another plastic one, with the address of Rosy Dawn's and Rachel's apartment.

'*Please return me to Miss Rosy Dawn Lopez at...*' the plastic disc began. It was just in case Kit got lost again. Kit smiled.

She went to her dressing table and took out some writing paper, an envelope, a pen and a stamp. Then she sat down at the kitchen table and began to write on the plain note-paper, omitting her address:

Dear Miss Lopez,

I feel I must write to you to let you know that Kit has found her way home, and returned to me just today. It was a wonderful surprise, as I hadn't seen her for these past months, and I was afraid something dreadful had happened to her. It is evident from the disc you fitted to her collar that you have been looking after her – and I thank you from the bottom of my heart. I can't begin to tell you how happy I am to see her back. She really had become a part of me.

I would have liked to thank you in person, but I am leaving New York today, and so unfortunately I am unable to do so. However, I hope you will accept the enclosed as a gift, a token of my deep appreciation for caring so well for Kit; we are both extremely grateful for your kindness.

With very best wishes to you and yours,

Catherine Woods.

Kit wrote out the cheque and signed it with a flourish. She put it with the letter inside the envelope, sealed it and stamped it, and without losing a moment, hurried straight to the mailbox to catch the first available post.

* * *

Neither Rosy Dawn nor Rachel could remember if they had left the living room window open. They were naturally concerned when Kit made no appearance on Tuesday. She had not returned by the following morning either.

"Perhaps she's just getting more adventurous now she's better," suggested Rachel to the anxious Rosy Dawn. "She'll probably turn up tonight."

Rosy Dawn nodded and sighed. Rachel was probably right.

"Look – a letter for you," said Rachel, her mouth full of breakfast cereal, as she sorted through the morning mail.

Rosy Dawn didn't recognise the handwriting. She withdrew the contents of the envelope, and as she read the letter, her mouth dropped open. The cheque fluttered to the table. Her eyes widened in amazement.

* * *

Kit was happy to think that money she had so wisely invested over the years was going to be put to good use. The cheque she had sent to Rosy Dawn would cover the mortgage on the apartment; she and Rachel would never be homeless. Furthermore, there was more than enough to cover Rosy Dawn's college fees and to set her up in her own veterinary business. Rosy Dawn would make the best vet the world had ever known.

Kit just *knew* it.

* * *

The strange inner prompting inside Kit had turned into a fierce desire – one which could only be assuaged now by immediate and purposeful action. After mailing the letter to Rosy Dawn, she spent the remainder of the day tying up some loose ends.

Finally, she lifted the telephone receiver and dialled the number she had scribbled on the notepad by the phone.

"Hello," she said in brisk and business-like fashion. "I'd like to book a ticket on the next available flight to London Heathrow."

The transaction completed, she went into the bedroom and took her suitcase from the wardrobe. In fifteen minutes she was packed. She picked up the phone again and rang for a taxi.

Dressed for the journey, she sat down to await its arrival. She looked out of the large window of her luxury apartment at the dramatic and magnificent New York skyline. It was dusk, and night was fast approaching. Millions of lights sparkled in the navy blue sky.

It was nearly half a century since she had first witnessed the sight, her first night in this huge, exciting land. It seemed only yesterday. Yet she had travelled the length and breadth of this continent; she had visited state upon state; seen deserts, mountains, prairies; small towns, big cities; lakes and valleys, cabins and mansions.

She had met and mingled with black, red, yellow and white. She had heard almost every language on the face of the planet. It had been a wonderful, kaleidoscopic experience.

The doorbell rang. The cab had arrived to take her to the airport. To the plane which would take her home.

Home. All she could see now in her mind's eye were hills, fields, valleys, forest.

And in the middle of forest, an old, old friend who had called her back; a friend with whom she had spent so many magical hours those many, many years ago: the great oak tree.

Kit seemed to have accepted Bess's inevitable journey to The Great Adventure. They sometimes spoke about how life might be in this new and exciting existence. But despite her daughter's emotional intelligence and extraordinary intellect, Bess realised that there was still some distance for Kit to travel before she was truly able to accept her passing.

Returning one day from visiting a friend, Bess had found Kit in her room, crying. She threw off her shawl and took her daughter in her arms.

"Kit! Whatever is the matter, my love?"

Kit sat up, her eyes red, tears streaming down her face.

"I'm crying because...because..." She couldn't continue, the sobs racked her body so.

"Oh, don't upset yourself, darling. What is it that distresses you so?"

"I'm...afraid..."

Bess was silent and let Kit find the words to express her fear and grief.

"I'm afraid that the day...the day that you leave me...oh!..." The tears and sobs came so hard and fierce that Bess herself felt distress threaten to overcome her. But she becalmed herself and said gently to Kit:

"You mean...when I go on The Great Adventure?"

Kit nodded through her sobs. Bess's voice was low and soothing as she stroked her daughter's wet and tangled hair.

"I promise you Kit, that when I go, you will not feel as you do now. You will be calm, and I will be happy. You will do what you have been born to do, and I will go where I have been born to go. Don't forget, my sweet, I will choose the time when I feel it is right; when I know you can do what needs to be done without fear, without pain or grief. And know this too; I shall always be with you. You may not see me, but you may sometimes hear my voice inside your head. Occasionally you may feel my presence. You see Kit, everything changes, but love does not. Love is forever. Whatever we have had, we will always have. That cannot be changed.

"*LOVE ALONE IS UNCHANGING.*"

1974...and after

Here is a child who clambers and scrambles,
All by himself and gathering brambles;
Here is a tramp who stands and gazes;
And there is the green for stringing the daisies!
Here is a cart run away in the road
Lumping along with man and load;
And here is a mill, and there is a river
Each a glimpse and gone forever!

Gone forever. Familiar faces and places she had loved flitted through her mind like scenes from an old home movie. So many memories. It was forty-six years since she had left her home for America, with its vibrant, cosmopolitan society. Of all the thousands of people she had known, two faces returned to her over and over. Berni Edelmann and Rosy Dawn Lopez had made their mark upon her soul. Wherever she was, they would always be a part of her.

Kit noticed her reflection in the train window and saw that she was smiling. She came out of her reverie and caught the eye of an elderly lady, who smiled back at her before returning to the book she was reading. The rhythm of the train was not quite as Kit had remembered it. She looked about her. The rhythm was not the only difference. The new electric trains lacked the charm of their predecessors; the elegant, muted colours of the seating had given way to more garish hues; polished wood had been superseded by tubular steel and plastic; cigarette butts littered the floor, and the smell of leather had been replaced by stale tobacco smoke. Kit sighed to herself and looked through the window at the passing countryside. Yes, there *were* more buildings to be seen for sure; but the sight of the familiar British landscape of rolling hills, woods and farmland contracted her heart and sent a thrill of excited anticipation through her being. Home again!

Home again, home again, jiggity-jig!

She glanced at the diagram of train routes on the opposite wall of the carriage. Five more stops to Woodhills Vale & Appleton. Kit remembered her mother having referred to 'the apple town' where the fruits of the local orchards were the beginnings of the market trading thereabouts. Bess had still called Appleton 'the apple town', for it was a habit formed long, long ago, before Kit's own birth. Fascinating how language changes over the centuries, Kit thought. And accents. Even over a period as little as fifty years, she had noted how vocabulary and expression had altered so radically. Travel and communications had, of course, speeded up the process during the twentieth century. She was amused at the thought of Jane Austen being dropped onto the streets of New York's Harlem today. This exquisite manipulator of the English language would surely need a translator.

Kit rummaged in her hold-all and retrieved the newspaper she had bought at Euston Station. She would catch up quickly on the main events. Flicking through it, she skim-read the bulk of the main articles. Only four stops to go. *MP In New Scandal*. No change there then. Some things *never* change. *Protesters Scupper Building Plans In Local Beauty Spot*. Good for them. More power to the people. There were a few inches of column space devoted to various items on the lines of *Pop Idols In Drug Busts; Vanishing Women – Religious Cult Suspected; Soccer Star's Battle With The Bottle* and other sensationalist copy. Kit yawned, stretched, then folded the paper and put it back in her hold-all. Three stops and she would be back where she belonged. Her heart beat a little faster.

She took out her make-up bag, and in her compact mirror, retouched her lipstick. It was a shade of deep coral, which reflected the colours of the flowers on the material of her long, smocked dress. A beige-coloured floppy hat the same tone as her peep-toe platform shoes, sat upon the seat beside her. Kit delved into her hold-all and took out her hairbrush, quickly running it through her long, brown tresses. She tidied everything away and zipped up the hold-all. The hat, she plopped onto her head, then gathered up the handles of her luggage in readiness for her departure from the train.

She watched with eagerness the approach to her old home town. Still rural – what a relief. Still beautiful. But things change. There were still a few miles to travel. What would she find when she finally alighted at Woodhills Vale & Appleton? A sprawling out-of-town retail outlet? Woodhills New Town? High-rise flats with washing strung like bunting to greet her arrival? Her heart beat even faster. Would the old forest still be there at all? For the first time, real apprehension threw a wet blanket over her excitement.

The train began to slow. A sign flashed past in her peripheral vision. Then another. Her carriage finally stopped next to one which read 'Woodhills Vale & Appleton'. She had waited so long for this moment. Kit felt a mixture of anticipation and impatience as she queued behind the other alighting passengers. *Oh, do please keep moving. Come on!!*

At last she stepped down onto the platform, and instead of walking purposefully to the exit like the other commuters, Kit put down her hold-all and her handbag, and stood shading her eyes from the glare of the sun. She gazed intently into the middle distance, searching anxiously for her heart's desire.

Oh, yes! Yes! Yes! Yes! The magnificence of the forest still dominated the landscape.

Not long now, Mother, I'm almost there!

* * *

The heat of the afternoon sun beat down upon Kit as she made her way to the taxi rank outside the station. As she waited for a cab to pull up, her excitement fused with an irritating feeling of fatigue, exacerbated by the heat of the day. Much as she desperately wanted to make her way to her beloved forest, her body told her it was in need of food and rest before she undertook the journey. Hearing Bess's advice about looking after herself properly ringing soundly in her brain, she heeded her body's request, and asked the taxi driver to take her to what he felt would be the most comfortable hotel in Appleton.

"Well," the cabby replied, "you could do worse than 'The Lucky Cat'. It's a hotel and restaurant on the main Appleton road. I hear it's pretty good – the restaurant does good business, that's for sure. That do you?"

Kit assured him it would. 'The Lucky Cat Hotel.' What more appropriate welcome could she have for her homecoming?

It was indeed a comfortable hotel. The décor, she was pleased to see, was traditional, with subdued lighting and deep, claret-coloured carpet in the lobby and restaurant. Her room was simply but tastefully furnished with mahogany furniture, peach walls and carpet, and cream paintwork. It looked onto the main Appleton road, but the sound of the traffic below was not intrusive. The en suite bathroom had a bath and wash-hand basin, and peach-coloured towels and bath mat. It would do very nicely until she found somewhere to live.

Her feline nature dictated first cleanliness, then rest. The soak in a warm bath was so welcome after her travels, she almost fell asleep, her hand still enclosing the peach-scented bath soap. She slowly finished bathing, then leisurely dried herself, enjoying the pleasant perfume of the toiletries of which she availed herself from the little wicker basket on the vanity stand.

Wrapping herself in the cream-coloured towelling robe which lay across the flowered bedspread, Kit at last lay down, her head on the plump pillows, and closed her eyes. She fell into a deep and pleasurable slumber.

* * *

Refreshed after her catnap, Kit rose from the bed and looked through the window to the street below. Diagonally opposite was a car showroom. A small forecourt contained an assortment of second-hand cars. Ideal, thought Kit. I'll need transport if I'm going to find somewhere to live hereabouts.

The cars seemed to be so much smaller than their American cousins. One model she recognised from the British movies she had seen on TV in the USA.

A small beige Mini sat on the front row of the assembled cars. Cute, but unobtrusive, Kit decided. We could get along well, you and I.

"Just stay right there," said Kit to the car. "I'm coming to get you."

She dressed quickly, donning a long, plain, navy-blue dress, with a sleeveless crochet waistcoat to match. The outfit would look OK to wear in the dining room tonight, too. Kit was travelling light.

She put on her hat and shoes, and ensuring her cheque book was in her handbag, she locked the door of her room, and ran down the stairs rather than waiting for the lift.

It was half an hour to closing, and the salesman wasn't expecting any further trade before the day was out, so he was pleasantly surprised to earn himself commission on the little Mini which had come in only the day before.

Kit's animal instincts told her that the salesman was a man she could trust. John Walker, announced the badge on the lapel of his charcoal pin-striped suit, Sales Executive. He was pleasant and knowledgeable, but not pushy. He lacked the avaricious glint in the eye that many of his associates in the trade possessed. Kit could tell a lot from a person's eyes.

A trial drive convinced Kit that the purchase would be a good one. Though it was such a very long time since she had driven in England, Kit managed the journey without a single hitch; after driving on the other side of the road for the last forty-odd years in the US, she now had to readjust to the British traffic system. The skills soon returned. She loved driving the little car. It was a joy. And surprisingly roomy inside for such a tiny vehicle.

Back at the showroom, the paperwork completed, Kit climbed into the driving seat once more. She wound down the driver's window and thanked John Walker, who handed her his card and told her not to hesitate to contact him if the car needed any attention. He would arrange for service and repairs – but he reckoned Kit would enjoy trouble-free motoring for some considerable time. The car was low mileage and only a couple of years old.

Kit thanked him again, and waved goodbye as she slid out of the forecourt and into the stream of traffic on the main Appleton road. She headed for the car park at the back of The Lucky Cat Hotel, and came to a halt near the rear entrance door, parking easily between a Hillman Minx and a battered Vauxhall Victor.

She locked the car and sighed with satisfaction. A good day so far.

She would have dinner at the hotel and then make the journey to her beloved forest. She felt the old excitement returning as she pushed open the hotel door and entered The Lucky Cat once more.

* * *

Kit chose a quiet table in the corner at the back of the restaurant, and settled down to read the menu. On the front of the red plastic cover was gold lettering which announced: *The Lucky Cat Restaurant* and *Menu*. Between these lines of information was the picture of a stripy cat, again in gold, sitting boldly upright, its tail curled about its paws.

Kit opened the cover, and on the first page was italicised writing.

Sheena and Malcolm Brearley welcome you to The Lucky Cat Hotel and Restaurant.

The hotel, which enjoys a reputation for comfort, fine food and good wines, has been restored by the owners to its present high standard since its purchase in 1965.

'The Lucky Cat Hotel' is so called, as it stands on a site of local historical interest, where legend has it, in 1723, a young witch was burned at the stake, but cheated her persecutors by turning herself into a cat and escaping the ties that bound her. Leaping from the stake, she fled the scene, and was never to be heard of again.

Kit's jaw dropped and her eyes widened. This was her story! It was about *her!!!*

She couldn't believe it. She was sitting on the site of her dramatic and life-saving transformation. The name of the hotel was a reference to an extraordinary and gruesome event in her own past. Kit was staggered. She tried to think of the geography of the place all those hundreds of years ago. There was the forest, there the old church...she glanced out of the window at the sprawling town and tried to work out the positioning in her memory. It was so difficult to see things clearly with all these new edifices on the landscape, built up hill and down dale...but yes, it must be true. How utterly amazing!

Her face evidently conveyed her astonishment, for the waitress who had appeared at her table with notebook and pencil poised, was grinning as Kit looked up.

"You readin' about our local history?" the girl asked. Kit nodded. "Funny to think that happened right here," said the girl. "Makes you shudder to think about folks bein' burned to death on this very spot."

Kit had to agree with that remark. It certainly did.

"Mind you, as for the turnin' into a cat bit," continued the waitress, rolling her eyes, "folks in them days would believe *anythin'* they were told, wouldn't they? That's how these old legends got started, I suppose. Somebody made somethin' up and it got spread about an' daft folks believed it. It's as well we know better than to swallow mad stuff like that in this day and age."

Kit smiled at her. If she only knew.

"Now, what can I get you? I hear the chef's special today is very good. Torna...Torna..." The waitress struggled to remember the name of the dish.

"Tournedos Rossini?" suggested Kit.

"That's it," said the girl.

"My all-time favourite," Kit replied, smiling and nodding her assent.

"I wonder how 'e knew to cook your favourite, eh?" laughed the waitress.

"I suppose I'm just lucky," said Kit.

* * *

The meal was indeed excellent. Kit eschewed wine in favour of mineral water, as she was going to be driving out to the forest. As she ate, she wondered how the story of 'The Lucky Cat' had survived the centuries. Word of mouth? A local historian's scribblings? It would be interesting to find out, one day.

But there were many other things that Kit planned to do. And none of them would she even attempt until she had completed her pilgrimage.

Her meal completed, Kit thanked the restaurant staff and went back to her room to collect her warm, black woollen serapé. She may need it later tonight as proof against the cool night air.

Outside in the car park, vehicles were arriving; more diners for the already busy restaurant.

Kit relinquished her parking space to an elderly couple in an ancient Morris Minor, and manoeuvred easily through the traffic onto the main Appleton road. She called in at a petrol station a little further down from the hotel, and filled up the tank before heading out at last into the cool of the evening, towards Woodhills Forest.

The lights and bustle of Appleton were soon behind her, the buildings becoming more sparse as she drove through the hilly landscape. It was now dusk; overhead Kit caught sight of a few tiny bats out for their evening meal. An old church loomed up on the left of her as she turned a bend in the lane. It looked unused, fallen into disrepair. A sign of the times in today's more secular society.

Kit switched on the headlamps, as darkness was rapidly approaching. She was almost there. The forest had been in view since she had arrived in Appleton. Soon she would be part of it, as she had been centuries before.

The road swept gracefully to the right and brought her to the edge of the forest. Kit took the car up onto a grassy verge, close to the stone wall which separated the forest from the road. There she would not obstruct any passing traffic.

She climbed out of the car, her heart pounding in her breast. The clunk of the car door closing broke the silence of the evening. Kit ensured the car was secure, then looked about her.

The wall was too high to be easily scaled. Overhanging branches from the trees on the other side were out of the reach of anyone without a ladder. But not of course, to a cat.

It was now dark and Kit was unobserved. In seconds she was up on the branch of an ash tree, her feline vision scanning the countryside around her. She could see the lights of Appleton in the distance, and to the east, the spires of the university town of Oakbridge towered over the buildings below them.

Kit turned her attention to the ground below. Her claws extended, she descended the ash tree and jumped softly down onto the forest floor. She stood for a second, sniffing the air, revelling in the perfumes of the forest, the familiar odours awakening memories of long ago. Then with sureness of foot, Kit made her way towards the epicentre, wherein her own heart belonged. She began to move at a faster pace, her heart beating with exuberance. Excited at the thought of the reunion, she bounded joyfully forwards, the shapes and scents of the trees well-loved landmarks; the route to her haven.

At last she sighted it. The huge oak stood firm in the clearing: taller, wider, stronger than ever. Kit stopped in her tracks and savoured the sight of her dear old friend. A cloud passed in front of the newly emerged moon, then left it behind, drifting into obscurity, leaving the brightness to illuminate the powerful and majestic oak and the slim young woman, at last reunited.

* * *

As she had done centuries before, Kit, supported by the great oak, sat on the leafy floor and listened to the sounds of the forest; watched the play of moonlight and shadow on the living landscape around her; felt the rough but friendly bark under her fingers, smelt the aromas of the night, and revisited her memories.

She knew that she was not alone that night. As she sat, leaning against the trunk, or lay in the hollow of the oak tree with her tail curled around her, she felt the presence of Bess; and it was as if they were transported back through the years, enjoying the scene together, sharing their happiness in nature, and in each other.

Hour upon hour Kit sat, and told Bess of her life since they had parted; of her travels and the people she had met; of her adventures; of the marvels of the passing centuries. Every now and again, in the silences in between, she heard Bess's voice in her mind, making reply. A laugh here, a gasp there, a wise remark, a pithy pun. And finally:

"Well Kit, my love, tell me some more tomorrow, for it's time for us both to get some rest."

Kit, concurring, rose and pulled her wrap around her. She lightly brushed her fingers once more along the bark of the oak tree, then tail held high, trotted back through the forest to the ash tree and the forest wall.

Kit felt a warmth and a calm inside her she had not felt for the longest time. This was what she had badly needed. She had been right to follow her instincts. She had been right to come back home.

* * *

It was well after midnight when Kit began the drive back to the hotel. The headlamps of the little car swept the winding lanes, lighting tall barns and low hedges, throwing up spectres of the gnarled remained of trees struck by lightning in years gone by.

Turning a bend in the lane, the old church came into view, and briefly lit from below by the light of the car's lamps, the faces of its stone gargoyles leered menacingly above her.

As she passed it, Kit thought she saw a flicker of light through the dingy windows, but put it down to the brightness of her own car's headlamps as she swirled on round the bend in the road. Appearances were so deceptive at night.

It was pleasant driving in the darkness, alone with your thoughts, the road to yourself. Well, almost to yourself. A large black van, a minibus perhaps, was parked some way along the road from the church, on the verge under a low hanging willow tree. Must be lovers – a clandestine meeting, thought Kit, and grinned to herself.

The street lamps of the main Appleton road could be seen in the distance. Not long to go now. She would soon be at the hotel, asleep in her bed. She needed rest, it had been a long and eventful day – and night. But a good one.

Kit collected her room key from the night porter in the lobby, and shortly after, her head was on the pillow. In her peaceful dream, she felt she was snug and warm in the hollow of the old oak.

"Goodnight Kit, my love," said Bess.

* * *

The next day, Kit began her quest for a home. She wanted to purchase a house, not to rent one. For some reason, she felt she wanted to put down roots. It was inexplicable, even to herself, that she should wish to cease her nomadic existence, and to finally come to rest in the simplicity of rural England, albeit it was her original birthplace, somewhere she had loved to visit periodically during her long and wandering life. Why here? She had loved everywhere she had been from New York to London, from New Orleans to John O'Groats, and could happily have stayed in any one of them. She had been strongly drawn back, and this time she instinctively knew she was to remain here. Why now? These were unanswerable questions.

After a good breakfast, Kit decided to drive around the area, explore it further, before deciding where she would like to live. She'd make a day of it, eat at the local hostelries, and visit her beloved forest before returning to the hotel again.

The day was warm and sunny. She looked forward to driving her little car. Dressed once more in her flowered smocked dress, freshly laundered at the hotel, she donned her sunglasses and threw her black serapé and her handbag onto the back seat of the car. She'd buy some new clothes soon, but first things first. She wanted a roof over her head. Her own roof.

With a light heart, Kit sailed out of the hotel car park. As she drove past the car showroom, she saw John Walker on the forecourt. She tooted her horn and waved at him. He waved back, then turned to continue his conversation with his customer.

The traffic thinned out and almost disappeared completely as Kit wound her way out of town and into the countryside.

Here and there were dotted smallholdings and farmhouses. The lanes were often quite narrow, but the nature of the hilly environs and the quaint old buildings lent a great charm to the landscape.

Having spent the morning exploring, Kit began to feel hunger gnawing. She looked out for a village pub, and found one which boasted a view of Woodhills Forest. Kit decided on a Ploughman's Lunch, and settled down in the dimly lit but cosy interior to enjoy her food. As she ate, she mused upon her venture. Anywhere in these parts would be excellent, she thought. A trip to an estate agent's is the next thing.

She asked a girl who was waiting tables if she knew of one in the area. The girl said no, she didn't, but maybe Elsie might. Elsie was an older woman, plump and bright-eyed.

"Well of course, there's Jackson's in Appleton, and Grady O'Farrell's there too...now let me see...if you go into Southvale Village – that's the village down the road from here – just go straight down that way," she indicated the direction with her chubby, freckled fingers, "you'll find a little property shop just opened – er...Leach and something it's called. They might be able to help you."

Kit smiled and thanked her, and leaving a tip on the table, went out into the afternoon sunshine.

She found Leach and Pollard quite easily, and gathered up a couple of brochures, which she perused in the car. Beech Cottage – that looked nice; The Mill, Asham, lovely. She would go and take a look at them – from the outside first, to see if they were worth an internal viewing. The way estate agents took photographs, you could never really tell where a house was situated. It could be on the edge of a quarry, or next to a pig farm, for all you knew. Oh well, it's a start.

Kit looked at her map. Quickest way would be to go through this Southvale Village and then out to Asham along...Kit turned the map sideways to read the name. Northpoynton Lane. OK.

She switched on the engine, and was soon out on the winding road again, following the signs for Asham. On the left she saw an entrance to a lane. It was her turning. Northpoynton Lane. That sounded somehow familiar. Then she heard Bess's voice in her head.

"Remember old Ma Benson? You do! You know, the one who lives on the north-pointing lane – remember we went down it when you were just a little one? The poor old dear has just died. Eighty-seven she was, a good age..."

Yes, the north-pointing lane. Now Northpoynton Lane. Kit looked around her. She didn't recognise the scenery at all. She continued on down the narrow, winding lane on her way to Asham. Suddenly, she spotted a small copse to her left, far back off the lane. She could see by another break in the hedge that a narrow track led to it. As she approached it, the bonnet of a red car appeared between the hedges, waiting to drive out onto the lane. Kit decided to slow down and let the car out; it would give her time to look at the scenery, which had become infinitely more interesting.

The fields at the southern end of Northpoynton Lane had given way to hills and woodland. The copse was set on the slopes and brow of a hill. Just visible from the car was a thatched stone building at the far end of the track, which was surrounded at the back and sides by the copse, its front screened by a few trees, and facing the lane. The driver of the red car acknowledged Kit's courtesy with a gesture of his hand, and turned out onto the lane, driving northwards in front of Kit's car. Kit, however, intrigued by the thatched building, did not follow, but turned hard left onto the track from which the red car had just come.

As she turned, she caught sight on her left, of a sign post, almost hidden by the branches of a tree, which read *PRIVATE PROPERTY*. On the right, however, was another; it read *FOR SALE, GRADY O'FARRELL, APPLETON*. Intrigued, Kit continued on up the track. The odd tree on either side lined the winding route to the building, which Kit thought might be a thatched barn. The *FOR SALE* sign might apply to it and the land surrounding it. Perhaps the farmer who owned the adjacent fields was selling off some of his estate.

As she drove nearer, Kit saw a low stone wall around the

building. She pulled up when she could drive no further. She had arrived near a wooden gate. Another *FOR SALE* sign was placed just inside the grounds, next to the gate.

She got out of the car and walked to the gate. What she saw as she looked over it made her gasp.

The thatched roof belonged to the most charming little cottage she had ever seen. It was a stone building with wooden framed windows of dark oak. The Gothic style oak door was set in a stone storm-porch. Set on the wall to the right of it, the name *Copse View Cottage* was inscribed in large Copper Plate lettering on a piece of wood fashioned from the section of a tree. Variegated ivy grew up one front corner of the house, Russian Vine up the other. Wild roses climbed a trellis, shaped over the storm-porch; honeysuckle joined it from the opposite side. A wide, crazy-paved pathway snaked round the garden and ended up, whether from north or south, back at the front gate. The lawn through which it wound its way was lush and green, though somewhat overgrown. On it was a stone seat to the right, a stone bird-bath to the left. The curtains at the window looked a little dusty, as if whoever owned the place was too old or infirm to clean them; but the overall effect was similar to that seen on the chocolate boxes of yesteryear. Kit looked up at the huge trees which protectively surrounded the cottage. A perfect setting for a perfect dwelling.

Kit was enchanted. Her heart did a somersault. *I must have this cottage! I must!!!*

Feeling very excited, she quickly climbed back into the car and drove at almost breakneck speed down the winding track to the entrance to the lane. She made a mental note of the telephone number on the *FOR SALE* sign, and ascertaining the road was clear, turned left onto Northpoynton Lane. The little car fairly flew along, until Kit spotted a red telephone box on the northernmost corner of the lane. She pulled up with a screech of brakes, and fumbled in her bag for coins for the telephone.

Out of the car and into the telephone box; Kit moved like she had wings on her heels.

"Hello, good afternoon. My name is Kathryn Woods. I'm interested in Copse View Cottage. Could you give me some details, please?"

The assistant at Grady O'Farrell gave her the price and other relevant information, including the age of the property. It was just over two hundred years old.

"I'd like to make an appointment to view as soon as possible," said Kit, hoping that the sound of her voice wasn't affected by the pounding of her heart somewhere near her throat.

The assistant replied: "When would be convenient to you? The keys are here in the office, by the way. The owners actually live abroad – they've just inherited the place and have instructed us to handle the sale. In fact our sign only went up this afternoon – you're the first to view it."

Kit's heart leapt again. "Would it be at all possible to see it some time this afternoon? I'm actually in Northpoynton Lane at the moment."

"Yes, of course," said the assistant warmly. "As soon as Mr Baker arrives back at the office, I'll ask him to meet you there – oh! he's just coming in through the door now." Kit could hear the murmur of voices, and then the assistant said, "He'll be with you in about fifteen minutes."

"Thank you so much," replied Kit. "I'll be waiting outside."

"That's fine. Goodbye for now."

"Goodbye." Kit replaced the receiver and punched the air. Then she got into the car and turned back down the lane, feeling so overjoyed she almost overshot the entrance to the track. The little car responded like a dream as she swung sharply off the lane again and headed towards the cottage. Once at the gate, Kit pulled up, and before the count of five was in the little garden, taking in the details of the plants and shrubs. She peered in through the windows of the cottage, shading her eyes from the sunlight. Through one window she could see beamed ceilings of dark oak, a flagstone floor, and a large, open stone fireplace. Lovely! She made her way around the back of the house. It was cooler there, more shaded, due to the thick copse behind.

She had just made the happy discovery of a small vegetable patch on the south side of the building, when she heard the sound of a car engine approaching. Kit went around to the front of the house, where the red car she had seen earlier drew up at the gate.

A middle-aged man in a navy suit climbed out, and slammed shut the door of the car. Kit went to the gate to meet him and introduced herself.

"Paul Baker," he replied. "You're quick off the mark, Miss Woods! I'd only just got back to the office after putting up the board."

Kit smiled. "I don't let the grass grow under my feet once I make my mind up," she said.

"So I see!" he grinned.

They walked up the pathway, and Paul Baker explained that the house had been cleared the day before, and the furniture sent for auction. The curtains had been left to make the house look inhabited, a ploy to discourage vandals; the curtains were included in the purchase price, as the present owners had no need of them.

He took out the keys from his pocket, and opened the large front door.

"After you," he said gallantly, and allowed Kit to enter ahead of him.

Kit went inside. From the moment she stepped over the threshold she knew the place was for her. It was as if the cottage had said "Welcome home, Kit".

* * *

Over the ensuing months, Kit set to, decorating and

furnishing her home with an enthusiasm that surprised even herself.

The hallway of Copse View Cottage was square, with wooden floorboards. A staircase with oak banister and spindles rose from the centre. It was dramatic, but welcoming. The walls Kit painted with a warm yellow-gold; a large, thick rug of the same shade, she placed at the foot of the stairs. She furnished this entrance with an oak hall table on the left, over which hung an oak-framed mirror in Gothic design. Huge aspidistras stood on either side of a full length, Gothic style oak-framed mirror on the opposite wall on the right.

In the kitchen, she chose cupboards of dark oak; the walls she painted a light terracotta. Garden herbs in terracotta pots were placed here and there on the windowsills. It was a disproportionally large kitchen for the age of the cottage; big enough to fit a round oak dining table and chairs. This pleased Kit, for there was no separate dining room.

Her sitting room was cool and peaceful with pale green walls. She furnished this too, in dark oak, with a brown leather Chesterfield suite; plush, olive green velvet curtains and cushions lent a touch of class. Large plants in huge pots were placed tastefully on either side of the stone fireplace, and here and there, smaller ones on the tops of cupboards and bookcases. Kit realised that what she had created was the feel of the forest. She was well content with the result.

For her bedroom, which caught the early morning sunlight, she chose a pale primrose, with claret-coloured rugs and curtains. The bed linen was of a pretty floral design, containing roses of the same hues.

Upstairs in the bathroom was a white scroll-top bath with claw feet. It was in very good condition. Kit built her bathroom around it in white, oak and gold.

There were two further bedrooms in the cottage, which, Kit thought, would perhaps come in handy if friends came to stay. For one, she chose a sky blue; for the other, a pale lilac.

Throughout the cottage, Kit had hung ornately framed

prints of her favourite paintings. On the galleried landing on the first floor, she hung in pride of place the famous picture of a steam train entitled *Gare Saint Lazare*.

Having completed the furnishing and décor, Kit added the accoutrements of the present age: TV, radio, music centre, tapes and records, and all the useful kitchen appliances necessary for life in the twentieth century.

Now settled in Copse View Cottage, Kit was thrilled with her new home, and spent as much time working in the garden as she did in the house. Autumn was approaching; there would soon be leaves to be gathered, too.

Kit had decided to take her time building her library of books. She had plenty of bookcases and methodically filed her collection as she went along; English literature, World literature, reference books, cookery books; books on languages, art, music, philosophy – every subject that interested her.

The nearby university town of Oakbridge was alive with book shops, as was to be expected. Kit went there on numerous occasions and drove back with her little car almost groaning under the weight of the tomes in the boot and on the back seat.

Appleton Library was also well stocked, and Kit was often there, taking out books, keeping up with the latest novels as reviewed in *The Times* and *The Guardian*. One or two she liked enough to purchase for her own collection.

Yes, life was indeed very pleasant. Kit had entered a new phase, one in which she was taking things at a different pace, recharging her batteries, as it were, allowing herself to enjoy the moment. Her untimely brush with death had given her a more relaxed and philosophic attitude to her existence.

> *What is this life if, full of care*
> *We have no time to stand and stare?*
>
> *No time to stand beneath the boughs*
> *And stare as long as sheep or cows;*

No time to see, when woods we pass
Where squirrels hide their nuts in grass;

No time to turn at Beauty's glance
And watch her feet, how they can dance;

No time to wait till her mouth can
Enrich that smile her eyes began?

A poor life this if, full of care
We have no time to stand and stare.

Kit could see WH Davies's poem in her mind as clearly as if it were printed on paper in front of her eyes.

And *Whatever's gonna happen*, sang Ruby Jean Rae in Kit's brain, *whatever's to be...*

In the meantime, thought Kit, I'll make a leisurely visit to Appleton library.

* * *

September was poised gracefully between the vibrant summer and the cool autumnal days to come. The sun still shone, though the temperature was naturally slightly cooler.

Kit donned clothing suitable for the season; a long-sleeved, ankle-length dress in a green which reflected the colour of her eyes, and a brown leather jacket, fitted at the waist. She checked her appearance in the full-length mirror in the hall, and satisfied that she looked presentable, took her car keys from the drawer in the hall table, and picked up the pile of books which had to be returned. She was looking forward to her trip to the library. Who knows what delights lay in store for her today?

Inside the large, bright, main reading room, Kit made her way to the librarian's desk at the centre. She put down her pile of books and received the six little ticket pouches on which her name and address were written in blue biro on the front. A cough or two, or the occasional tap of footsteps were the only sounds to break the silence in the huge, book-filled room. Kit went over to the modern fiction section and selected a few titles which she recognised as newly arrived on the shelves.

She took the books over to an empty table, and sat down to look at them more closely, in the comfort of the well-upholstered seating. The first looked rather interesting, judging from the reviews on the back cover. Kit read the first page and liked the opening paragraph. It was intriguing. She resisted the temptation to read further, and put the book on one side. That one she would definitely take. The second one, she decided, was not the slightest bit intriguing. The syntax was self-indulgent and obtuse. Far too irritating to get beyond page one. She pushed it to the far side of the table. As she did so, she glanced around her. A few students; a housewife or two; several elderly people. Kit was shifting to a more comfortable position to continue her reading, when her eye fell upon the single occupant of a table on the far side of the room, evidently reading through a number of large newspapers.

Her heart missed a couple of beats. She stared. She couldn't help herself. She was riveted.

He was handsome, no doubt. About thirty-five years old, he looked to be tall, slim and tanned; but what arrested Kit's attention was the luxuriant head of grey hair, so unusual in a man of his years. An extraordinary shade of grey. He must have felt the intensity of Kit's gaze, for he looked up, and directly across at her. Her heart leapt into her mouth. His eyes were the bluest blue she had ever seen. He smiled at her. Kit instinctively smiled back and then lowered her eyes quickly back to her books again. She thought she would melt. She felt like she had turned to gelatine, that she had become transparent, that he could read her thoughts through her gaze. She daren't look up at him again – not so soon at any rate. He would think she was a flirting, flighty kind of woman. Oh, but she desperately wanted to look at him again. And again and again. She had the oddest, most insistent feeling that she had seen him somewhere before. That feeling was as strong as her attraction for him.

The attraction got the better of her. She looked up, as nonchalantly as she was able, sweeping the room with her gaze, trying to appear as if she was thinking deeply about something else. Her eyes finally came to rest upon the spot he occupied. Her heart thumped. Her eyes widened. He was no longer there.

A panic, a desperation took hold of Kit. She looked wildly about the room. To no avail. She got up quickly, her chair scraping the floor as she did so. Leaving the books on the table, she almost ran from the library, pushing the revolving door so hard she almost missed her exit.

On the street outside she looked right and left, and across the road. No sign of him. Kit's disappointment was palpable. Dejected, she went straight to the car park and began the journey home. No point in going back to the library now. She couldn't concentrate on words in books. All she would see from now on would be those refined features, that thick, grey hair. And those deep sky-blue eyes.

* * *

There had of course, throughout the centuries, been men with whom Kit had sustained a relationship over a period of time. She liked to get to know interesting people; for some, she felt a genuine physical attraction. But somehow, there was always a piece or two of the jigsaw missing. It may have been a lack of consideration, humour, maturity or perception; sometimes integrity, gentleness or a sense of adventure were the essential qualities which were not in evidence. And of course, none of these suitors could she trust with her great secret of The Gift. Like Bess before her, she would live two parallel lives.

This would not be an insurmountable problem, thought Kit, if like her mother, she found her true soul-mate. But two and a half centuries had passed. Was there any reason to think that life would not continue just as it had before? Despite these thoughts, over the ensuing weeks, while out and about in Appleton, her eyes sought the head of grey hair, a glimpse of the deep blue eyes. She would return home disappointed after each trip.

This is ludicrous, thought Kit. I'm behaving like a fool. I probably won't ever see him again. It happens, you know. You see somebody; then you don't. Get wise, she told herself. Pull yourself together and start to live your life to the full again.

And although the picture of him refused to leave her mind, she followed her own advice and decided to concentrate on other things. She would begin by making a shopping trip to Oakbridge and treating herself to a new pair of boots. Brown leather thigh-length ones, with the highest heels she could find. *That* should make her walk tall again. She could go out and meet some new people, see what the world had to offer.

So despite the fact that it was raining hard, Kit sallied forth into Oakbridge, and scoured the shoe shops with gusto, until she found what she was looking for. The price was as high as the boots themselves – the leather was soft and luxurious. There was an embossed design which began at the ankle and petered off halfway up the calf. They were a beautiful, rich, chestnut brown, and Kit could not have resisted them if she'd had to starve for a month to buy them – which fortunately, she didn't have to do.

Pleased with her purchase, she strode out into the rain once more, her shoulder bag slung across her long, beige raincoat, the carrier bag in one hand, her umbrella in the other. It was a very heavy downpour. The rain bounced six inches back up from the pavement as it fell; the sound of the water hitting her umbrella was almost deafening. A wind had got up, and blew the rain in the faces of the shoppers, many of whom muttered curses as they went by, losing their battle with the elements.

Kit lowered her umbrella in front of her to ward off the wind and the lashing rain against her face. She could see none too clearly, but the other pedestrians managed to avoid bumping into her as she bulled along the pavement towards the parking lot at the end of the High Street.

As she was passing Watkin's huge book shop, she suddenly collided with someone who had evidently just come out of it onto the street, for the impact dislodged a few of the books which had obviously been purchased there. They fell onto the wet pavement at Kit's feet. Dismayed at the possible damage to the pristine books (one of which she noticed was *Far From The Madding Crowd*) and the equally possible harm to the owner, Kit, still holding onto her umbrella, threw down her carrier bag and apologising profusely to the stationary black raincoat (which was the only thing visible to her at the time), scooped up the books and stood up to hand them back.

"Oh, I do hope I haven't done you any damage," Kit said, proffering the books, and moving back the umbrella, the better to see the person to whom she spoke. The rain pounded her face, but she was unaware of it. Her heart lurched. It was *him!*

His blue eyes sparkled with humour. He was shaking his grey head to indicate that she had not harmed him. Then he simply laughed as he took the books and said, "We must stop meeting like this," and stepped across the pavement, in through the open door of a waiting taxi. The last thing she saw was his amused smile at her as the taxi drove off.

Kit stood dumbfounded on the wet pavement as the other shoppers made their way around her. There was only one thought in her mind.

He's still around. He's still here. *He's still here!!!*

* * *

It was no use. Now she had heard his voice, too – a soft chocolate-y baritone, the music of which still played in her memory, like a favourite piece.

We must stop meeting like this.

But Kit never wanted to stop meeting him. She felt once more that it was what she was living for. She wanted to meet him over and over for the rest of her life. She wanted to wake up every morning and meet him again, have his grey hair next to her brown, his blue eyes looking into her green, his body strong and warm and close to her...

She was like a woman possessed. In love. In love for the first time, and she didn't even know him. It made no sense at all. Stop this, she told herself, in denial. It's infatuation. He's probably the greatest cad on the planet. There's got to be something wrong with him, some huge imperfection. And you know you can't deal with anything other than Perfect, Kit. Not when it comes to the love of your life...

Would the thought of him leave her in peace for one single moment? No, it would not. Would she be able to live without him, the thought of him an immovable factor in her life? No, she would not. Could she do anything about this intolerable situation? No, she could not.

Now, her little house felt empty. She was no longer contentedly alone; she was lonely. It felt like her heart was torn out, and that she was left with a huge, black hole in her soul. So this is what it felt like to be lonely.

She had never known what loneliness was before. It was a terrible, desperate thing. A bereavement. Why did she feel bereaved? You had to have lost someone very dear to feel bereaved. Kit was ashamed of herself, cross that she was thinking this way, debasing the feelings of those who genuinely had loved and lost; the thousands who had spent a lifetime together, living and loving, separated at last by death. Her feeling of loss was as nothing compared to theirs. Why therefore should she feel this way? Kit was unhappy and confused by her feelings. She felt out of control, rudderless, useless. Under the circumstances, there was only one thing she could do.

She made her way to the old oak tree in the middle of the forest.

* * *

The autumn leaves made a thick, comforting carpet on the forest floor. Kit padded her way into the hollow of the oak and lay down, her tail curled around her, warm against the chill of the night.

She listened to the rustle of the branches in the night breeze, and watched the gentle descent of the leaves; down, down, down, where they lay content with their companions, quiet and still at last.

The moon was full again, a silvery orb, its place in the world continuing unchanged; unfazed by the tumultuous feelings of the inhabitants of the planet below it. No blue bruises appeared upon its face tonight. It was pure, clear, like an innocent heart.

Kit's eyes began to flicker, and then she slept, her breath coming slowly and evenly, her ears, at first her sentinels, relaxing their hold on the world. She drifted into a dreamless slumber, her troubled spirit and thrashing thoughts seeping silently into the earth below her.

* * *

How long she remained thus was impossible to say. When she awoke, it was well after midnight. The early hours of another day.

She opened her eyes and began to gather her thoughts. Although his face and his voice were first to enter her mind, she felt refreshed, able to continue. It was time to resume her place in the world.

Kit turned on the engine of the car and started her journey homewards. She began to experience the physical enjoyment of manoeuvring her little car, just as she always had. This was a good sign – her spirit was healing. She concentrated on feeling the rapport with her vehicle, both of them on the same mission, to glide and turn with effortless skill, their tempo unimpeded by any other presence on the winding road. Kit felt as if she was moving forward, physically and metaphorically. It was good feeling. Her thoughts began to be more positive, her mind more alive. Her time in the forest had again renewed her.

She swirled the car eastwards, the headlamps illuminating the old church with its grim-faced gargoyles. As she straightened up to drive past, her attention was caught by a flickering light in the lower windows of the church. She drove past, remembering that she had thought she had seen this happen before in the disused building. But this time she had *definitely* seen the light in the windows. This time she stopped.

She drew her car over to a grass verge – under the willow tree where she had before seen the black van with the imagined courting couple. It was some distance away from the church, and unseen by anyone who may be in the building. Criminals with a drugs cache? Or it could be youngsters in there, larking around. They should be at home and in their beds by now, thought Kit. Courting couple on one of their illicit meetings? Or just plain vandals? At any rate, at this time of the morning, it was likely to be somebody up to no good.

Instinctively, Kit changed to feline form. She would watch, listen and learn.

From the lowest sill she could access, Kit peered through the dusty glass. She could make out the shapes of people – two in the centre of the floor, several on the right, apparently seated, some of whom, she deduced, must be holding candles. The flickering flames made it difficult to see clearly, so, curious to find out the purpose of the gathering, Kit jumped quietly down to the ground and crept through the graveyard to the rear of the church. All was still. There was no one around.

Kit resumed her female form and tried the handle of the door at the back of the building. Surprisingly, it turned noiselessly, and the door was soon ajar. The door then, and the church, were in regular use.

Kit slid inside and closed the door silently. Back in feline form, she trod softly, the stone floor cool on the pads of her feet. Another heavy door was ahead of her. It was slightly ajar. A voice was heard, though the words were indistinct. The green eyes took in the scene through the narrow slit.

A man, in some kind of red-hooded, priestly garb stood facing the door behind which Kit was hidden in the shadows. He was addressing a girl in a chair opposite him. Her back was towards Kit; her hands appeared to be tied behind her. Along the left hand side of the room were a group of ten or so other people, dressed in hooded, black robes, sitting on a long pew facing the middle of the church. Every other one of them held a candle. They were watching the proceedings from under the long hoods which obscured their faces. There were only four pews in the room, each on one of the four walls, facing the centre. Apart from the one occupied by the people in black robes, the others were empty. The remainder of the pews in the church appeared to have been removed, to clear a space for the scene taking place in the middle.

Kit slid through the gap in the door, into the dark interior. She hid in the black shadow underneath the pew at the back of the room. There she could see and not be seen.

It was not long before Kit realised that this was some sort of religious interrogation. The girl's hands were tied by ropes to the back of the wooden chair on which she sat.

Kit shivered. The scene was exactly like the one she herself had taken part in, centuries before. Without even hearing a word, Kit's sympathies were with the girl, helpless against those who would oppress her.

Whatever the girl had just said evidently caused consternation amongst the onlookers. They shifted in their seats and muttered angrily.

The man in red robes drew himself up and looked haughtily down at the girl.

"You dare to question the authority of the Primus, The Supreme Head of the Union of Saints?" His tone was one of controlled anger.

"I dare to question anyone who simply assumes authority and then uses it unwisely."

The onlookers gasped at the girl's audacity.

"You think because you are educated that you are qualified to bandy words with your superiors?" He delivered the words sarcastically to belittle her attempts to subvert his authority.

The girl answered him evenly. "I think because I am educated."

There was a silence. Evidently those present were awaiting the conclusion to the sentence, but then in the silence, the words hung like swords in the air and made their point. The meaning was not lost upon her inquisitor. Angered that she had left him no further opening in that line of discussion, he changed tack.

"It is the intention of this hearing that you are given the opportunity to make clear your position regarding the doctrine of The Union of Saints. You have been accused of heresy by members of The Council; by your own words you shall convince them of your guilt or innocence."

"I am well aware of the intention of this hearing." The girl spoke dryly, then continued her silence, again leaving him no alternative but to look for another avenue by which to attempt his attack. It was not long before he found another one.

"It has been said that you have expressed a negative attitude to the campaign designed to bring The Tainted to heel. It must then be assumed that you ally yourself with the enemy, those who do not follow the paths of righteousness. What say you to this?" His mode of expression, Kit noted, occasionally slipped into antiquated phraseology – probably a deliberate ploy to lend ancient authority to his doctrine and position. It sounded somewhat ridiculous in this day and age – but its resonance to Kit gave it a sinister quality.

"If by a negative attitude you mean I have actively discouraged young children to perpetrate violent actions against those they do not know, simply because of doctrines conceived by thoughtless, intolerant and dangerous adults, then I am proud to say that I must be guilty of a 'negative attitude'. Though I am sure that secretly more than a few women of the Union of Saints whose ten year old sons may otherwise have been killed or injured whilst engaged in handling mines and bombs, may look upon my exploits in a more positive light than does The Council."

The Council members muttered again. The Primus drew closer to the girl, and his eyes narrowed.

"These women make a sacrifice, perhaps the greatest sacrifice of all in order to rid the world of The Tainted, making the world a more spiritual place, one in which the evils of other so-called religions no longer hold sway. And those children, even at their tender ages, show a spirit and a courage which cowards such as yourself obviously lack."

He retreated, obviously pleased at his performance, as The Council uttered their approbation.

"In response," said the girl calmly, "on the subject of courage; I see no courage in hiding behind a front line of small children, who, unable to think for themselves, take risks which the esteemed members of The Council and The Primus find unacceptable to take themselves. Indeed, the very fact that you all hide your faces from the world, and your whereabouts from the press, seems to denote to me a most deplorable lack of courage. And I am to respect this?"

There was an uproar from The Council. Kit's eyes widened in anxiety for the girl. The Primus looked riled enough to strike her. But his hubris regarding his intellectual prowess got the better of his anger. He held up his hand and signalled for silence. Order restored, he continued coldly:

"I am surprised at your using the word respect. I think you have ably demonstrated that this is patently not in your repertoire of thoughts or actions. For you have shown no respect for the authority of the hierarchy of The Union of Saints – your superiors, elders and betters."

Keeping low, Kit moved slightly, shifting her position, her

green eyes keenly taking in the expressions of the faces which had now become more visible to her. There was real hatred glinting in the eyes of The Council members. Her heart beat faster still.

The Primus was not finished with the girl on the subject of respect. He was determined to be the victor in this battle of words; to gain further credibility with The Council and maintain his unassailable position as their leader. He would use any argument at his disposal to do so.

"Regarding the subject of respect," he snarled, "you show none even to the woman who bore you. By the fact that you are here and accused of heresy, you have betrayed her – and she, a loyal member of The Union of Saints and an Officer of The Council."

The girl's answer had a distinct note of bitterness.

"Respect is not due by virtue of authority, heredity or blood ties. It can only be earned. If it is not earned, it shall not be given." She turned her gaze to the woman sitting at the far end of the pew, who, by the indication of The Primus, was obviously her mother. "I have little to say about betrayal," she continued flatly, "despite the fact that I am an expert on the subject, being the victim of such betrayal as would sicken every right-thinking mother on this planet." Her eyes pierced those of her own mother, who, under her hood, and dimly lit by her flickering candle, pursed her lips and averted her gaze.

The members of The Council roared their disapproval.

The proceeding of the arguments were not going as The Primus had planned. He tried again.

"Has your own mother not taught you obedience? Has she not, over many years, as a loyal and true member of The Union of Saints, undertaken with maternal devotion the task of encouraging you in your acceptance of our doctrine?"

"Oh yes," replied the girl with utter contempt, "indeed she has. Had she not, I would not be here, bound to this chair, but elsewhere, living a free, open and happy life."

An outraged roar erupted from The Council. And once

more The Primus was not met with the subdued shame he required.

"Furthermore," continued the girl bravely, "your doctrine promotes division from others, intolerance which breeds belligerence, which ends in injury, murder and chaos. I want no part of it. It troubles my spirituality. And indeed my own sense of morality. I would expect that any great deity would be sorely disappointed at the pettiness, cruelty and arrogance of those who purported to act in its name."

The uproar at this last gave The Primus the impetus to do what he had really sought to do from the start: to seize upon the girl's statement as proof of heresy from her own mouth, as indisputable evidence of her guilt. Her open opposition to The Cause would leave no room for mercy.

But he had not vanquished her spirit. He had not defeated her intellect. Anger rose inside him like a mighty ocean. His only consolation now was that he had the physical advantage of her – and the approbation of The Council for what he was about to do. He would savour the vengeance he would wreak upon her.

Kit knew it. The girl knew it. But they both knew she could not have acted otherwise.

The Primus held up his hand and nodded to The Council. They subsided into silence.

"From what we have seen and heard in this place, this night, it is evident to me that the accused is indeed a heretic, and a danger to our Cause. How say The Council? Raise your hands if in agreement."

Twenty hands were silently raised. The girl and her mother exchanged a glance – a picture that spoke a thousand words.

"So be it." The Primus drew himself up and spoke in a solemn tone. "I will now ask The Council to take their leave, whilst I attend to the grave matter of the spiritual welfare of this woman, and attempt to retrieve her soul and place her once more upon the road to righteousness."

This was what Kit had feared most. Her heart beat

violently.

There came the sound of The Council members rising, and their feet shuffling on the stone floor as they exited through the front door of the church, their candles flickering as they left. The chamber was darkened further, now lit only by a candle on the altar and one in the hand of The Primus.

There was a dreadful silence.

It was broken by his soft, menacing voice.

"It seems that you have been found guilty," he said, with ill-concealed satisfaction.

"Was there ever any doubt the outcome would be otherwise?"

The girl's voice was equally soft, but she was contemptuous in her delivery.

The Primus walked slowly towards her. By the light of the candle, Kit could see the expression in his eyes. The girl could see it too. For the first time, she looked uneasy. She was very, very vulnerable. Kit watched and waited, her feline instincts preparing her for what may lie ahead.

"Guilty." The Primus was an inch away from his prisoner. Their eyes were locked upon each other. "You will not get the better of me," he said, his lips curled in a sneer, his body bending downwards, the candle held aloft, illuminating them both in its eerie, flickering light. The girl began to fear what was to come, though she remained silent, keeping her eyes always on him.

"You never will. I am The Primus," – his head was now level with hers, "and you," – he swept his eyes over her, "you are a mere...girl."

With a sudden movement, which caused the girl to cry out, he produced from his robe a curved, gleaming, knife, and put it to her throat.

Kit's muscles poised for action. But The Primus just laughed in the girl's face, as he withdrew the knife, and taking a lock of her black hair, cut a swathe down the shaft, causing her hair to fall into the darkness below. There was a sharp intake of breath from the girl at the nearness of the weapon to her face; she leant as far back in the chair as she could. Her eyes began to show real fear.

Kit's muscles began to twitch. She began to move.

"You will call upon The Great Deity to save you – body and soul," he intoned in declamatory and priestly fashion, walking away from her a few steps, the better to make his next approach the more frightening. He was enjoying tormenting her. He was clearly deranged.

The girl's heart pounded furiously.

Kit inched forward as The Primus loomed towards the terrified girl.

"Cry to your Deity!" he suddenly shouted as he reached forward and caught up the girl's long, black hair in his hand, "beg His forgiveness, Tainted One!"

Suddenly, without warning, he brought the candle flame down to the hank of hair he held in his hand. The girl screamed as the smell of the burning hair hit her nostrils. She kicked out with her legs and caught The Primus on his thigh, making the chair fall backwards and extinguishing the flame on her hair as she fell upon it to the stone floor, unconscious.

There was a scream of pain and horror from The Primus as the cat's claws scored the flesh on his face, the warm, red liquid spurting from his eyes, his cheeks, his throat, his chest. He staggered blindly in the darkness of blood, falling heavily as his foot came into contact with the leg of the upturned chair. His head hit the stone floor and he lay bleeding in the darkness; the candle guttered as it fell from his hands. There was the smell of smoke and candle wax. Then silence.

The Primus moved not a muscle. His eyes were closed, the lids torn, the blood from his wounds oozing onto the flagstone.

Kit, now unobserved, changed back to human form. Her heart drummed in her ears. The smell of burnt hair had brought back memories to haunt her. She breathed slowly in order to regain her calm.

She felt for the candle, and found it some feet away. There

was now no means of lighting it, however. The last remaining lit candle, on the altar, extinguished itself as she picked it up. Clouds floated by in the night outside, suddenly leaving the moon hanging in the sky, clear and luminous. Its beams shone through the filthy windows of the church and lent enough light to enable Kit to ascertain that The Primus was alive but unconscious – as was the girl. Kit picked up the chair in which the girl was bound and pushed it upright. Then she untied the girl's hands. Her head, still smelling of burned hair, lolled to one side. Kit lifted her up and carried her over to a pew, where she laid her down, and placed an old kneeling cushion under her head. It was musty and dank, but it would afford the girl some comfort at least.

A sudden movement drew Kit's eye to the front door of the church. It had opened, a breeze from outside coming into contact with her skin. Her heart pounded. She froze. She could see no one. She peered into the dark corner of the church where the front door still stood slightly ajar. A shape moved low in the corner. Kit dared not breathe. But soon she was able to make out what it was.

It was a cat. Relief flooded her. She breathed again. Then her heart jumped once more. The cat spoke.

"We really *must* stop meeting like this."

* * *

The cat came out of the shadows and stood in the shaft of moonlight which pointed like a finger into the dark chamber.

Kit could not utter a sound. She stood and stared. The cat was large and handsome, with thick grey fur and the bluest eyes she had ever seen. The old feeling of déjà vu swept over her like a great wave, taking her breath with it. Her thoughts were in tumult. She fought for control.

Suddenly, in a blinding flash, it was 1928, and a pair of blue cat's eyes shone through a slit in a basket on a station platform...through its grey fur, Kit could have sworn that it smiled.

It was smiling now.

We really must stop meeting like this.

IT WAS HIM!!!

Disbelief, wonder, awe. And joy. Such joy!!!

He stood in front of her now, transformed, six feet tall, his deep baritone voice the essence of dependability, yet the old amusement dancing in his eyes.

At first, Kit could not formulate a reply. Then, still gazing in amazement into his eyes, she said: "It's you! You're..."

He moved towards her and put a finger on her lips.

"Later, Kit. We'll have lots of time to talk later." He looked about the room. "You've managed all this very well," he said approvingly, indicating the scene which surrounded them. "Now we have more to do."

There was an electric moment when his warm skin touched hers as he took her hand and said: "Come on, Kit, we've got some wrongs to right."

As they moved through the darkness of the chamber, her hand was in his, and it felt like it had always been there.

* * *

THE OAKBRIDGE TIMES October 29, 1974

...continued from page 1

...and newspaper coverage has been extensive throughout Britain since freelance investigative journalist Thomas Grey exposed the workings of the cult religious group The Union of Saints in *The Guardian* last week.

More of the missing women have been discovered, in addition to those whom Grey found imprisoned in the crypt of the disused church of St Anne's in Southvale, in the early hours of last Wednesday morning. They had also been kept in the crypts of other churches which had fallen into disrepair.

The women had apparently been found guilty of 'heresy' or

'sedition'; attempts were being made by the cult to brainwash, or simply force by imprisonment and torture, any of their women who tried to challenge doctrine, or indeed leave the cult.

Some of the women were less fortunate than those who were found alive; their bodies were discovered buried in the undergrowth which surrounded some of the disused churches.

The cult members known as 'The Council', together with their leader or 'Primus' (who calls himself Mah-Lek) apparently travelled by night in a black van to the disused churches, taking the accused women for 'trial' and 'sentencing'.

Mah-Lek, who upon questioning refused to give his real name to the police, has since been discovered to be Peter Charles Pitman, the son of Headteacher Michael Pitman, of Millhurst School in Bedfordshire.

Pitman Snr declined to speak about his son's activities, other than saying he was "shocked and dismayed".

Grey, having read initially about the cult, did research in the areas in which the women had begun to be registered as missing, working undercover, and in various disguises, in order not to arouse the suspicion of the cult members.

He was able to supply the police authorities with documents and forensic evidence pertaining to the cult's practices, though due to the nature of his profession, declines to say how he obtained some of his more remarkable finds. It has since come to light that he is now able to produce evidence which links the cult to the bombings in Leicester, Glasgow and London in which twenty-seven people were killed.

Pitman and other members of 'The Council' are remanded in custody until their trial, which is due to take place at The Old Bailey in December.

Kit closed her scrapbook containing the newspaper cutting. They had had so many adventures together since that fateful night in the dark chamber of the church. They had been a good team.

As she often did, Kit cast her mind back to that night. Down to the crypt they went and freed the tortured women...both of them working together to break the locks on the cage doors, Kit herself a picture of efficiency on the outside, a maelstrom of emotion within...the relief and gratitude of the poor creatures half-starved, injured, filthy and unkempt, almost at their wits' end...the calling for, and arrival of the police and the ambulances...Tom had done a wonderful job in breaking the hold of the evil cult.

And after their night's work was over, and the church was empty once more, Tom accompanied Kit back home, and they talked and talked until daylight.

They each recalled the first time they saw each other at the station. Tom had never forgotten Kit's face. She had never forgotten the blue eyes in the basket. Fate had decreed that they went their separate ways to do their work in the world; but Fate had brought them together once more.

Tom of course, had recognised Kit in the library. He engaged in some investigative work of his own, of a more personal nature; he knew where she lived, and where she shopped, and how she loved her garden.

That very night, Fate had taken the lead once more, and Tom had tracked down The Primus and The Council to the disused church, where, as he stood in the shadowy recesses of the vestibule, he had seen Kit transform, and overcome The Primus.

They marvelled at the way their lives had become intertwined; that they should meet in this tiny piece of England, forty-six years after they first saw one another. And that they were both Gifted, and returned to the place of their birth.

That meeting was the beginning of their partnership. There were many other cases they worked on together: the slave-trading of the immigrant children...the case of the primates stolen from the zoos across Britain...the government minister involved in racketeering...the financial scandals of the misused charity funds...the dreadful case of the chimera, illegal genetic engineering of the worst possible kind...Kit shuddered at the remembrance. Other cases, countless ones; too many to remember now...

The Lucky Cat Hotel. That's where they had their first dinner together. It had somehow seemed more than appropriate. They had discussed books, both of them being great readers. The first of course, had been *Far From The Madding Crowd*. Tom had surprisingly not read it before the day Kit bumped into him in Oakbridge. He had been amused at Kit's vehement denouncement of Sergeant Troy, and the apparent stupidity of Bathsheba Everdene. How could Bathsheba not have noticed how wonderful Gabriel Oak was? He was right under her nose; it was *he* who was working like a Trojan (Tom had laughed at the intended pun); with a name like Oak, how could she not have seen how strong and dependable Gabriel was? And at any rate, a man who makes the proposal:

And at home by the fire, whenever you look up, there I shall be, and whenever I look up, there will be you,...

just *had* to be a better bet than some jerk with a sword-swinging routine who chopped off bits of her hair, treated her badly, then took a hike in the opposite direction.

Tom agreed, and entertained by Kit's exuberance, sat back and listened with great amusement while she continued her lively critique. She quoted the sentence about Oak 'feeling balanced between poetry and practicality' – a jolly good mix, in her opinion.

Here Tom ventured the observation that Gabriel Oak sounded like a cross between Wordsworth and Superman, and sketched on his paper table napkin a hilarious cartoon of the poet Wordsworth dressed as a caped crusader, complete with outsize belt and lycra tights. Kit laughed until she nearly cried, then called the waitress and asked for coffee. Then she asked Tom why it was that it took so darned long for Bathsheba to see what was good for her, and Tom chuckled and said she'd had to otherwise there'd have been no darned book, and then the conversation descended into great silliness and mirth as they drank their coffee...

And so they dined, and went to the cinema, attended concerts and art exhibitions, comedy venues and theatres; and betwixt and between they worked on cases together, keeping mind, body and senses alert and in good working order. And they had fun. Lots of fun. They were good times.

They'd gone to the odd football match too, but Kit said it wasn't really for her, so Tom cheerfully went on his own and left Kit to do Kit things.

Then there was that Saturday night. The moment that Tom turned Kit's world upside down. She remembered the devastation she had felt...

He had, she noticed, been much quieter than his usual self that day. He had been away for a few days, and Kit had missed him greatly. Tom was rather introspective. Kit asked him if he was feeling all right, and he said yes, there was nothing wrong with him; but Kit started to be a little worried. He was always playful, but today he was much more serious. He told her he had to go away again that night. He would call her when he got back. He was evasive about where he was going, and for how long.

Later that night, as they walked down the path to the gate of Kit's cottage, where Tom's car was parked, he suddenly turned to her and said: "Kit, we can't go on like this. Not any more. It's..." He stopped, searching for the right words.

Kit's heart fell with a thud. Tears sprang unbidden into her eyes. No! It couldn't be! No, Tom, no! We've been so perfect together...what have I said?...what have I done?...He's been away...he's going away...has he – the thought brought the tears into her throat and almost strangled her – is he in love with someone else? *Oh, Tom!*

Through the dreadful blackness in her soul she became aware of his words registering at last in her brain, his voice, low and serious:

"It's time...it's time we thought about getting married."
"*OH, TOM!!!*"

* * *

Tom had intended to ask Kit to marry him for some time. But she was so independent, so happy with her life in its present form. What if she refused him? What if she didn't want to make such a huge commitment? Tom didn't think he could stand to hear her voice, soft in its delivery, searching for soothing words to gently let him down...

But he wanted to marry her. He wanted to so very badly. It wasn't enough, the way things were...it was more wonderful than he could ever have imagined, being in her company...but it wasn't enough...

He felt compelled from within his heart to take that final step, as proof of his love. Not to do so would be construed as an indication that his love was not strong enough for this most sacred and binding of ties.

For all that women now proposed to men, Kit would not be one of them. He knew she would think that a man may perceive a proposal at best, as a tender trap; at worst, forward and predatory. Kit was an old-fashioned girl at heart, much as she was a strong and capable modern young woman. These were certainly strange times for the mating game. Except that it wasn't a game. It was a serious step to take; not one to be undertaken lightly.

Away from Kit, for these few days, he thought and thought about it. Then he made a decision. If he didn't ask, he'd never know her answer, and she would never be his wife. He would have to ask her.

If she said yes...if she just said yes...

He would find a wonderful place for their honeymoon, one which would surprise and delight her, provide her with unforgettable and idyllic memories...

And if she said no...If she said no...

He would leave for a few days and lick his wounds. But he would have to come back to her. He couldn't live without her.

This is ridiculous, he told himself. I'm acting like an idiot.

He had the reputation of being strong and courageous. And yet here he was at five hundred and twenty-seven years of age, taking so much time to summon up the courage to ask the only woman he had ever truly loved to marry him. Ridiculous.

So he would ask her. He would ask her on Saturday.

* * *

It was part of the pleasure of living, to indulge in the odd bout of nostalgia about events in their past, and then to look out through the window and see him once again, part of her present. Kit felt incredibly lucky.

They still lived today, all these years later, in Copse View Cottage; she loved it so. Tom said that to take Kit away from the cottage would be like parting Scarlett O'Hara from Tara; he would be happy to be wherever Kit wanted to be.

They married in Oakbridge; but what they considered to be their real and special ceremony took place, just the two of them, beneath the great oak in the middle of the forest.

It was a warm June day. The dappled sunlight shone through into the cool shade, its shafts of light like a million candles on an altar, as Tom and Kit made their vows to each other.

They would be loyal, loving and caring; respectful and considerate; their watchwords would be humour, integrity and creativity. Their love would last throughout their lives, here on Earth, and throughout the Great Adventure. The old oak tree looked down upon them, and heard their vows completed with the words of Thomas Hardy: Gabriel's Resolve from *Far From The Madding Crowd*:

And at home by the fire, whenever you look up, there I shall be and whenever I look up, there will be you.

They kissed each other long and tenderly to seal their commitment; then with their arms around each other's waists, they wandered slowly through the forest, in silent commune, each knowing that of all their Gifts, their love was the greatest Gift of all.

Far into the wooded place they went, and in step with one another, returned at last to the great oak, where, filled with quiet and tenderness, they sat among the woodland flowers upon the forest floor.

They looked deeply into each other's eyes, sitting in silence under the leafy canopy.

Still at nightfall, they remained in their beloved forest, inside the great oak, the grey fur curved around the circle of tabby stripes, the purrs of deepest contentment echoing from the walls of the woody hollow.

And at last Kit knew why she had been called home.

Diary Entry, 8 June 2010

I'll never forget this day.

It's been the biggest day of my life so far. It was an exciting one for our parents – how could it not have been?

When we got back around 12:30, my brother Tommy and I got out all the family photo albums, something we do every now and again. It seems funny to see us when we were tiny, all wrapped up in baby shawls, me in a pink one and Tommy in a blue one. And then there's the one taken on our fifth birthday showing heaps of cards with '*Happy Birthday Twins*' and the big cake shaped like a cat's head with '*Tommy and Caitlin 5 Today*' and kisses in icing all round the edge. Tommy and I are pretending to play a duet on the piano. Tommy's fingers are all chocolate-y.

Then there's the one where we're all out in the garden on the night Tommy and I had completed our first mission. We were twenty at the time. We're looking really pleased with ourselves. Mum and Dad are looking even more pleased. Tommy looks good in this one. He's the big grey cat on the right, standing next to Dad. I'm the small tabby on the left of the picture, next to Mum. Mum and Dad were there of course, the night of our first mission, but it was Tommy and I who did the job. But we couldn't have done it, we couldn't have done anything we've done since, without their amazing knowledge and their encouragement. That's the best thing parents can ever do for their kids, give them lots of confidence and know-how. And lots of love. We've always had *lots* of love.

Since they were married, Mum and Dad have been inseparable. They weren't about to change that when their time came.

This morning, with the strangest mixture of joy and sorrow, Tommy and I put their remains in one casket, hewn from the big oak tree in the forest. Then we buried them underneath it, near Grandma Bess, like they'd asked us to.

There they'll be together forever, in the dappled light of day, and the moonlit beams of night.

BIBLIOGRAPHY

Chapter: 1723

Excerpts from the Bible

Chapter: 1900

Macbeth, William Shakespeare

Henry V, William Shakespeare

The Merchant of Venice, William Shakespeare

Chapter: 1928-29

View from a Railway Carriage, Robert Louis Stevenson

Song, *O Tannenbaum, O Tannenbaum,* German carol, August Zarnack, Ernst Gebhard Anschutz

Macbeth, William Shakespeare

Chapter 1974...and after

View from a Railway Carriage, Robert Louis Stevenson

Leisure, WH Davies

Far from The Madding Crowd, Thomas Hardy